ReVamping the Gestalt

Book 4 of The Behemoth Gestalt

A Novel In Behemoth's Shadow

Chad W. Knox

ALSO BY CHAD W. KNOX

In Behemoth's Shadow Universe

INTERESTED IN MORE OF THIS UNIVERSE'S INSANITY? CHECK US OUT ON FACEBOOK AT

"MUGZ INK BOOKS"
&
"REN SILVER, AUTHOR"

Copyright 2025 Mugz Ink Books LLC

For more information, follow "Mugz Ink Books" on Facebook.

Paperback: ISBN 978-1-967333-02-8
Hardback: ISBN 978-1-967333-04-2
E-Book: ISBN 978-1-967333-05-9

Edited by: Wouldn't be prudent...

DEDICATION

For those who continue to get up every morning and get it done.

CONTENTS

ACKNOWLEDGMENTS

Pat – I invoked her name, hope you don't mind.

Thanks for turning the pages.

Author's Note

Hmmmm….what to say….Rhi's too busy to be bothered right now, so I can say whatever I want.

Sadly, I got nothin'.

Oh! Actually, the end of this book sets up a collab crossover with another book series for Book 5. So, there's that…but there'll be more details on that later.

Prologue

RHI

Why are you making me do this? I don't get paid for narrations, bud. Actually, you don't pay me squat. I mean, it was nice to let you write your little author's note(nice cop-out, by the way) without even commenting on it. Now you've got me prologueing. Prologuing? Seriously, that's how that's spelled? Whatever.

Hello and welcome! For those who are joining our show already in progress, welcome some more! Why the hell are you starting with Book 4? I mean, seriously, who does that? Go read the other books first!

Seriously? You're not gonna. You're actually going to make me recap the other books for you? Do you want me to just recap this book for you, too? I mean, we're never getting an audiobook. Could you imagine someone trying to voice me? Yeah right.

Fine...bunch of lazy fuc...

Grumble. Grumble.

Yeah, I actually said grumble grumble, what of it? OK, let's see if I can Luis this bitch.

(Deep inhale)

Book 0 starts with me, but not really, as the author sorta pushed my character to the side, which pissed me off to no end, but it really didn't affect the story cause that story wasn't about me. It was about this 300-year-old vampire named Shae who'd been dared to pick up a high schooler to be her personal tap boy/girl/naked squirrel by her best friend Shelby, who also happens to be a vampire. But that's not really relevant cause she's just in the story so the author could help tell the tale from Shae's point of view. I'm also a vampire, but not during this story, but that's beside the point cause the author's a dick. Shae meets up with James (who just happens to be of legal age, thanks to some contrived garbage the author made up to avoid legal action). They have a series of on-off moments over 3-4 years (I can't remember which because the author kept bouncing back and forth on ages). But, by the end of the book, James proposes to Shae-OH! James didn't know Shae was a vampire this whole time because he's a moron, but he figured it out when he proposed to her due to...plot. Shae is wishy-washy about giving him an answer, again, because of plot. In the end, Shae doesn't say yes or no and disappears the next day, ending the book.

Whew, saved you $11 there...unless you're one of those digital book readers. Print is better. Remember, you only rent digital content.

(Deep Inhale 2)

Book 1 - Fourteenish years later, James comes home on leave from the US Air Force for his mother's funeral. While home, he finds out from his sister that Shae is in town (she's been missing since Book 0) and he goes to the Boffer park to find her, but she just beats the crap out of him and runs away. Weird ass signs have been showing up that eventually turn into the beginning of a zombie apocalypse later that day. Shae also follows James to confront him, and it turns out she has no memory of James. There sure are a lot of memory problems in these books, huh? Fucking hack writing. Anyway, James gathers his friends and family to try and flee the city from the outbreak, and Shae tags along because she gets flashes of James's memories that she's in, but she doesn't remember them happening. Also, it turns out James is on some military super-soldier serum that he's run out of and is slowly going crazy from withdrawal. Shae guesses it's a blood derivative, and James starts trying to choke down blood to try and stave off his withdrawal. Everyone flees to a ranch in the hill country that they fortify after robbing a Walmart. A quick trip to the secret super-soldier lab in San Antonio, and we meet Travis, who's also like James. We find out James is gonna die from withdrawal because they can't make his serum. Once back at the ranch, they call "The Hacienda," James goes nuts and accidentally kills himself, but Shae brings him back as a vampire. Bells and Whistles and all that. But James is showing weird signs and doesn't appear to be a regular vamp. Our duo make a trip to Austin to try and find Natalie, a blood worker who is the one who robbed Shae of her memories at the vampire Pagoda's orders 14 years ago. Nat restores her memories and the tri bang for two days(but not really).

Meanwhile, I make my entrance and follow the pair back to The Hacienda, where I'm captured. Why'd I follow? I had a crush on James back in Book 0. Why'd I get captured when I'm the most badass fighter in this whole series? Fucking Nat put the whammy on me. Come to find out, James and Shae are trying to take over Pagoda's compound, nicknamed The Alamo, to use as their zombie apocalypse clubhouse. BTW, Pagoda is Shae and my master. He's an ass. James comes up with some contrived plan, and we end up killing Pagoda in a ridiculous fashion, and suddenly Mark, one of James's friends (and a normal human), is in charge of all the vampires somehow. Don't ask. Oh yeah, James and I hook up, and Shae's down with it, but I'm not telling you the details cause...read the damned book. This book ends with James, Shae, and Pete about to head off to Houston to try and find Pete's mom, because James promised to in exchange for Pete's help getting into the Alamo. OH, and Nat has somehow linked James, Shae, and my mind together in some weird ass group mind thing we've never heard of called a gestalt, hence the book's name.

(PANT PANT)

Still with me? Good.

Book 2 kicks off with James and Shae slaughtering a bunch of rapist scumbags on the way to Houston. Even though the dead guys are garbage, the whole thing adds to James's already overflowing PTSD basket of snakes. They find Pete's mom at a military base/refuge camp run by a dictator asshole. Then they head to the Drakes in Houston because the magic portal to Drakes from Austin is broken, and Drake asked them to look into it. BTW, Drakes is a freaky bar that doesn't follow the rules of physics, reality, or common sense. The duo fight their way into the Drakes, which is full of zombies, and rescue two soldiers who'd been trapped. Come to find out, the two female soldiers aren't from this world but some parallel world that's similar to ours, and one of them, Beth, is a mega-pop star who once quasi-dated James back in the desert. Of course, this is a different Beth who doesn't know him (more memory shit, right?) and just confuses things.

MEANWHILE, my ass gets sent to another weird-ass Renaissance

Festival-looking world where I join up with a bunch of D&D types, one of which is a gorgeous red-skinned, tail-having, fang-sporting, red-eyed hottie named Tara who smells so damned good we end up getting married. Don't ask, read the book. After a year of shenanigans on that planet, I return to my new Drakes franchise and get sent back home to the Drakes in Houston along with Tara. Yeah, Drakes bars are all over the place (there's a reason). We arrive and save James and crew, but it turns out that instead of being gone a year, I've only been gone a week. Fucking weird ass dimensional time-traveling nonsense or some shit. I leave that to the geeks to figure out. Then we visit one of James's friends at NASA and save their asses from getting overrun by zombies. Beth and Rachel return to their world. We visit some of Shae's adopted family and not-good shit happens. Then we find another of James's friends, Liam, who has been bitten by zombies and dies. OH, and there are these flying mech things that attacked us in Tara's world, again in Houston, and then again when we finally get back to Austin. We managed to mostly fend off the first two attacks, but during the third, we're about to get our asses handed to us when a new flying death MacGuffin shows up and saves us. It's being piloted by Beth, who looks ten years older than we'd seen her a week ago, is battle-scarred, and says we have to come with her cause "Behemoth" says so...whoever the hell Behemoth is.

Whew, man, I skipped a lot of Book 2; oh well, buy it and read it if you want to know more.

(**WHEEZE** I guess that cigar I had in Houston is getting to me.)

In Book 3, we come to find out our planet is actually inside some massive megastructure/space station called Behemoth. When I say massive, I mean it, as it houses over 100 planets (called Bio Habs.) All of the Bio Hab's inhabitants are unaware they're actually just living in giant zoos for making soldiers for some ancient war. We're recruited by the Daemon Corps (DC) to fly the big giant robot mech-things and protect our Bio Hab from the Angel Guard (AG). The AG are the assholes that kept attacking us and it turns out they were the original protectors of Behemoth but went rogue and were replaced by the DC. Now, the AG and DC are trying to kill each other and rogue factions of both keep blowing up Bio Habs because they're terrorist fucks! Oh, and Tara is a Daemon, the race created to protect Behemoth, who make up the DC and AG. It's a whole mess. Then we get captured by the AG, who explain their side of the story, and it turns out we might be working for the badder of the bad guys. Both sides are dicks. Oh, and Beth? Beth was plucked off her Bio Hab to serve in the DC and is an ultimate badass who's been away from humans so long she'd kinda turned into a robot. Something Shae, our new leader, btw, took upon herself to try and fix. Then, some bullshit happens and Tara ends up being accidentally/on-purpose murdered by the AG and the rest of us are torn up pretty badly...I lost my legs! They were my favorite legs! Granted, they grew back, but they weren't original anymore. Oh yeah, did I mention I'm a vampire now too? That happened back in Book 1. That's how my legs grew back. More crap goes on, I meet the author of this shit show, but it seems he doesn't know what the fuck he's doing either. What's left of our gestalt tries to figure out whose side we're really on. Both sides suck. But we can't go home cause they'll erase our memories of everything and for some reason, we can't have more memory fuckery going on. Then, after a year of playing Space Ace, Book 3 ends with our Bio Hab burning and us losing Shae...and I'm kinda torn about it cause it had been her plan that got Tara killed...and I'm really conflicted about how I felt when I watched her die cause I wasn't sure if I should have tried to help her, or even if I could have. But James and I survived.

Now, here we are with Book 4 and I just had to spout off all that crap for you lazy assholes. If you knew all that already, cause you took the time to support the author and read the other books...I'm not calling you an asshole. You know who you are.

Oh yeah, I guess I should have mentioned, I know who you are, I know where the fourth wall is, and I like to break it. Sometimes for comedic effect, sometimes just for the hell of it because I don't have anyone to talk to about this shit anymore.

OK, let's get back to it.

Chapter 1

RHI

"Get off your ass!" I yelled, entering the room for the third time today. I was out of patience.

"Still not interested," James said, not looking up from the video game he'd been engrossed in for the last four hours.

I stopped, hands on my hips, and stared at the back of his head. He'd been like this ever since we got back; actually, he'd gotten worse. He didn't have an interest in doing anything. He just wanted to be left alone. The fact that he'd taken an interest in this video game last week was an improvement. The problem was, it was all he was interested in. I'd had to drag him to eat and, like now, drag him to practice.

"James," I said, stepping between him and the TV.

James moved to look around me.

This must be what having a teenager is like, I thought to myself before plucking the controller from his hands and tossing it over my shoulder.

"Hey!" James protested. "Those are hard to come by now."

As he tried to reach around me, I lifted him easily and put him on my shoulder.

"Seriously?!?" he hollered.

"Yes," I retorted. "You haven't been off this couch in a week, and you need to practice. And maybe a shower...no, definitely a shower."

At first, he tried to struggle, but my iron grip didn't allow him any leeway, so he eventually settled into a limp pout.

"Had you kept up your practice, you could have stopped me." I chided.

"Whatever," James mumbled.

∞∞∞∞∞Ω∞∞∞∞∞

<u>RHI</u>

"Tuck in your damn elbow!" I said for the umpteenth time, my foot connecting once again with James' outstretched elbow, sending him staggering back off balance. I settled back into a neutral stance as James recovered.

Shaking his arm, James cautiously advanced back into striking distance and feinted before following with a series of punches designed to get him in close enough for a throw.

I sighed, blocking each of his half-hearted strikes and taking a simple step back, which caused James to overbalance as he reached out to grab me.

James found himself teetering on the brink of falling forward as his arms flailed in the general direction of where I had been. He looked up at me as I frowned at his awkward position. A heartbeat later, my hair brushed his face as my reverse kick caught him in the gut and sent him flying.

"At least try to recover when you find yourself overcommitted like that!" I growled, my frustration palpable. His half-committal to the session was chipping away at what calm reserve I had left. I figured pounding him into the mat would have sparked some sort of reaction from him, but so far, nothing.

It had been two years since we'd survived our escape from the living fire. There were things I refused to let myself deal with, as I had to focus on putting James back together.

It seemed that my "persuading" of James during the escape from our dying Bio Hab, AKA a brick to the back of the head, had caused more damage than I thought—a lot more.

At first, he hadn't been able to speak. That went on for six months before suddenly coming back without warning. But then there were gaps in his memory and the oddest of abilities. Like he forgot what a fork was or how to use it. He could use a spoon and a knife, but just stared at a fork on the table. That never came back, and he had to learn how to use it all over again.

What took the cake was the fact that he didn't remember Shae or Tara at all. Anytime I brought them up, he didn't know what I was talking about. When I tried to walk him through memories, the parts with either of them were foggy, and he had trouble remembering any specific details.

At first, I thought he was faking it. I knew amnesia, and this wasn't it. If it weren't for the other things he'd forgotten, I would have said someone had tampered with his head. But the only two people I knew who could do that were dead.

[Hey, look, more memory issues...fucking hack writer. --Rhi]

The funny thing of it all, though, had this been five years ago, I'd have been ecstatic. I'd had that schoolgirl crush on James, and the thought of having him alone, all to myself, would have been amazing.

Now, with everything that had happened and his current state, any thought of a romantic interest in him was gone. I refused to let myself "take advantage" of the situation...I just couldn't...not after abandoning Shae.

Besides, every time anything romantic popped up, it was Tara who—

NOPE! Not going there, I yelled at myself inside my head.

James looked up at me from the ground, where he was pulling himself up to all fours.

I snapped my fingers, and a towel appeared in the air beside me. I lifted my hair and wiped the back of my neck as I watched James. My hair was finally growing back out after having cut it short during our Behemoth war year. While the maintenance was a chore, there was something calming about combing out the hair that now hung below my shoulders. I missed Tara brushing my...

No! I scolded myself again and shoved the memory away with venom.

I watched as James was still breathing hard after the sparring session. Even after all this time, I outmatched him on so many levels. He was usually happy on the days he could get me to break a sweat. Today, he just didn't seem to care. I figured he was just going through the motions until the session was over and he could get back to his video game.

"Mr. Sable?" A security guard stuck his head in, breaking the uneasy silence that had fallen between us.

James looked up. "Yes?"

"They want you at the front gate," the man said.

"The front gate? What for?" I asked.

"Yes, ma'am," The guard said. "He has...a visitor."

James and I looked at one another as the guard made his escape.

"Looks like they still fear you," James said as we walked down the hallway of the Alamo and out into the sun. Every person in the house was ducking out of sight as we passed.

I shrugged, "It has its uses."

"We're not dealing with vamp politics anymore. We haven't heard from another community in years now," James said.

"True, but it's a lot easier to maintain respect than to earn it back," I said, tossing the soiled towel into the air, and it vanished.

James shook his head in amazement. "Sure wish I knew how you did that."

I frowned, not looking at him. "Magic," I mumbled.

The main gate of our "Alamo" compound was a pair of ancient wooden doors, having survived from the mission's original founding. In modern times, with zombies now walking about, they had been paneled with steel plates and reinforced hinges. With this being one of the perimeter wall's weak points, the three-meter doors needed as much help as they could get.

Four guards at the main gate stood in a circle, talking in low, excited voices. They broke as we approached; three moved back to the gate shack, and the fourth turned to face us.

"I don't know what this is, ma'am," the guard said to me. "We were on watch as normal, keeping an eye outside. One minute, the clear zone was empty; the next, she was standing next to the gate."

A 100-meter clear zone around the perimeter had been established at James's recommendation when we first took the Alamo from the vampiric asshole Pagoda. Even a vampire moving flat out couldn't clear 100 meters unnoticed. It had been a lot of work, but now nothing could get within striking distance of the compound without the sentries knowing. At least, that's what we'd thought.

"She?" I asked.

"Yes, ma'am, and she asked for Mr. Sable," the guard said, pointing towards the guard shack next to the gate.

I looked at James, who shook his head and shrugged.

As James approached the small building, a high-pitched voice came from within, and a small white blur knocked him to the ground. His head hit the ground hard enough to make me cringe.

"Did she say, 'Daddy?'" I asked.

∞∞∞∞∞Ω∞∞∞∞∞

<u>JAMES</u>

When my eyes finally regained focus, I looked down to find a mess of red hair and freckles hiding large green eyes that were peering up at me. The little girl, who couldn't be more than 12 years old, was wearing a strangely clean white dress and sobbing uncontrollably. I stared down at her in shock.

Rhi reached down and tried to remove the child, but the little girl started to yell and fight, recoiling away from Rhi and clinging to me that much tighter.

"It's alright, Rhi," I said as Rhi reached to remove the girl's hand from my shirt. Rhi backed off but eyed the child wearily.

Carefully, I stood up, the child stubbornly refusing to let go of me. Children were not my strong suit. I'd never really dealt with children before, especially not one that was sobbing and calling me daddy.

It took a few awkward minutes, but I managed to get her calmed down. After a bit more persuasion, I managed to get her to exchange the bear hug she had on me for simply holding hands, albeit with a white-knuckled death grip.

"What's your name?" I asked, kneeling in front of the girl.

The little girl remained silent, staring at me. After a moment, her eyes darted to the circle of guards who'd gathered from the commotion. I took the hint and stood up, glancing at Rhi.

"Alright, we'll take it from here. Get back to it," Rhi snapped her fingers at the guards.

A chorus of "Yes, ma'ams" replied to her order.

I glanced around, "Hey, let's head over this way." Leading the girl over to some old rot-iron patio furniture beneath the shade of a large pecan tree, we sat down together. I started to say something but noticed the girl was still eyeing Rhi, who'd refused to sit.

"Rhi, could you give us a minute?" I asked.

"Yeah, right," Rhi snorted, crossing her arms and refusing to move.

"Rhi," I said flatly.

"Fine." Rhi took a few steps back and turned her back to us, but didn't move any further.

Sighing, I turned back to the girl. She leaned against me on the bench, her hand still stubbornly in mine. Her warmth and the smell of humanity on her told me she wasn't a vampire. As far as my senses could tell, this was just a normal little girl.

"So, what's your name?" I started.

"Viola," she whispered, still eyeballing Rhi.

Glancing at what Viola was looking at, "Don't worry about her, she's a nice lady." I briefly saw Rhi's shoulders minutely moving up and down in laughter. "Where'd you come from, Viola?"

Viola remained silent.

"Are you hurt?" I asked, giving her the once over, noticing her bare feet for the first time. There wasn't a scratch or even a mosquito bite on her that I could see. The bottoms of her feet were dirty, but that was it. If she'd been walking through the Texas hill country, it didn't show.

Viola shook her head.

"Where'd you come from?" I asked but was met with more silence. "Where's your mom?"

Her grip tightened enough to make my knuckles pop, but she remained silent.

After a few minutes of fruitless questioning, I sighed.

"How about we get something to eat? That sound good?" I asked.

Viola didn't reply but didn't resist as I led her into the main house.

Rhi followed and took up a post by the door to the deserted kitchen.

Sitting Viola down on a stool at the counter, I managed to get her to let go of my hand.

"Now let's see." I looked around the kitchen. "What would a little girl want? You wouldn't mind telling me that much, at least, would you? Of course not," I sighed when she failed to reply. "I got it!" I pulled out a fresh loaf of bread and sliced off two pieces before rummaging in the pantry and pulling out a glass jar.

"We're all out of crunchy, so you're going to have to settle for creamy. But Sam makes some pretty darn good peanut butter." I paused, "You're not allergic to peanuts, are you? Guess we'll find out," I muttered when she remained silent.

I retrieved another small jar from the cabinet and placed it on the counter. "You're going to have to trust me on this one. The best thing we've got to make the J in your PB&J are these mustang grape preserves." I assembled the sandwich quickly and put the plate in front of her.

She eyed the plate with suspicion.

Finally, I pulled a plastic jug out of the fridge and poured a glass of cold red liquid.

"And what kid doesn't like Kool-Aid?" I put the glass down in front of her before putting the jug away. When I turned back, Viola had eaten half the sandwich already.

"Guess you were hungry after all." I grinned.

She held the other half of the sandwich out to me.

"No, that's alright, you finish that one," I said.

She continued to hold the sandwich out.

I reluctantly took the sandwich and took a bite before handing it back. I had to admit it was good, but I'd pay for it later. Solid food had been off my menu for ages. I still preferred to avoid the after-effects of "regular" food by sticking to a vampire's strictly "liquid" diet.

I stole a drink from the glass to wash down the sticky sandwich, purposely letting the red liquid touch my upper lip.

Viola giggled upon seeing my Kool-Aid mustache.

I couldn't help but smile at the sound of her giggling. Before long, she had a matching mustache and was picking the crumbs off her plate.

"Feel better?" I asked.

She nodded and yawned.

"Tired? Come on, you can lie down over here," I said.

When I came around the counter, she held her arms up to me. It took a moment to realize what she wanted. Awkwardly, I picked her up and she wrapped her arms and legs around me before putting her head on my shoulder.

I glanced over at Rhi, who was stifling a laugh at my awkwardness.

I carefully carried Viola up to my room and lay her down on my bed. She was out before her head hit the pillow. I stood there watching the girl sleep until I felt Rhi touch my mind.

James.

I jumped at the touch but turned and joined her at the door. *Should I just leave her there?*

It's a room without windows and only one door. I think she's OK, come on, Rhi said, pulling me back and closing the door.

I plopped down onto the couch I'd been on earlier while playing video games. The living room was small, but it met my needs. Like the bedroom, it was void of any windows.

"OK, what the actual hell?" Rhi started.

"You're asking me? You know as much as I do," I said.

"How many other illegitimate kids you got running around

out there?" Rhi said.

"What? None...that I know of. We don't even know if she's mine. And why is this making you so mad?" I could see her literally seething as she accused me.

Rhi seemed to realize this and took a breath to get herself under control.

"She's obviously human, so I'm not too worried on that front," Rhi said.

"You were worried about the security risk of a 12-year-old little girl?" I asked. Rhi was paranoid, even by my standards. But that was a bit much.

"With everything we've been through, yeah," Rhi said. "Security said they searched her and she was unarmed."

I looked at Rhi.

"That's their job, James, little girl or not. Strangers get searched," Rhi chided.

I held my hands up and nodded.

"At the moment, the only thing I can think of is she's some sort of diversion," Rhi said, making a sour face.

"Diversion?" I asked.

"Something to keep us occupied so we're not paying attention elsewhere," Rhi said.

"Or she could just be a little girl," I countered.

"Claiming to be your daughter," Rhi scoffed. "James, we're a couple of years into a zombie apocalypse now. A little girl wandering into the compound clean as a whistle and wearing a brand-new dress?"

"Fair enough." I sighed. "So...what should we do?"

"Well, I'm going to go talk to security and have them keep an eye out for anything unusual," Rhi said.

"Unusual?" I laughed.

"Yeah, and then I'm going to take a stroll outside the compound and have a little look-see," Rhi said.

"What about me?" I asked.

"You?" Rhi smiled broadly. "You're going to stay here and look after your daughter."

Chapter 2

JAMES

"How about this?" I started. We were in one of the gardens, pulling weeds. It wasn't something I did often, but I was running out of things to do with the child. "What if I tell you something about my family? Then you can tell me something about yours?"

Viola had slept for a few hours, and it was now early afternoon. I looked to the young girl for a nod of affirmation. When she didn't respond, I did it for her by saying, "Deal."

"So, my mom was really nice. She died before the outbreak, so she's not around anymore. That's happened to a lot of people here." I yanked an unusually difficult weed from the ground. "She had a difficult time taking care of my sister and me, so we all lived with my grandparents. My grandparents passed away a while before the outbreak, and my sister not long after the outbreak. So yeah, family is something precious and worth hanging onto. Even if it is only their memory."

I didn't even get a blink out of Viola.

"My mom used to make this weird tuna casserole thing. She used a whole bag of potato chips to make it and smothered it in cheese!" I smiled at the girl. "Not healthy in the slightest, but it sure was tasty. Has your mom ever made anything tasty?" My attempt at being sly fell flat on Viola.

I'd been pulling my hair out trying to figure out any way to get the litt...to get Viola to talk about herself. I was quickly running out of activities to share with her. At this rate, we'd be thumb wrestling soon.

Luckily, one of the other moms in the compound saw me and took pity on me. She had a girl about Viola's age with her and suggested we head over to the family area.

The family area had been built up in the past few years out of necessity. After Z Day, Pagoda had taken in as many families as his compound could hold. He wasn't being compassionate; he was building a feeding herd. But it had worked out in the end, thankfully.

There was a small playground with a make-shift jungle gym made from old construction equipment. It may not look pretty, but it was solid and all the rough spots had been filed down. It was still safer than some of the playgrounds I'd played on as a kid.

The woman sat on a bench beside a tree while her daughter tried to get Viola to come with her to the playground. But Viola was refusing to leave my side. Eventually the girl shrugged and headed off to join the few other children playing.

I looked down at Viola and found her watching the other children with keen interest. She looked like she really wanted to join the other children.

"Viola, I promise I won't leave this spot. You can go play if you want," I said.

Viola adamantly shook her head.

"You can see me from the playground," I said.

"It's alright," the woman beside me said. "She doesn't have to play if she doesn't want to."

This seemed to satisfy Viola as she sat silently beside me.

I frowned, wondering just what I'd gotten myself into this time.

∞∞∞∞∞Ω∞∞∞∞∞

RHI

Closing my eyes, I listened. The house was quiet. I shook my head as I could hear James snoring loudly. It was comical that he still breathed, even while asleep.

Viola was breathing deep and slow, indicating she was in dreamland. The girl never shifted in her sleep, no crying, no calling out, no nightmares. Nothing to show she had any sort of trauma. She just lay there, curled up against James. It would be kind of cute if she didn't give me the screaming willies.

I didn't think the day was ever going to end. Viola had shown up in the morning, and after her nap, James had kept her busy the rest of the day. Every attempt at prying more information from the child had failed.

I'd managed to lift fingerprints from Viola's Kool-Aid glass, but got nothing back from the limited databases we had access to. Now they were all asleep, and I could finally try to get some answers.

Sighing, I stood up from my bed and approached the wall. My hand paused next to the light sconce as I checked one last time for anyone nearby. My eyes darted back from the hallway behind me and narrowed as I pushed my way through the "wall."

The real wall appeared 10 meters away. The wall extended left, right, and up, disappearing into darkness as I moved forward. The fury I'd been keeping in check began to bubble to the surface as I strode purposely on.

A section of the wall moved aside at my approach, revealing another room beyond.

"What's with the kid?" I fumed as the wall slid back into place behind me.

The walls of this room were lined with multiple computer panels, screens, and readouts. It was a five-year-old's button-pushing dream. Its sole occupant looked up at me with a bored expression.

"No idea." The AG, known as Cr'eon, said, not taking her feet off the console before her. Seeing my expression, "It's not us," she said defensively.

"Then who?" I asked.

Back when Cr'eon had been part of the DC, she'd manned one of the observation posts of my Bio Hab. Their job was to monitor Bio Habs for unusual incidents and to watch for AG incursions. Due to a series of mistakes, she was demoted multiple times and became disenchanted with the DC.

I first saw her when she hosted our newcomers' briefing to Behemoth. She didn't give a shit about anything back then. Then she was recruited by the AG and found she hated them a little less than she did the DC. She wasn't a happy Daemon. That's why we got along.

"The computer?" Cr'eon ventured cautiously.

My temper was well known amongst the AG. While a Daemon was supposedly stronger and more powerful than a vampire, it had never been put to the test. I knew that Cr'eon had zero fucks left to give, so me going off on her didn't help. But I didn't have anyone else to vent at.

"Listen, we've been running this simulation for you for over two years now," Cr'eon began, "and James hasn't shown any signs of recovering his memory. The higher-ups have already given up on him."

My expression hardened.

After the living fire, I'd basically bullied the AG into providing this safe space for us while James recovered. I'd recreated the Alamo complex, but I'd removed his friends and family as he already knew they were all dead from the living fire. Plus, I doubted the computer could recreate them well enough to fool James.

I realized my mistake too late, though. We'd already begun the simulation with him when I remembered the living fire destroyed everything on our Bio Hab, not just people. The Alamo was gone, but for some reason, James never said anything about it. I figured his mind had latched onto its security after all the trauma we'd been through. I'd had to go with it at the time.

"I'm just being honest with you," Cr'eon said. "The fact that my command left me here to monitor this...what did you call it, 'the store?' The fact I got stuck with this shows that....they hate me," Cr'eon finished with a long sigh.

"Cr'eon..." I growled.

The real reason the AG gave in to my demands was that they wanted to study James. They desperately wanted to know about his ability to break Behemoth's "rules."

After the first fruitless year, they'd pretty much given up on it, but I convinced them to let me continue. This place was safe and protected from Behemoth and the DC. The AG agreed but pulled all staff except for Cr'eon, who had apparently drawn the short straw.

"It had to be the computer," Cr'eon held up her hands defensively. "The sub-mind must be getting desperate after all this time. The medbots have repaired all the physical damage to James's body. There's only so much they can do for mental damage. Maybe the sub-mind thinks this child will stir something in him. At this point, it can't hurt."

"Of course it can. James can't have..." My voice trailed off, seeing Cr'eon's chiding expression. "You know what I mean. If he can't remember anything, how's he going to remember that Tara..." My voice trailed off again as I tried to push the encroaching memory away.

Cr'eon put her feet down and stood up. "Listen, I know you don't know it well, but this sub-mind has been helping our cause for longer than I can remember. It's brilliant. If it has introduced this child, then there's a good reason. Maybe it will help him remember Tara. Maybe that will be the breakthrough he needs. Behemoth knows you've tried using Shea enough times. Give this a chance."

I shook my head. "It doesn't feel right." After a long moment, I sighed. "What can you tell me about Viola?"

"Nothing. I've checked the system and the only thing I've got is..." Cr'eon turned and accessed a computer screen with a look. A few mental commands and an image of Viola appeared. The only text that accompanied the image was:

Viola – a child

"That's it?" I examined the screen.

"There's nothing else." Cr'eon shrugged, a human expression she'd picked up from watching humans for so long.

I stared at the image for a long moment before sighing and turning back to the wall from which I came.

"Let me know if anything else comes up," I said.

As I left the room, I heard Cr'eon mutter, "I don't know what I did to deserve this, but it had to be something spectacular."

Chapter 2.5

BETH

The Bio Hab swung first one way, then the other as I smoothly maneuvered my AUG through a series of lazy turns on my rambling journey towards my destination. I wasn't thinking about anything, just letting my mind wander, and the massive flying powered armor followed.

We were on patrol in high orbit above this green-tinted Bio Hab. There wasn't a sense of urgency; there never was here.

I hadn't seen real action in over four years. Even Behemoth's amazing simulators couldn't replicate the feeling of facing down a real opponent. I had lost my edge a long time ago and found I didn't care anymore.

"Colonel?" the voice of my second rang out in my virtual cockpit. "Everything OK?"

Behemoth had returned me to command of a wing after I left Shae and her crew. I'd been afraid I'd be sent back to the schoolhouse to train up more Chosen Army recruits. But I didn't have to worry about that, I'd been sent back to the line.

Of course, I wasn't given back the wing I'd trained and tuned for years. Instead, I was given a whole different set of Daemons and assigned to a Bio Hab that had never seen an AG incursion.

"Just checking my stabilizers," I said as I straightened up my course and stopped daydreaming.

My new wing wasn't bad. They just hadn't worked together before. It took years to establish the rapport I was used to, and my patience was running thin.

I think you need to reexamine what we talked about before, the voice of my minder spoke in my head. But this voice didn't come through the tactical net keyed to my virtual cockpit. This voice lived in my head and sounded like Phil Hartman.

I'm not retiring! I said for the millionth time.

A minder was a sort of AI that Behemoth assigned to "special" cases like me. It was part friend, part shrink, and lived inside your head. It was supposed to always look out for you, even if it wasn't in the best interest of Behemoth. But I never believed that line of bull.

And for the millionth and one time, why not? my minder asked.

I have no Bio Hab to return to. And I'm not having my memories erased! I said.

If you were part of Behemoth's Chosen Army, that meant you were recruited from your Bio Hab to serve and protect Behemoth. It was a voluntary service, but if you ever quit, all memories of your service were erased, and you were returned to the Bio Hab you came from.

Well, my Bio Hab was dead, so I wasn't going back there. This, plus I'd been serving for over 15 years now. I didn't want to lose those memories.

What if it were possible to retire and remain on Behemoth with your memories intact? the minder asked.

Impossible, I snapped. *It's not allowed. You can't just wander about Behemoth like that.*

It's done all the time, the minder said.

Not by the chosen, it's not, I countered.

True, but you're not exactly a standard chosen member now, are you? the minder said.

This was true. I was the only non-Daemon to ever be promoted to Colonel, the same rank as base Daemons. This was because I was an AUG pilot prodigy. I could out-pilot any chosen member and most of the DC. This didn't earn me many friends, though.

Will you at least think about it? my minder asked.

Can't think now, got a gate point coming up, I said and pushed the conversation to the back of my mind.

Sounds about right, my minder grumbled.

But as with everything my minder said, it sat in the back of my mind and slowly gnawed at me. It wasn't until I was back in my quarters that the dam finally burst.

"Retired...I mean, what the hell would I do? Get an RV and take up fishing? I'd rather slit my own throat," I said in disgust.

I'm sure there are plenty of non-fish-related hobbies you could pick up. What about your music? the minder asked.

Back in my home Bio Hab, I'd been a musician. A rather popular musician, if I'm being honest. I'd sold tons of albums and gone on multiple tours, and it had all been fun. A lot of work, but still fun.

Until the zombies showed up and destroyed everything.

When I'd first been "rescued" by Behemoth and recruited into the Chosen Army, all I'd cared about was being a better soldier. Music had been the furthest thing from my mind. My life had been easy, free of distractions. My mission to protect Behemoth kept me going.

Then...they showed up and turned everything upside down. How a handful of lunches with Shae had twisted me up was still beyond me. All I knew was that after they'd been lost, my creative block had cleared.

An idea for a song would creep into my head every now and again. I'd jot it down and start trying to work on it, but it always managed to elude me in the end. I'd get frustrated and toss my PDD across the room. Then, a few months would go by, and another idea would pop into my head.

If you were retired, you could focus on your music without being interrupted by your duty, the minder offered.

I picked up the PDD in question and thumbed through it. There were dozens and dozens of entries. As I skimmed the subject of each one, nothing sparked my interest.

"Give it a rest," I said, and tossed the PDD back on the desk with my other work. I then went to take a shower.

Thankfully, my minder laid off and let me shower in peace.

Ever since I came to this unit, I'd been stuck in Groundhog Day. I'd wake up, study, patrol, workout, shower, and sleep. Repeat. The routine was simple, but it ended up giving me way too much time to think.

I checked my schedule. Thankfully, it wasn't one of my feeding days, so I lay down and started skimming manuals.

I'd read everything there was to read by now. It didn't stop me from reading them again. By this point, I knew each of these manuals backwards, forwards, and sideways. My eyes robotically began scanning the page without me actually taking in any of the information.

The next page was an illustration of a couple caught in a compromising situation, but they didn't seem to mind the attention.

Seriously? I said to my minder. It sometimes did this, messing with my manuals to test me.

Just checking to make sure you were at least looking at the screen and not mindlessly flipping through the pages, my minder said.

I sighed and thumped the PDD that was still displaying the pornographic image. The image disappeared and was replaced with a schematic of an AUG's leg.

But my minder was right, I was stuck in a rut.

Maybe I should request a transfer? I offered.

To what? my minder asked.

I don't know, anything that's not AUG related, I said.

Back to the schoolhouse? he said.

That's AUG related, I said.

Then what? he asked.

I don't know, I started. *Construction? Clerical? Ambassador?*

My minder didn't outright laugh at my suggestions, but I could sense he was barely holding his mirth back.

What? I finally said.

I'm just trying to picture you as an Ambassador, he said.

Not so much, huh? I said.

*I mean, it's more entertaining than a clerk. I doubt you'd

last 10 minutes as a clerk. As an Ambassador, I'd say you could at least make it through the first day,* the minder said.

A day, huh? I said.

You'd be arrested at the beginning of the second day for trying to strangle someone for sure, my minder chuckled.

Right, I sighed.

It's better than you being a clerk. You'd have shot someone the first day, he said.

Oh really? I asked, feeling a little better. *And construction?*

Oh, that you'd be great at. But where's the fun in that? he said.

Goodnight, I said and flicked off the lights.

Night, he said quietly.

But it took a long time for me to get to sleep that night. My brain wouldn't turn off once I'd started thinking about other jobs. One thing after another popped into my head even as I scolded myself that no one was allowed to retire here.

It wasn't done.

Chapter 3

JAMES

"Why is it so fucking hot?" Viola asked, tugging at her sweat-drenched top that kept sticking to her.

"Watch your language," I said, glancing at her just in time to catch her eye roll.

"Dad, I'm 18 years old."

"And?" I retorted.

"I'm a bit old to be worrying about 'potty' words," Viola said.

"I think I liked it better when you didn't talk," I said with a smirk.

Viola's reply was to roll her eyes at me again and shake her brilliant red hair. As she grew, Viola never lost the fiery red hair, nor the freckles that covered nearly every part of her. They just seemed to multiply under the Texas sun.

"Trust me, once you get comfortable, it's impossible to break the habit. Just ask your Auntie Rhi," I said.

"She's not my Aunt, Dad," Viola said.

"Well, I'm not your father either, so..." I countered.

The first few days after Viola showed up at the Alamo were awkward. I'd never babysat before, and then I was a full-time father. Rhi had suggested possibly placing Viola with one of the other families in the compound, but something wouldn't let me do it.

Instead, Viola and I spent a lot of time hanging out with those same families. While Viola was playing during these "play dates," I was frantically trying to learn everything I could about being a parent.

Before I knew it, I had a young adult on my hands instead of a child. It was as if time had gone fast-forward, and there was nothing I could do about it.

Rhi was with me at every turn. Sometimes, it felt like she was watching me as much as she was watching Viola. Even after six years, Rhi still watched Viola as if waiting for her to pop open like some Trojan horse. Despite this, Viola and Rhi had developed a good relationship. It had taken some time, but it eventually happened.

Viola would seek Rhi out anytime she had a problem she didn't want to talk to me about. This usually concerned "girl stuff" or Viola's string of teenage relationships. The fact that Rhi was the one keeping Viola out of trouble on that front amused me to no end.

Throughout this whole time, though, Viola had remained tight-lipped about anything before the day she arrived at the Alamo. Anytime someone brought it up, Viola simply refused to talk about it. After a while, I stopped asking.

"Oh, don't start on that again," Viola said in exasperation. "But really, what's with the heat?"

We were halfway up "the hill" now, and the Texas sun was high in the sky. The cinderblock walls to either side of us had quickly turned into an easy-bake oven.

It had taken us over a year to complete "the hill," but when it was finally done, we had a safety corridor between the Alamo and the local mall. For the past four years, residents of the Alamo have been able to safely walk from the compound all the way to the mall.

It had taken several months to clear out and brick up all the entrances. The building maintenance was a pain, but the mall now served as a huge multi-purpose building. We used it as a school, housing, training facility, storage area, and all-around go-to building. With the increase in population, the Alamo was getting too small and needed to expand. The mall had been the perfect vessel once we got to it. Plus, you had to have a mall in every zombie apocalypse; it was the rules.

"Are you out of breath?" I asked, looking at Viola's flushed face.

"Shut up. Just because you don't have to breathe doesn't mean—" Viola started.

"Alright, alright." I surrendered. I walked a few more yards, listening to her labored breathing. "I'm just saying you might want to get a bit more exercise, that's all."

Viola's look shot daggers at me, and I promptly shut up.

We crested the hill a while later and stopped to look down on the mall complex.

"I still can't believe we've held onto this place for so long," I said, looking at the sprawling complex.

"Well, you did fortify it like a god-dam—"

My scowl caused Viola to pause.

"Like a gosh-darned military bunker," Viola finished with a smirk.

I tried to hide my smile but failed.

Viola punched me in the arm. "Shut it."

Twenty minutes later, we were inside, finally out of the sun. Large fans had been set up to help circulate air, but it was still stuffy inside the two-story mall.

"Still wish we could run the AC," Viola said.

"It draws too much power. Even with the solar cells up top and the backup from the thermal tap, we couldn't maintain it for more than an hour or so," I said.

"I know, Dad," Viola said with the typical sigh of the exasperated teenager that I'd come to recognize. "They taught us all about it in school."

We threaded our way through various partitions and eventually came to the storefront we were looking for.

"You know I don't need this, right?" Viola practically stamped her foot.

"School is school," I said.

"But I already know everything they're teaching," Viola said.

"Bookwork is only part of school. There are still other things you need to learn," I said.

"True, there's biology," she gave me a knowing grin.

"Stay away from Jimmy Hanson," I frowned.

"But he's my...biology partner," she dug at me.

I knew nothing had happened between the two. Rhi's "chat" with the boy had made sure of it. But Viola knew what pushed my buttons and took every chance she got to be a teenager.

"You know, if I didn't have to go to school, I could avoid all these bad influences," Viola suggested.

"Really? And who was influencing who when Rhi found you and Suzy Chan at the bottom of the Grotto, huh?" I shot back.

"Suzy Chan, Dad? She doesn't count!" Viola said with a wave of her hand.

"Oh? And why is that?" I asked.

"Because Rhi stopped us before anything happened," Viola mumbled.

"Sorry, I didn't quite catch that?" I cupped an ear towards her.

"But...I...just..." Viola knew she couldn't win this argument; she never did. She accepted defeat with an overdramatic teenage sigh and entered the school room.

"See you after," I said.

Viola didn't look at me; she just waved at me over her shoulder in a "whatever" motion.

"Still fighting school?" The voice came from behind me.

"Yeah." I sighed and reluctantly turned to face Rhi.

"We all did at that age," Rhi nodded. "Why don't you tell her about your five-year plan for high school?"

"Oh, shut up." I shook my head.

"Who knows, maybe she'll meet someone who just got dumped, sitting across from her at lunch and grab them before somebody else does," Rhi said.

"Hey, just because—" was as far as I got before I completely lost my train of thought.

"James?" Rhi asked, concern on her face, as I just stood there pointing at her. "You alright?"

I shook my head and said, "Hey, you're supposed to help me keep that from happening!" I glared at her.

"I never agreed to that," Rhi said with a frown on her face.

"But—"

"I just said I'd help keep her out of trouble," Rhi said as she sighed.

"Exactly," I said.

"So, I taught her how to be careful and not get caught," Rhi said.

"Not get caught? Even from you?" I asked.

"No one can pull one over on me. I know everything that goes on here," Rhi shrugged.

"Everything?" I asked.

"I know she dated Suzy Chan for four more months after I caught them. I also know she lost her virginity—"

"Nope! I don't want to know," I said, turning away from her and covering my ears.

"Really?" Rhi grinned evilly. "You don't know that she slept—"

"Not listening," I said as I fled, my face hot.

This was Viola's final year of school. The father inside me hoped that when Viola "graduated," everything would settle down.

Yeah right.

∞∞∞∞∞∞Ω∞∞∞∞∞∞

<u>JAMES</u>

The Alamo and adjoining mall complex had taken on a life of its own. With Rhi and me being the only vampires still living on site, we'd stepped back and let the rest of the populace take things over. The humans had formed their own council to oversee everything, and aside from the occasional squabble, got along rather well.

I'd been rather impressed with how well they were doing. From all the zombie apocalypse fiction I'd read or watched, people tended to turn on each other at the first chance they got. I was happy to see the fiction remained just that, fiction. It would have restored my faith in humanity had I ever lost it.

Rhi and I were now just ordinary citizens, for the most part. Her reputation remained as she tended to keep up the hard-nosed enforcer act around the general populace. Anytime there was a serious threat to the Alamo, we helped to ensure the place stayed safe. Had we not been there, a lot of people would have died. In appreciation, there were still a few who volunteered to provide us with blood. With how many people there were now, someone rarely had to donate blood more than once every six months or so.

I wiped my forehead for the millionth time today as I approached the mall entrance. It amazed me that I still sweated, despite being a vampire. None of the movies had prepared me for sweaty vampires. On screen, they all looked cool and dry. Maybe that's why all the movie vampires lived somewhere other than Texas.

Rhi told me I sweat so much because I kept my blood level "topped off" all the time. If I lowered my intake, some of those more pesky 'human' characteristics would go away. The problem was that I liked being human, just not the sweating part.

When I rounded the corner into the mall's food court, my mind was still lost in sweat-soaked ideas. It was Halloween, and the older kids were planning activities for the younger ones who'd never actually had a pre-Z Day holiday.

Since Z Day, there has been a not-so-surprising increase in the number of younger children. The safety of the Alamo had allowed enterprising couples the opportunity to start repopulating the Bio Hab, and they were going at it like rabbits. Thankfully, we had qualified medical personnel on-site.

"Hey, Dad, check me out!"

I looked up to see Viola standing between two people with her arms stretched towards the ceiling. The two had paintbrushes and were finishing up painting Viola's body a deep red. While the skimpy outfit she wore managed to hide the more private areas that no father wants to see on his daughter, it managed to make the getup seem worse than if Viola were naked. In addition, she wore some sort of makeshift tail and a headband with two small black horns on it that sat atop a wig of jet-black hair.

"So, what do you think? Is it devilishly good enough to win the costume contest tonight?" Viola asked, turning to face me, revealing all red eyes with black irises/pupils.

I didn't even feel it when my knees hit the tiled floor. My head seemed to crackle and pop like it had been filled with Pop-Rocks.

"Dad?" Viola left her painting duo behind and hurried over. She knelt beside me and placed her hands on either side of my head. She stared deep into my eyes as her own seemed to go blank.

"Well, it's about fucking time," Viola said as she sighed with relief. She kissed my forehead and stood up. "Dad, it's time to wake up."

"What the?" Rhi gasped, appearing from thin air beside us. "Where am I? What's going on?" she asked as she looked around.

"Relax, he's done," Viola soothed.

"What do you mean he's done? I was just in my room and—" Rhi started, still looking around in confusion.

"His brain finally repaired itself," Viola said in a casual tone.

"His...brain?" Rhi turned and looked at me before looking at Viola. "What do you mean, and why are you dressed like...like that..." Rhi's already unsteady self struggled with what she saw.

"It took a lot longer than I thought it would." Viola stretched and delicately scratched her nose, trying not to smudge the red paint. "It should have only taken a few months, a year at the outside. But you know, Dad, he's got to be difficult in all things." Viola finally turned to face Rhi.

"I'm sorry," she said, indicating her costume. "I know it's in bad taste, but I was getting desperate at this point. It seems dressing up as Tara was the final thing that helped trigger his memory."

"But..." Rhi's face was still a mask of confusion.

"Rhi?" My voice came out softly. I felt that if I spoke too loudly, my head might come apart.

"Yeah?" Rhi knelt beside me, Viola forgotten.

"My head...it doesn't hurt anymore." The constant headache

I'd had for the past several years was gone. I'd had it for so long I'd gotten used to it. "I remember."

"What do you remember?" Rhi asked excitedly.

"Tara died at that volcano...I remember her. How'd I forget something like that?" It was weird. Things I'd forgotten were suddenly coming back. It started small, with one image or one word. But that would trigger another and then another. It was a chain that seemed to be pulling one memory after another back into my head from somewhere else.

I was so distracted with this feeling growing inside me that I almost hadn't noticed Rhi shudder when I spoke Tara's name.

Biting her lip, Rhi's voice was unsteady, "Tara was killed at a volcano, yes."

"And Shae..." Countless moments with Shea flooded my head as I spoke her name. My skin started to prickle as I looked up into Rhi's face. "Shae's dead too, isn't she?" My voice was a whisper.

Rhi placed her hand gently on my face, her touch causing my prickling skin to practically spark. "Yes, she died when the Bio Hab burned, James."

Multiple emotions shot through me, causing an uncomfortable warmth to begin filling me. "Wait, my family, my friends...if the Bio Hab burned..." I looked at my surroundings in confusion.

I had somehow forgotten my sister, her husband, and my friends who'd been living at the Alamo. No, that's not right. I remembered they were dead, but it was like it had happened to someone else.

"All this, Dad," Viola cut in, "is an illusion." She snapped her fingers, and the world froze, save for the three of us.

"An illusion?" I looked around at the now-frozen people.

"Yeah," Rhi said softly, turning away from staring at Viola in shock. "After your...after our Bio Hab burned, you weren't right in the head." Rhi caressed my cheek.

"I went to the AG, and they built this safe place for us while you healed," Rhi said. "We're still on Behemoth, just hidden away from the DC."

"And you sure took your time doing it!" Viola scolded me.

"But, my family...my friends. They're all gone?" A fresh wave of pain washed hot through me.

"Nothing can survive a Bio Hab being recycled," Viola said. "Nothing. I'm sorry, Dad."

I nodded, realizing I was slowly rocking back and forth. "Some part of me already knew that. It was as if I was in mourning all this time, but couldn't figure out why."

Rhi wrapped her arms around me and buried her tear-streaked face in my shoulder.

"Why are you crying?" I asked her.

"Shut up," was all Rhi said.

"What is going on around here?" A grease-stained woman in overalls rounded the corner, a lit cigarette hanging from her lips.

"Good, glad you're here, Hess. It saves me the time of tracking you down," Viola said.

"Fine, but what is going on? One minute, I'm checking the thermal tap tie-ins downstairs; the next, everything froze!" the woman known only as Hess said.

I'd seen the woman in passing. She was an engineer who worked on the thermal plant at the Alamo, but I didn't know her beyond that.

"Don't worry about it right now. We've got more important things to deal with." Viola turned to Rhi and me. "Dad, we gotta get going."

It took me a minute to pull myself together. "To where?" I asked in a ragged voice. I felt exhausted all of a sudden. I rubbed my face and ran my hand down the short beard I'd grown over the past few weeks.

Viola snapped her fingers again, and the world dissolved around us, revealing a massive, empty metal room. One wall had a large window and a single door that led into what appeared to be a control room of some sort. A strangely familiar Daemon stood staring at us with her mouth agape.

"Let's move in there for now," Viola pointed at the door. "I've been in this room too damned long."

"Language," I said out of habit.

"American, Dad," Viola retorted the same way she always did when I got onto her.

We left the empty room and slowly made our way to the room containing the lone Daemon.

"What's going on?" Cr'eon demanded as our group filed in.

Viola said something to Cr'eon in a language I didn't understand.

After a moment of what appeared to be shock, Cr'eon prostrated herself on the floor before Viola.

Rolling her eyes, Viola continued in the strange language and shooed Cr'eon to her feet.

"What was all that about?" Rhi asked.

"They all get starstruck the first time," Viola sighed.

The fog in my head seemed to clear as I approached Viola. Placing my hands on her shoulders, I gently asked, "Who are you...really?" I stressed the last word.

Viola stared at me as she took her time replying.

"I'm your daughter." Viola then smiled at Rhi, "And I'm your daughter."

"Our daughter?" Rhi cocked her head.

"I'm actually the daughter of all four of you," Viola said.

"How can that be?" I asked, drawing her eyes back to mine.

"This," Viola stepped back and indicated herself. "This is...think of it as a modified Blank. It was created using DNA samples from all four of you."

"A Blank?" I asked, confused.

"Remember that thing they sent us after Tara di...after...Tara?" Rhi stuttered. "They sent us that android thing as a 'replacement.' It said it had been programmed to be compatible with all our personalities."

"Yeah...Lou. I remember you nearly took his head off several times," I said, not taking my eyes off the girl I'd been raising for the last six years.

"It should have minded its own business and stayed out of my head," Rhi growled.

"I'm not a blank, not by a long shot. It would be like comparing a toaster to a starship," Viola offered.

"Wait," I took Viola's hands in mine. "I've watched you physically grow up."

Viola nodded. "I have a limited ability to change the physical attributes of this body."

"You're a shapeshifter?" Rhi asked.

"Not really. I can only make so many changes before a new body must be created to represent my next stage in development." Viola smiled. "I just transfer to the new unit as needed."

"So, you are a robot?" I questioned her.

"Wait, if you're a robot, why'd I have to teach you about pads?" Rhi complained.

Viola chuckled, "Not a robot...and not an android before you ask. You don't really have a word for what I am. For all intents and purposes, I'm a living, breathing being."

"What happens to your old body?" Rhi asked. "You know, when you 'outgrow' it."

"It is recycled into parts for other units," Viola offered.

"What if—"

"Listen," Viola said, cutting me off with a gentle hand on my cheek. "We can 'what if' all day long, and there will be plenty of time for those types of questions later. Right now, you have more important things to be concerned with."

"Like what?" Rhi asked.

"Like getting mom back," Viola said.

Chapter 4

JAMES

Several moments passed, allowing for Viola's bombshell to settle.

I finally broke the silence. "What do you mean, get your mom back?"

"How does Behemoth—that's not its real name, by the way," Viola started.

"What's its real name?" Rhi asked.

"You couldn't pronounce it. Anyway, how does Behemoth create new DC?" Viola asked.

"It doesn't," Rhi provided. "It uses clones of its current DC. When the primary dies, a new one is cloned and brought up."

"Sort of," Viola said. "Each DC's memory is continuously monitored and backed up in the core system. This way, when a new clone is made, it doesn't have to be taught everything from scratch. Behemoth just downloads the most recent mind copy into the new clone."

"Wait," I started. "If it's so easy, why doesn't Behemoth just create armies of DC instead of using us?"

"Yeah...here's the thing," Viola said. "Only one of those mind backups can exist at a time. For whatever reason, if two clones are created using the same mind backup, even from two different time periods, both clones end up going nuts."

"Nuts?" Rhi asked.

"Well, it ranges from going comatose to psychotic, uncontrollable rage. It's never in the middle. It's either one extreme or the other," Viola explained.

"Why doesn't Behemoth just create new personalities or something?" Rhi asked.

"I'm sure by now, you've seen that Behemoth isn't creative," Viola said. "I know that's a gross oversimplification, but it's true. Behemoth's creators purposely limited its 'imagination' as it were."

"Wait, Behemoth was created as a troop-building station for a war," I said. "It had to have the ability to come up with new things in order to create a variety of troops. I mean, look at all the different types of Bio Habs."

"Segregated subsystems." Viola shook her head. "I know it doesn't make sense, but hear me out. The best I can figure, Behemoth's creators tried to put some sort of limiting governor on Behemoth to keep it in check...to keep it from turning on its creators and such."

"Then just have one of the creative subsystems manage it," Rhi offered.

"Can't," Viola said. "The subsystem administrators are so compartmentalized that it doesn't allow for it. I know it doesn't make sense, but you must remember: Behemoth isn't just some computer. It's an ageless entity that controls essentially a small galaxy."

"A galaxy?" Rhi scoffed. "Everything we've been shown only shows a hundred-plus Bio Habs."

"Say that again," Viola said.

"Everything we've been shown—" Viola's look cut Rhi off.

"Exactly, everything you're been shown," Viola said. "The size Behemoth has become is...incomprehensible. It's just too big. I mean, Behemoth had to design a faster-than-light system in order to simply function. Otherwise, something would happen on one end of it, and the 'brain' wouldn't find out for a millennium or two."

"But, how can something that big be created? I mean, the raw material requirements alone are unimaginable," I said. "That's always been something that bugged me about the size of this place."

"True," Viola agreed. "Behemoth is a living entity, but every living organism has limits. To make that kind of mass, you still need energy to create it. It's all proportional," Viola trailed off into that strange language she'd used before when talking to Cr'eon. It seemed she was still trying to explain things, but didn't have the words in our language to do it. Soon, she realized we were staring at her blankly, and she stopped.

"Sorry. Went off on a bit of a tangent there," Viola said. "Also, understand the things I'm explaining to you...don't take offense to this, but it's like trying to teach particle physics to a garden slug. I'm actually lying to you about some things just so you can get a basic understanding of what's going on. Again, I'm not trying to insult you."

"What has all this got to do with Tara and Shae?" I asked, ignoring Viola's ramblings. "Everyone knows only Behemoths' DC are cloned, and I'm pretty sure Tara wasn't included in that lot," I said.

"Yes," Viola hesitated. "That's the rub. Behemoth only 'backs up' its DC...and...any of its special interest projects."

"Special interest projects?" Rhi asked. "What's that mean?"

"It means," Viola started. "I found evidence that you, James, are one of Behemoth's projects."

"Wait, are you saying Behemoth created me?" I asked. "I mean, I know Behemoth took a special interest in me because I was this 'chaos engine' or whatever. But created me?" I asked.

"No, no, no." Viola shook her head. "Behemoth didn't create you, James. It's taken an interest in you because everything you touch changes."

"So? Everyone does that. The whole butterfly effect and all that," I said.

"Look at it this way," Viola said patiently. "A computer is programmed to count from 1 to 100. That's it; that's all it does—day in, day out, counting from 1 to 100. It's done this countless times over hundreds of years without fail and without error. It's 100% reliable.

"Then you come alone and sneeze on it," Viola continued.

"The next time, instead of counting from 1 to 100, it makes a soufflé instead. It doesn't know how to do that; it doesn't even have the materials. But somehow, someway, at the end of the day, there's a soufflé sitting on the console. The only thing different is your sneeze. You do this to almost everything you come in contact with."

"Everything I come in contact with?" I asked.

"Well, that's a bit of an exaggeration. From what I've been able to learn, it's basically anyone you've exchanged bodily fluids with since you became a full vampire," Viola said.

"Bodily fluids?" Rhi snorted.

"You're saying everyone I've ever—" I started.

"Kissed, sucked, fucked, spat on, bled on, pissed on—" Viola rattled off.

"I get it!" I said, holding up my hands to cut off Viola's rambling list.

"Don't forget your Fleshlight. It's probably trying to figure out how to plant a cabbage patch right now," Rhi couldn't help herself.

"Nice." I frowned at Rhi before turning back to Viola. "But, to what end?"

"Hmmm, let me think," Viola said, tapping her chin. "A computer that has no imagination suddenly has a random chaos machine at its disposal. Simple to use, just point and shoot, and suddenly, a new variant is introduced. I can't imagine why Behemoth would be interested in that," Viola's teenage sarcasm was dripping from her voice.

"Alright, smart ass—" I started.

"Better than being a dumbass, Dad," Viola shot back.

"Touché. I did teach you that one," I muttered. "But..."

"The AG tried to replicate your 'ability' for nearly ten years to no avail. They tried using DNA from all four of you, but they still couldn't replicate it," Viola said.

"Why would the AG want it?" Rhi asked.

"The AG want anything that Behemoth wants, if for nothing else, to figure out how to deny it to Behemoth. It's the main reason they've gone through all the trouble of this setup," Viola said, motioning to the room around us. "While the AG doesn't have access to cloning facilities, Behemoth does. We all know Behemoth doesn't throw away anything if it can help it."

"Behemoth cloned Tara and Shae?" Rhi had sobered up and become serious now.

"From what I understand, Behemoth cloned all four of you," Viola said.

"All four...but if that's true, why didn't Behemoth bring Tara back when she died?" I glanced at Rhi, who suddenly became still.

"That, I don't know." Viola frowned. "Speculating on Behemoth's reasoning is like playing darts in the dark, on a merry-go-round...in space."

"I get it." I held my hand up. Viola tended to ramble. A habit I couldn't imagine where she'd gotten it from. "So, where is this cloning facility?"

"It's in the most heavily guarded and secret part of Behemoth," Viola said simply.

"And where's that?" Rhi asked.

"I haven't the foggiest," Viola said.

Rhi and I both looked at her in stunned silence, our faces rising in agitation.

"But I know who works there," Viola smiled.

$$\infty\infty\infty\infty\infty\Omega\infty\infty\infty\infty\infty$$

JAMES

"So, where are you from?" I asked Viola as we moved through yet another empty hallway. I noticed the dust on every surface and wondered the last time someone had been in here. So far, every room and hall we'd come through had looked long abandoned.

"I was...uh, created by the AG," Viola said, her voice straining as she opened some sort of pressure door.

"Created? So, you're an AI?" Rhi said.

Viola smiled. "Calling me an AI is like calling you a walking stew. The AG needed something to replace Behemoth. I was it."

"Wait, I remember this story," I said. "One of the first AG we met mentioned it. But you lost the fight."

"Brilliant deduction, Dad." Viola rolled her eyes. "Yes, that coup failed miserably. About the only thing I managed to do was remove Behemoth's ability to easily recycle Bio Habs. It must work for it now."

Viola had us on the move and kept us moving nonstop. She said we needed to keep moving, but didn't say where. Apparently, she needed to get somewhere but wouldn't tell us more than that.

In addition, Viola said that now that she was becoming an active participant in this little quest of ours, Behemoth might take notice. As such, we needed to stay off the radar, hence us now using the empty 'backrooms' and corridors that Behemoth didn't actively monitor.

"Why does Behemoth really recycle Bio Habs anyway?" Rhi asked.

"Behemoth is insane if you hadn't noticed," Viola said, then glanced at Rhi. "You know, you've met him."

I glanced at Rhi, who just shook her head and waved me off.

"Anytime Behemoth perceives a Bio Hab in rebellion or infested with AG, it recycles it and starts over," Viola said.

"But doesn't that go against its primary purpose?" I asked.

"What, troop creation?" Viola asked. "Nope. Behemoth considers the Bio Hab as contaminated stock and a failure."

Viola stopped in front of a large pressure door.

"Watch your eyes when I open this one," Viola said as she entered several commands on a console and then opened the door, allowing a blinding light to stream into the darkened corridor.

After a few moments, my eyes adjusted, and I saw rolling prairie as far as the eye could see.

"Don't worry, we'll hit a town or something and pick up some transport there," Viola said, stepping into the sunshine.

"Where are we going anyway?" Hess said from behind us. She'd hardly said a word since we'd left the simulation room.

Viola sighed heavily. "Talus Junction, now will y'all stop asking?" Viola said, closing the door behind us once we were all inside. The door vanished without a trace into an outcrop of rock. Now, it looked as if we were all standing in the middle of nowhere.

"Talus?" Hess said. "That's only a few transport slides away."

"True, and if we had access to the primary grid, we could use the slides. But we don't, so we make do." Viola headed off, and we followed behind.

Rhi, Viola, Hess, Cr'eon, and I had set off from the control room several hours ago. Viola had warned us that to stay "off the radar," we'd be travelling through several non-humanoid sectors. This meant we'd probably be seeing some things that were going to be disturbing, but she wouldn't elaborate further.

"Why my daughter?" I asked an hour or so later.

We were still walking across the prairie. The sun was warm, but not burning. The grass we trooped through was about 20 centimeters high and the brightest green. Every now and again, the wind would shift the grass, and it would shimmer an almost iridescent color. We hadn't seen any animals, people, or vehicles. There was nothing here to show that this place was inhabited at all.

"Hmm?" Viola said.

"When you showed up, why pose as my daughter?" I asked.

Viola glanced back at me, "Truth?"

I nodded.

"Because I knew it would work," Viola said simply. "I mean, no one is going to turn a 12-year-old out into a zombie-infested Bio Hab. As long as I could keep Rhi from killing me, I knew you'd take me in." Viola shrugged.

"I could have placed you with one of the families," I said.

"Yeah, but you didn't," Viola said. "You've got that protective streak because you're a good person. Plus, you needed something to bring you out of that funk you were in." Viola glanced at me to see my reaction.

"That was true," Rhi admitted.

"It let me get close to you so I could monitor your health and try a variety of things to make you better. I honestly didn't expect to be in there as long as I was." Viola sighed.

Viola's sigh sounded just like Shae's.

"What's your story, Hess?" Rhi asked.

"Me?" Hess's voice was deeper than expected, with a touch of an accent I couldn't place. "Not a lot to tell, really. Viola brought me in a while back to help keep an eye on things."

"Viola brought you in?" Rhi asked. "When did you come into the simulation? Cr'eon never mentioned anything about someone else entering," Rhi said as she turned and glared at Cr'eon.

"Hey, don't look at me. I didn't know about it either!" Cr'eon said in her defense.

I was surprised when Viola insisted on bringing Cr'eon with us instead of sending her back to the AG. When I asked why, Viola said it was necessary and left it at that.

"Cr'eon didn't know," Viola said. "I brought Hess in the same way I came in and kept her hidden."

"But why?" Rhi asked.

"Just in case I needed help," Viola said. "She's good at a lot of things."

"This is true," Hess said, taking a long pull from the cigarette in her mouth. Hess had the same cigarette since leaving the simulation. It acted like it was lit, but never seemed to burn down. Or emit smoke, for that matter.

We walked for several more hours, but the sun never seemed to move.

"Ah, new plan. Let's go this way," Viola said as she stopped and stared at nothing. A moment later, she took a step up, then another.

"Uh," I started as I watched Viola climb some sort of invisible staircase. When I got to the spot she'd started up, I felt around but didn't find anything.

"Just put your foot out like you were going to take a step up," Viola said.

I tentatively raised my foot, and as I lowered it, something kept it from touching the ground. I looked, and my foot was about five centimeters off the ground. I moved my foot around a bit, trying to judge the size of the step, but with every movement, the "stair" seemed to move with my foot.

"Don't think about it. Just look at me and climb," Viola said from four meters in the air.

I shifted my weight onto the foot in midair and found it solid. I raised my other foot, and it found another step higher in the air. When I took another step, I discovered they weren't standardized. It seemed that whatever height I stepped up to, I found purchase.

I looked down and found myself five meters in the air. Looking down caused me to lose my balance, and when I reached out, my hand found some sort of handrail.

"Don't look down," Viola said, now thirty meters in the air.

"Now she tells me," I mumbled.

"Just keep your eyes on my ass and climb," Viola said without looking back.

I frowned. "Not really appropriate, Viola," I said.

"Well, it's either that or you're going to trip," Viola said. She hadn't stopped climbing this entire time.

With my hand firmly on the invisible handrail and my eyes glued to Viola's...waist, I started to climb. As long as I kept looking up, the climb was relatively easy.

I was doing fine until Hess climbed past me. The invisible stairs she climbed weren't the same as mine. They went off at a different angle and height than mine.

"This is so trippy," Rhi said as she also climbed past me, her face almost giddy as she appeared to be enjoying the climb.

"Don't think about it. Just climb towards where you want to go. The stairs will do the rest," Viola said.

I watched as both Rhi and Hess seemed to swirl around in the air as they caught up to Viola. I tried, I really did, but I couldn't get my mind off the fact we were now uncomfortably high in the air.

I did manage to figure out how to "steer" the stairs in the general direction I wanted to go, but if I thought about it too hard, the stairs wouldn't turn.

"Almost there," Viola called down to me.

The trio had stopped and were standing together a few meters above me. When I finally arrived next to them, I was drenched in sweat. It wasn't the climb that got me, but the small fear of heights I had.

"You're not going to have a heart attack on me, are you, old man?" Viola grinned.

"Old man? Aren't you supposed to be like a million years old or something?" I asked.

Viola motioned to herself, "Do I look a million years old to you?"

"Good genes." Rhi nodded.

"Come on." Viola rolled her eyes again before taking a step and disappearing.

The others vanished in front of me one by one. When it was my turn, I tried not to look at the countryside far below and took a step.

The world disappeared, being replaced by a blessedly solid corridor. The others waited for me a few meters down the hall.

Rhi patted me on the shoulder as we moved forward, coming to another door. Several other corridors wandered off in different directions, but we ignored those.

"How is this so easy for you?" I asked Rhi.

"It's not," Rhi said, smiling at me.

Without a word, Viola opened the door.

The town beyond sat beneath a star-filled sky. The weather was chilly, causing me to shiver involuntarily. The buildings around us seemed modern, with several stories, but were made to look old. Vehicles I'd never seen before transported what looked like box fans to and fro. More box fans seemed to float in and out of the buildings. A pair of them passed us, humming softly as they went.

"I'm going to fall asleep if we stay here too long," Rhi said.

"Are the people here box fans?" I asked, staring rudely at the closest ones.

I didn't see eyes, ears, limbs, or anything. There were different types of fans; some were singular with large blades, and some were twin with small blades. The longer I looked, the more variations I saw. I even saw a large box fan being followed by several smaller fans about the size of computer fans.

"Yeah," Viola said as if it were the most normal thing in the world. "This way."

I tried to keep up, but every corner we turned brought something new. My brain swam as I tried to figure out how a society of box fans would work. Every time I saw something I didn't understand, I'd stop until I could figure out how it fit.

Viola eventually got tired of stopping for me, took my hand, and dragged me forward.

We finally stopped in front of a large metal shutter that Viola banged on with her fist.

A moment later, the shutter rolled up, revealing a large mesh screen with a massive three-meter box fan beyond. Its blades lazily turned, hypnotizing me. A sharp pain in my ribs from Viola got my attention.

"Stop staring, it's rude," Viola hissed.

I tried looking anywhere except the fan, but it kept drawing me back to it.

Viola sighed, then caught herself. "No, I'm sorry, I wasn't talking to you," she said to the fan. She then proceeded to make several hand gestures and exhaled in a variety of ways.

The large fan didn't seem to move, but I did feel gentle gusts of wind come from it as it appeared to be having a conversation with Viola.

"OK." Viola turned to us, "Follow me," she said before stepping forward into the mesh screen and disappearing.

I blindly followed as my brain was starting to overload again.

I reappeared in a small room that appeared to be made of soft yellow plastic. The floor and walls were pliable, squishing as I touched them. It took me a moment to realize it was one of Behemoth's transport slides.

Two doors parted, sliding to the side as a third dropped into the floor before us. Beyond was a type of corridor I recognized. This was a Bio Hab halo.

We exited the lift and approached the massive window. The corridor curved to either side of us for as far as the eye could see. The outer wall was metal, but the inner wall was a four-story window. This windowed corridor ran completely around a Bio Hab, hence the term "Halo." If you had enough time, you could literally walk all the way around a Bio Hab without taking your eyes off it.

The Bio Hab within appeared frozen in the act of exploding. Massive chunks of the Bio Hab were already ripped away, revealing a glowing core that pulsed in blinding flashes. A partially built artificial ring surrounded the Bio Hab. One of the larger chunks of the Bio Hab had struck and shattered the ring.

"What the hell?" Rhi whispered.

"You got me on this one," Viola said. "Last I knew, this was a perfectly fine Bio Hab."

"There are still people in there," I said, pointing at what appeared to be several spacecraft frozen in flight around the Bio Hab.

"No living fire," Hess said matter-of-factly. "It's not being recycled."

"No, something else is going on here." Viola frowned.

"Looks like it's a local phenomenon," Cr'eon said.

Everyone turned to look at her.

"I mean, it's not something Behemoth does," Cr'eon said.

"How is it frozen like that?" Rhi asked.

The longer we watched, the deeper Viola's frown got.

"We need to go...now!" Viola said as she moved off.

We reluctantly followed. Even Hess was slow to leave the sight of the doomed Bio Hab.

Once Viola got us out of sight of the catastrophe, we picked up the pace. Viola led us through a true maze of corridors, access shafts and empty rooms. Even with my acute sense of direction, I was lost in five minutes. We didn't stop or even slow down as we continued forward.

I stifled a yawn and glanced at my watch. To my surprise, we'd been on the move for 30 hours now. I glanced at Rhi, who was also showing signs of fatigue. I shook myself in an attempt to snap out of it and became aware of our surroundings.

We were in what I could only describe as a giant ribbed tube. The ceiling was at least 20 meters high, and I could just barely step over each rib with one stride.

"Viola, my dogs are neighing," I finally said as I curled my toes in an attempt to relieve my aching feet.

"Neighing?" Viola gave me a quizzical look.

"Yeah, cause they've been barking so long they went horse," I said, giving her a tired grin.

"You're an idiot," Viola said, rolling her eyes. "Besides, we're almost there, then you can rest." Viola didn't look back as she was studying the wall to our right. Ten minutes later, she was pushing another part of the wall open, and we followed her inside, not realizing the floor had become a ramp downward.

The next thing I knew, we were sliding down this pink ramp covered with 10-centimeter nubs. The nubs seemed to grab onto us and push us faster down the ramp until it felt like I was in a bobsled chute from the Olympics.

We were unceremoniously dumped into a small room that appeared to be an office. A figure at a desk sat in a chair with its back to us. It opened the bottom drawer of the desk and, without a word or a glance at us, stood and left the room.

Viola was on her feet and across the room in a flash. She glanced into the open drawer of the desk and then looked at us.

"Everybody inside," Viola ordered.

Hess and Cr'eon didn't hesitate, but Rhi and I looked at each other. I wasn't sure if I was hallucinating from exhaustion or not as I watched Hess put first one foot and then the other into the desk drawer and disappear.

"Anytime now." Viola frowned at us.

I was too tired to argue, so I walked to the desk. Looking into the drawer, it looked like an average desk drawer.

"Just go," Viola said more softly this time.

I glanced at her before stepping into the drawer. The office faded, and a new room with six sides appeared.

Every surface of the room was covered in what looked like mattresses. As I looked at the mattresses on the ceiling, my head started to hurt.

Rhi and Viola appeared then.

"OK, we're safe here," Viola said.

"Thank God," Rhi said. "I don't think I could have handled one more weird sight today."

"Don't look up," I said, pointing at the mattresses on the ceiling.

"I don't care as long as I can sleep," Rhi said.

"Pick any one you want," Viola said as she touched a

mattress on the side of the wall and climbed onto it, her body sticking to the wall as if gravity had shifted for her.

"Bathrooms are through there." Viola pointed. "I'll get us some food in the morning. Sleep as long as you want. The room will wake us all at the same time, regardless of how long you sleep."

I was too tired to ask how this latest weirdness worked, and to be honest, I didn't care. I flopped onto one of the mattresses on the "normal" floor and was asleep a moment later.

Chapter 5

JAMES

"OK, so what is with all the weird things we saw yesterday?" I asked, taking a long pull from the pouch of not-blood Viola had provided. I didn't recognize the pouch at all. It was covered in strange symbols and writing, and tasted faintly of plastic.

"Yeah, we spent over a year on Behemoth and never saw anything like what we saw yesterday," Rhi said as she sat, leaning against a wall and sipping from her own not-blood pouch.

True to her word, we had all woken at the same moment this "morning." Viola had wasted no time in retrieving food for us from a cabinet built into the wall. Either it hadn't been there yesterday, or I'd been so tired I hadn't seen it.

Viola laughed. "Let's see, you're humanoid, from a humanoid Bio Hab. You're plucked off your home and dropped into a new, strange world. If you'd done the plucking, would you want to put the new arrivals somewhere so alien they couldn't make sense of it? No. You'd put them somewhere as similar to their home as possible to make the transition easier."

"Makes sense," I had to admit. I shrugged and slurped. The liquid, while not the best tasting, revived my body and filled me with energy.

"They did tell us the further we went from our sector, the

weirder it would get," Rhi said between slurps. "I guess we just didn't go far enough out."

"Yeah, prepare yourselves because it's only going to get weirder for you from here on out. Try to keep an open mind and not freak out, OK?" Viola said.

Rhi gave her a thumbs up, and I nodded, my mouth full.

Later, after several hours of strangeness that would give a sci-fi writer a migraine, we stood in front of a large set of three doors.

Viola clapped her hands together and turned to face us with a wide grin on her face.

"What?" I asked and braced myself as I recognized her 'you're not going to like this' face.

"OK," Viola hesitated a moment, trying to pick her words carefully. "This next part is going to be...rather difficult."

"How so?" Rhi asked.

"This next section," Viola said, patting the door. "This next section is shut down."

"Woah," Hess said grimly.

"Oh, hell no!" Cr'eon exclaimed.

"What does that mean?" I asked.

"It means this next section is empty. It doesn't have an active Bio Hab in it. As such, the whole area is powered down. No lights, no power, nothing," Viola said.

"We see pretty well in the dark," Rhi offered.

"Your vision still requires some sort of light for you to see. Once we pass these doors, there are no light sources. We're going to be in windowless corridors and rooms. It will be pitch black," Viola said.

"The dark doesn't scare me," Rhi said defiantly.

"It won't at first," Viola said. "But true darkness for as long as we're going to be in there can have some wonky effects on people."

"Why not use a flashlight or something?" I asked.

Viola took a moment to pat herself down. "Left it in my other pocket, I guess."

"How long?" Hess asked.

"Three days," Viola said. "It should take us about three days to get through this section. But we won't have to worry about anyone finding us. Behemoth doesn't patrol dead sectors."

"Dead sectors?" I asked.

"Sorry, bad choice of words. So, once we get in there, it's going to be dark, and it's going to be cold," Viola said.

"How cold?" Rhi asked.

"And there's not a lot of air," Viola added.

"Not a lot of air?" I asked.

"Don't forget the crawlers," Cr'eon offered.

"Oh yeah," Viola said, shivering involuntarily. "The crawlers."

"Wait, wait, wait!" Rhi said. "What the hell?"

"OK. So, the environmental systems are not currently running in this section. That means there's only the air leftover from before, plus the air currently being cycled in, so we can open these doors," Viola said.

"That's not a problem; we don't have to breathe," Rhi said.

"Unless we want to talk," I said.

"Environmental systems also control the heat, which means there isn't any. Now, the corridors we'll be moving through are part of the central network, so they're well protected from the outside. But eventually, everything cools. So, just be prepared and try not to touch anything with your bare hands. You might stick," Viola said.

"What's a crawler?" Rhi asked suspiciously.

"Yeah," Viola started. "Crawlers are harmless."

Hess snorted.

"What are they?" I asked.

"Think of them as caretakers. They are small biomechanical creatures who continuously monitor the area. They are usually inert unless they detect damage to the area, or a pressure loss, things like that," Viola said.

"What do they do then?" Rhi asked.

"They go fix whatever it is that's broken. You may feel them crawl over you while you're in the area," Viola said hesitantly.

"What do these things look like?" I asked.

"It'll be dark, you won't be able to see them—" Viola started.

"They're basically a cross between a cockroach and a spider,"

Hess offered.

"Robot cockroach-spiders...cockders? spiroaches? And they'll be crawling across us in the dark?" Rhi said as her eyes got big.

"They're not really robots—" Viola started again.

"Not really helping," Rhi said.

"They're harmless," Viola said.

"Yeah, right," Hess and Cr'eon said in unison.

"They are. If you feel one crawling across you, don't panic. Just leave it be. They don't care about us, just the area," Viola said.

"What if we don't leave it alone?" Rhi asked.

"Then it'll be damaged and another will come to try and repair it," Hess said.

"So...pitch black, freezing cold, no air, and scary spider-roach-things we have to let crawl all over us. Is that about it?" Rhi asked.

"Uh, yeah," Viola said.

"How are y'all going to do without air?" I asked.

"I don't need it," Viola said.

"I can cope," Hess shrugged.

"Uh..." Cr'eon said slowly. "My warskin probably doesn't have enough power for three days."

Cr'eon was wearing what looked like an old AG warskin. It had been repaired so many times that it looked like a quilt. I was surprised it could provide life support at all.

Viola sighed and pulled a small mask from her pocket before handing it to Cr'eon.

"Thank you," Cr'eon said reverently before touching the mask to her face, where it stuck by itself.

"So, you could remember a mask, but not a flashlight?" I asked.

"She needs this. You don't need a flashlight, you big baby," Viola said.

"And you need a spanking," I countered.

"Why, Father," Viola said in a slightly sultry tone. "Right here? In front of all these people?"

It was my turn to roll my eyes. I could hear Rhi chuckling behind me.

"Right," I said. "In space, no one can hear you scream," I muttered as I eyed the doors.

"Nope, we won't be able to hear you scream like a little girl once we're in there," Rhi said with a nervous chuckle.

Oh yeah you will, I said mentally.

We heard a loud clicking sound coming from the doors before they started opening on their own.

Viola took my hand and nodded to Cr'eon, who took Rhi's hand.

"Stick together, and if you get separated, just stay put. We'll find you," Viola said, making eye contact with each of us. "Ready?"

"If I said no?" I asked.

Viola just smiled and turned to the now-open door.

Light spilled in from this side and illuminated the corridor beyond. It looked like every other corridor...well, I take that back. It wasn't one of the themed corridors. It was the plain metal ones like what we'd been travelling through so far. The light from this side of the door only made it maybe forty meters down the corridor before darkness swallowed it.

A gentle tug from Viola, and I started forward.

We were halfway down the lit part of the corridor when the doors behind us closed, taking all light with it.

I've heard the phrase, it's not the dark we're afraid of, but what lingers in the dark. I had to agree. The first hour of walking wasn't so bad. It was mostly just adjusting to being led.

It was the second hour when things started getting wonky. It felt like the darkness was now a presence, pressing in on my face. I'd reach up and touch my face just to relieve the sensation, but it would return shortly after.

I'd been through a few nasty sandstorms in the desert, including one where I couldn't see my hand in front of my face until my fingers touched my goggles. That had nothing on this.

I hadn't expected the silence. No matter where you went on Behemoth, if you stopped and listened, you'd hear some sort of background noise, whether it be people, machinery, or just a low hum. There was always something.

Here, there was nothing. Only the sound of our footfalls

broke the silence.

After the second hour, Viola sensed my unease and started humming. It was like having your music player on shuffle. She ran through song after song. Some I knew, some I didn't.

By the fourth hour, the cold had begun creeping in.

I'm sure you've been told that vampires are tough creatures, and it's true. But just because the cold might not damage us as easily, doesn't mean it's not uncomfortable.

Rhi and I touched base with one another mentally every hour or so, just to have something to do. Sometimes we'd talk a bit, but mostly it was "you still OK?" "Yup, you?" "Yeah." And that was it.

Ten hours in, and the dark was starting to get to me.

It wasn't so much the dark that was doing it, though. Back home, we had places that didn't get light for days and even months. But these places still had residual light from sources other than the sun. They also had nature sounds of some kind.

Here, there was nothing.

The anxiety that I thought Behemoth had gotten rid of when I first came here was starting to creep back. I would hear something, or imagine I heard something, and my head would snap towards it. Then, later, I'd stop and turn towards it. Finally, I was tensing as if for a fight at every imagined sound.

"Hess."

I flinched at Viola's voice. Even though she said it softly, the word hit my ears with the power of an explosion.

I thought I was hallucinating when a dim light began to illuminate the hallway. I turned and found Hess holding her cigarette above her head, a tiny flame coming from it. It couldn't be much larger than a standard lighter, but it blinded me with its brilliance.

I rubbed my watering eyes.

"What?" Rhi asked as she shielded her eyes.

"She can't do it for long, so let's keep moving," Viola said.

True enough, five minutes later, the light died, and darkness returned. But even those five minutes seemed to have "reset" my anxiety clock.

Eighteen hours in, we had our first run-in with a "crawler."

I thought I was imagining the skittering sound and tried to ignore it. But then I felt something brush my pant leg, and I stumbled.

"You alright?" Viola asked.

"Something touched my leg," I said as I reached down and rubbed my ankle, trying to get rid of the sensation.

"Just a crawler," Hess said from behind me.

"Best to ignore it and keep going," Viola said as she tugged me ever onward.

My senses, which had already been starting to get to me again, were now on hyperalert. Every little sound made me think another crawler was coming.

A few hours later, we finally stopped.

"This looks good," Viola said.

I, of course, couldn't see anything but stopped when her hand rested on my chest. The sound of scraping and then a clunk was followed by something sliding across the floor.

"OK, everybody inside," Viola said as she pulled me off to the side.

I followed blindly, trying not to trip over my own feet.

A bunch of shuffling feet was followed by another scraping sound.

"Cr'eon, come here," Viola said.

More scraping followed, then a loud sigh from Viola.

"You've been running your heater?" Viola chastised.

"It's cold!" Cr'eon protested.

"You're as tough as they are; act like it!" Viola said with some vehemence.

"Yes, ma'am," Cr'eon replied in a small voice.

A moment later, the room filled with warmth as a few door indicator lights came on. They weren't enough to illuminate details, but we could see our silhouettes now.

Hess's tiny flame appeared in the center of the room.

The room looked like a storage closet. It was tiny, but we didn't need much space.

"OK, Cr'eon's warskin will provide enough power to heat this compartment for a few hours. Get some rest while you can," Viola said.

I hadn't realized how cold I was until my hands started tingling. I tentatively touched a wall, and it wasn't freezing, so I slid down it and sat on the floor.

A wave of exhaustion washed over me. While all we'd been doing was walking, the stress of the dark had taken a bigger toll on me than I thought.

I glanced at Rhi and found her sitting down against the opposite wall. I considered curling up with her, but I hesitated.

In all the years since our escape from the living fire, she'd never once approached me. All the flirting and innuendo of our earlier times had been absent. Now that I thought about it, the only time she ever touched me was during sparring. I know I'd made advances at some point, but she'd never accepted, always keeping me at arm's reach.

She'd kept her mind closed from me as well. Whenever we shared mindspeak, it was direct and focused on surface thoughts only. I'd have to ask her about this when we had time.

Right now, I was tired. I leaned over and curled up on the floor, using my arm as a pillow. I was out before I could think of something else to worry about.

"Time to wake up, Dad."

The whispered words caused me to jerk awake violently.

"Easy!" Viola's strangled voice came from under my chin.

At some time in the "night," Viola had weaseled her way into my arms and was curled up as the little spoon with me. My reaction to her waking me up had caused me to squish her a bit.

"Sorry," I said as I relaxed.

"It's OK. I forgot how you get sometimes," Viola said softly and began wiggling back against me in a way no daughter ever should.

"Uh..." I managed.

"Relax, I'm just stretching," Viola said, continuing her makeshift grind against me a moment longer before rolling to her feet with nimble ease.

The cold came rushing in from where her body had been keeping me warm only a few moments ago. I instinctively groaned at the loss of her warmth.

"Don't be like that," Viola said as she offered me her hand.

"We can do it again tonight." Her grin was sinister.

Viola had always been playful, bordering on flirty. I'd always taken it as harmless, until now. I wondered if, now that she'd revealed herself, things had changed in her mind.

I shook my head, trying to clear the wandering thoughts, and took her hand as she helped me to my feet.

Hess's tiny flame illuminated the room as everyone got to their feet.

You, OK? I asked Rhi. She didn't look OK. She had circles around her eyes and what looked like red streaks across her black eyes.

Ever since she married Tara, Rhi's eyes had been black. Only her irises were red. It was the exact opposite of how Tara's eyes were. In all this time, I'd never seen Rhi's eyes change like this.

Bad dreams, was all Rhi replied in my head. *I'm fine.*

I could guess what she'd been dreaming about and nodded in sympathy.

A minute later, we were back in the darkness, accompanied by the sounds of yawns and groans from people as they stretched and came awake.

The darkness made me feel like I needed to be quiet, as if there were something out there hunting us. One loud noise was all that stood between us and being eaten by teeth in the dark.

Needless to say, my mind was wandering all over the place by the time we needed to rest again. We'd been walking in the dark all day again. The fact I'd woken up tired hadn't helped any either.

Viola said one more walking cycle should bring us to the other side of the section and finally back into the light.

It had gotten colder "today," and the air was getting stale when I tested it. We'd been going through doors regularly, so the fresh air we'd let in with us was long gone by now, having been spread through each compartment we opened. All there was to breathe was air that had been in here for Behemoth knows how long.

Did you just substitute Behemoth for God? Rhi asked as Viola was sealing us in another small room for the night.

Beth used to do it, I said.

That's because Behemoth was an actual god on her Bio Hab, Rhi countered.

It was true. Somehow, Behemoth had become a god on Beth's Bio Hab. It wasn't the machine Behemoth but some multi-eyed and limbed monstrosity that was supposed to oversee their universe. I guess, in a broad sense, they could be considered the same.

By the time I lay down, Viola had warmed the room up, making it easy to rack out. I was so tired I didn't protest when Viola wiggled her way into my arms again. I didn't mind; she was warm, and I was only interested in sleep.

Something brushed my cheek, and I swatted at it in my sleep. The crash didn't wake me, but when something else skittered across my face, I bolted upright, swiping at my face frantically.

When I was a kid, I'd spent the night in the trailer of one of my mom's friends. They had one of those flip-out cushion chairs that could be used as either a chair or a small bed. Waking up in the middle of the night with roaches crawling on my face had been nightmare fuel for me ever since.

I was reliving that nightmare now as I could feel things crawling all over me in the dark. It would have been one thing if I could have at least seen what was going on. But with no light, my mind quickly spun itself into a frenzy.

I was on my feet, brushing at every part of my body and yelling. I'm not proud of it, but I was.

"Dad?" Viola called out to me groggily.

"James? What the?!" Rhi called out.

I could only imagine she had monsters crawling on her as well.

"Calm down!" Viola yelled. "They're only the crawlers. They're harmless!"

I couldn't hear her through my screaming.

"Cr'eon, emergency lights!" Viola ordered.

Cr'eon hit the emergency lights on her warskin, starting to drain what little battery life it had. Yellow light filled the room, revealing that every surface was moving.

"Oh shit!" Viola hollered and bolted to the door.

I didn't see any of this as I was still in a blind panic, trying to get rid of the hundreds of crawling nightmares on me.

"Out!" Viola's voice called out just as a pair of hands grabbed me and tossed me outside the room.

I hit the deck hard and rolled until I hit a bulkhead, knocking me senseless. On the plus side, the impact also knocked the wind out of me, ending my screaming like a small child with a skinned knee.

Hands picked me up and carried me down the yellow-lit hall.

"It's alright; they'll leave the further away we get," Viola said when my head finally cleared.

I looked from the bouncing deck to Viola, who had me over her shoulder and was trotting down the hall effortlessly. I didn't feel any more of the creepy crawlies and started to calm down.

"You good now?" Viola asked as she slowed to a walk.

"Yeah, you can put me down," I said, and Viola delicately put me on my feet.

I looked around and found everyone was here. Most seemed rattled, but fine. I watched as Rhi flicked her hair, and a small metal creature dropped to the floor before scurrying back the way we came.

Viola ran her hands across my body, searching for more crawlers. When she was satisfied there were none, she turned to the group.

"I'm sorry, that was my fault," Viola began.

"What was that?" Rhi asked.

"That was a crawler node. They look identical to the other rooms," Viola said.

"What's that?" I asked.

"It's where they...it's their home," Viola finally said.

"I guess that's one way to get rid of squatters," Rhi said.

"Sorry," Viola seemed embarrassed.

"Everybody OK?" I asked. When everyone said they were, I continued. "Well, I think I've had as much sleep as I'm getting tonight," I shuddered.

"Yeah, let's get moving," Rhi said as she threw a look over her shoulder.

"Honest guys, they really are harmless," Viola said.

"Uh-huh," I muttered.

"OK, let's go. Cr'eon, save your batteries," Viola said and took my hand, grumbling.

"What's that?" I asked as we were plunged into darkness once again.

I felt Viola pat my hand.

"Don't worry about it, Dad," Viola said. "Most men can't dance, and I don't think anyone else saw your freak out."

"Oh, we saw it," Rhi chimed in.

"Are we there yet?" Hess asked.

Several more hours passed. Between Viola's hummed showtunes and Hess's occasional flame breaks, we were settling into a routine.

"Is it getting brighter in here?" Rhi asked.

I looked around but didn't see it. Then I realized I could see slight movement in the darkness.

"It is," Viola said, her frown practically audible.

We continued forward, and the light grew until it was twilight.

"There shouldn't be anything here, so be on guard," Viola whispered.

You hear that? Rhi asked me.

I could just barely make out a low hum coming from up ahead.

Generator? I asked.

Maybe, Rhi said.

We slowed to a crawl as we approached cautiously. We couldn't see the source of the light, but it seemed to be coming from around the curve of the passage far ahead of us.

"What the hell is giving off that much light?" I whispered.

I saw Viola's shrug, testifying to just how bright it was getting in here.

After two days in darkness, the new constant light was hurting my eyes. The light was Cameron Blue, and it didn't help to soothe my nerves. Every time we passed a dark side hall, all I could think about was a slime-dripping monster waiting to pounce.

Then we started hearing banging sounds, grunting, and an angry voice that was shouting in a language I didn't understand.

"Hurry!" Viola said and ran ahead.

I gave Rhi a quick glance before following.

When we reached the source of the light, the scene was chaotic.

Several light stands were set up in a large room, illuminating one wall. Cables and machinery of all kinds were strewn about the room in disarray. Some were dark, some still humming with lights, and others had sparks shooting out of them.

I stopped when I saw what else was in the room.

There was a three-meter-tall...for lack of a better word...hedgehog beating on the wall with a shovel.

Viola didn't hesitate as she picked up another shovel off the floor and began pounding on the wall as well.

"Don't just stand there, help!" Viola called over her shoulder.

I grabbed another shovel-looking instrument from the small pile on the floor and approached. The shovel was more like a three-sided battle axe. Each edge looked sharp enough to do some serious damage. I made sure to keep clear of the two already swinging.

The wall had a large tear in it where it looked like someone had cut a large opening. The problem was that there were crawlers desperately trying to repair the tear while the hedgehog was trying to make it bigger.

And the hedgehog was losing.

I saw movement inside the tear and realized there was someone inside the wall who was about to reenact the Cask of Amontillado!

I swung and hit the pile of crawlers on the wall, sending them sprawling, only to watch as more appeared from inside the wall. There were crawlers on both sides of the wall trying to seal the hole. I failed to control my shudder of revulsion as several dislodged crawlers landed on my shoes.

Rhi joined a moment later, but it was obvious this was a losing battle. Whoever was in there was about to be sealed up inside the wall!

There was a crackling sound behind me, and suddenly, the crawlers scattered...like flipping on a light and sending the cockroaches running.

I shuddered again.

"That should do it," Cr'eon called out from behind us.

I glanced back and saw Cr'eon and Hess both reassembling the knocked-over machinery and reattaching tangled wires.

A loud crash drew my attention back to the hole in the wall.

Now that the crawlers weren't opposing the hedgehog, he was making short work of widening the hole from his side. Meanwhile, the glow of hot metal was coming from the other side as whoever was inside was cutting their way out.

A moment later, the hedgehog dropped his shovel and reached into the hole. He pulled out one, then two, then six total "hedgehogs" from the small hole.

Once back on our side, the seven sat down on the floor, breathing hard. They chattered to each other, but I couldn't understand a word.

You catching any of this? I asked Rhi.

Nope, just noise to me, Rhi said.

Viola knelt next to one of the newcomers and chattered at them in a series of nasally grunts.

"Is everyone OK?" I asked.

"Yeah. These guys just disconnected their scrambler somehow," Hess said.

"Scrambler?" I asked.

"It keeps the crawlers away," Cr'eon said.

"How can we take that with us?" I asked only half-jokingly.

The sound of Cr'eon's voice caused all seven of the newcomers to stop and look at her.

Cr'eon noticed the silence and looked up from the panel she was still working on.

Her glance caused the newcomers to backpedal until their backs hit the wall.

Viola jumped between the two, waving her arms and making all sorts of noises now. After what sounded like a heated argument, the newcomers seemed to relax slightly.

"I guess seeing a Daemon is the last thing a bunch of thieves would want to see," Cr'eon grinned.

"Thieves?" I asked.

"They're scavenging," Viola said over her shoulder. "They're from one of the outliers."

"That explains it," Cr'eon said.

"Explains what?" Rhi asked.

"Outlier colonies exist within the...what you'd call the back alleys of Behemoth. The box fan city we saw? Outlier," Cr'eon said.

"Since they're not part of Behemoth, they usually have to scrounge for parts and such to keep their colony going," Viola said.

"They sneak into Behemoth proper, take what they need, and then the crawlers fix whatever damage they caused," Cr'eon said.

"Seems like a pretty good system," Rhi said.

"It would be better if they could just live within Behemoth proper without having to sneak around," Viola said.

"Where'd they come from, though? I mean, originally," I asked.

"Varies," Cr'eon said. "Most are from Bio Habs. There are rumors of those who are leftovers from the early days of Behemoth, when they still had regular transports running back to the main systems. Each colony has its own story."

"And Behemoth doesn't bother them?" Rhi asked.

"There's no need," Cr'eon said, shaking her head. "As long as they stay off Behemoth's radar, Behemoth ignores them."

"And if they get on the radar?" I asked.

"Behemoth wipes them out utterly," Cr'eon said. "There are stories—"

"For another time," Viola said as the hedgehogs returned to the hole they were working on. "They're grateful for our help and offered compensation if we were planning on sticking around."

"Compensation?" I asked. "Aren't they scavenging?"

"The hospitality of the Rhrodn is well known. But I declined as they are planning on being here another week or so," Viola said, then turned to me. "I figured you wouldn't want to spend that much time in here with the crawlers."

"As long as they have that machine, I don't mind," I said,

pointing at the anti-crawler boxes.

"Huh," Viola said, then turned and went back to the Rhrodn. After a few moments of grunting and snuffling, Viola returned with two of the Rhrodn in tow.

"They said we can rest here until we're ready to move on," Viola said.

I was tired. Having not slept last night when we were attacked in the crawler node, willpower was pretty much the only thing keeping me moving.

"Sleeping in a construction site?" Rhi asked, nodding to where they were noisily making the hole in the wall larger once more.

"They should be done making noise in about ten minutes, then they'll make sure we're not disturbed," Viola said.

"And these two?" I asked, looking up at the...they were friggin hedgehogs! They were standing on two feet right now but had been on all fours while moving around. The shovels, once turned on, cut through metal like butter, so they didn't have to do much with their tiny arms. But they were surprisingly limber.

"These two are for warmth," Viola smiled.

"What?" Rhi asked.

"If we wouldn't come back to their colony, then the Rhrodn are going to provide us with as much hospitality as they can, here. This includes us using them as pillows/blankets," Viola said.

Hesitantly, we all settled down, and the Rhrodn curled up around us. It was strangely comfortable...and warm! I was surprised steam wasn't coming off the Rhrodn with how warm they were. Plus, they made a sort of thrumming sound that lulled me to sleep despite the room being so bright.

Several hours later, with more sleep than I was expecting, we were bidding the Rhrodn farewell and moving back into the darkness.

"Why couldn't we understand them, Viola?" Rhi asked once we were away. "Behemoth's auto-translator is usually pretty good."

"Couldn't help with the box fans," I added.

"There are some languages that are so foreign, they don't or can't translate," Viola began. "Then, there are others that Behemoth hasn't incorporated yet, such as the Rhrodn."

"If they're so old, why hasn't Behemoth added them?" I asked.

"The Rhrodn are unusually talented at...evasion. If they don't want to be found, they usually won't be," Viola said.

"Were those gray boxes back there oxygen producers?" Rhi asked.

"Very good," Viola said, her voice laced with just a touch of sarcasm. "Yes, the Rhrodn make their own air, so they won't have to use suits while working. It requires large machinery to keep the supply up in such an open area."

We trooped on through the dark in silence for several more hours without incident.

By now, I'd become used to the quiet dark. I could recognize when my body was reaching its limits and would ask for light or sound, whatever I needed.

Rhi never asked for help; she just soldiered on, only taking her breaks when I did.

"Hold up," Viola said just as I was about to ask about a camping spot.

We'd been going much longer than we usually did in a "day."

"Cr'eon, give me some light," Viola said.

Painfully bright yellow light erupted around us. It wasn't the first time since the crawler node that we'd had to use Cr'eon's emergency light. We'd had to traverse several stairwells or shafts with ladders where light was essential. But we'd always kept it as short as possible.

It turned out Cr'eon's AG warskin didn't have much of a battery and tended to draw heavily on the wearer to remain functional. I didn't know how it worked exactly, as my DC warskin had never drawn energy from me that I knew of. But for her, we'd usually have to take a break each time we used the emergency light so Cr'eon could rest and recover.

As my eyes adjusted, I could see three more doors like the ones we'd passed through coming into the dark zone. I glanced around the group and found everyone looking as ragged as I felt.

It took a few minutes, but the doors finally began to click and open.

Fresh light and air washed over us from the new zone, and our group hurried forward without the need for Viola's prodding for once.

Chapter 5.5

BETH

I hated biopods with a passion. Whoever invented them must have been a fish. Don't get me wrong, I know they have saved countless lives and have been designed to be near-perfect for body augmentation. But why do I have to breathe fluid? Why do I have to drown before they can start saving my life?

I've read the specs. I know how it works, how it provides a perfect conductor for all manner of transmission, and how my body started out breathing fluid before I was born, so it's a natural state.

But that doesn't mean I have to like it! They have to give me a double dose of sedatives each time I go into the tank. I wish they'd just knock me out, but they say it's better for my body if I actively transition. Garbage!

I don't mind it as much once I'm in. Usually, you're either fading in and out of consciousness or your mind's thrown into an AR simulation to keep you stable.

My favorite AR sim was always flying. Nothing crazy fast, just a nice slow, lazy flight above the treetops. Occasionally dipping into a canyon or something simple. Nothing requiring quick turns or anything.

You know you bitch about the biopods every time you're in one, right? It's always the same complaint, my minder said.

You don't have to listen, you know, I replied.

You know I have to, the minder said. *I listen to everything you think.*

Voyeur, I muttered.

Instead of being so negative, try being positive for a change, the minder said.

Oh yeah! I get to drown again! Yippie! I said.

How about the fact that this augment is going to take care of those nasty aches you have in your shoulder, back, and knees? the minder said. *How about how this is going to get rid of the slowly growing mass in your brain that would have killed you back on your Bio Hab? How about how it's going to knock off a couple of decades from your biological clock? How about—*

OK, I get it. Biopod good. Cut it out already, I muttered. *How much longer?*

Sixteen hours, my minder said cheerfully.

Great, I muttered and settled back to wait as I returned to my game of digital solitaire.

You know— my minder started.

No! Don't start, I said. "Just because you have a captive audience doesn't mean you can start torturing me about the whole retirement thing.*

Well...can I just say—

No! You can't, I said, cutting him off again. He'd been hounding me nonstop for nearly two years now about retiring. We both knew it was impossible.

Actually, my getting this body augment was a compromise to try and get him to stop bugging me about it. If he wasn't talking about retiring, he'd been talking about this augment.

I mean, I didn't need an augment. I'd been in service for what...16 years now? My reflexes were still top tier, my PT scores were maxed, and my reaction time was the same as an 18-year-old.

Of course, all those things he mentioned were true. I did have some aches and pains, not that I'd ever complain. Besides, those pains were what your body did to remind you that you're still breathing. They weren't so bad. After a while, you got used to it...and the meds.

So, I guess, with this magical "cure-all" augment, I'll have a whole new body to get used to. No more meds to help me get through this or that. I'll have to break in new muscles, but the techs promised me they'd start off top-notch, so I shouldn't lose my edge.

The fact that Behemoth could take your body and "fix it" so that you literally regained your youth had been the stuff of myth and legend in my home Bio Hab. I guess the fact that I was living it makes me a part of those myths now.

OK, OK, don't get ahead of yourself, my minder said. *It's just a rejuvenation, not the magical rebirth of a goddess!*

You saying I couldn't pull off a goddess? I said indignantly.

My minder wisely kept his mouth shut.

I still wish I understood what my deal was, though. I mean, I was a vampire. We're supposed to stop aging once we're created. But I'd kept right on aging, gray hair and everything.

The bio-techs couldn't explain it either. They had the vampire template for my Bio Hab and went through it with me. Right at the top of the list was the slow aging boon.

But then again, I hadn't been created in the traditional fashion either. Having my blood drained and drinking from my master wasn't how I was made. I was made from a bloody kiss.

You know, moms always warned that kissing led to babies. Man, was that not true in my case!

I was hoping that with this augment, I'd finally stop aging. I mean, I had to drink the fucking blood, why couldn't I get all the benefits?

Well, at least you're finally calling them benefits and not curses, my minder said.

Stay out of it, I chided him.

I didn't blame James for it anymore. I had, for so long, focused my hatred on what he'd done to me. Even with everyone telling me there was no way he could have known, I still used him as the scapegoat for my wrath. It gave me something to focus on instead of wallowing in self-pity.

I wish I hadn't been so hard on him. I know that before the

end, I'd softened a bit towards him, but I'd never gotten around to "forgiving him" for what wasn't his fault to begin with. Now it was too late.

They were all gone.

First, Tara in that fake control point terror attack. Then the rest when their Bio Hab burned in yet another terror attack. Those four hadn't had an easy time of it. Hopefully, wherever they were, they could finally rest.

Chapter 6

JAMES

"Exactly how long are we supposed to wait here?" I asked as I stared out the window at the neon city. "I'm sick of 'resting' and 'relaxing'."

Knavan was the "high-tech shit" city I'd been expecting when we first arrived on Behemoth. It had glimmering skyscrapers, streets painted with neon lights, holographic advertisements everywhere, and sleek vehicles sliding through the perfectly maintained roads. That last part should have told me everything here was a lie. No city this busy had zero potholes.

We'd been in Knavan nearly two weeks now, and my patience was running thin. Now that I knew there was hope of getting our family back, I wanted to get on with it already.

"We wait for as long as it takes, James," Rhi said for the umpteenth time from her place at a small table. She was carefully honing a knife while a pistol sat in pieces beside it on the table. Both were new acquisitions from this place.

A knock on the door interrupted my rant before I could get started.

I looked at Rhi, who looked back at me.

In a flash, her pistol was reassembled and at the ready. She nodded at me, and I approached the door.

I carefully touched the panel beside the door, and the image from the hallway outside appeared on the display. Viola, Cr'eon, Hess, and someone with their back to the camera stood waiting for me to answer the door.

"Yes?" I spoke into the panel.

"Blah, blah, blah," Viola said our passphrase.

The group filed in after I opened the door. Once inside, I secured the door and turned to stare into amethyst-colored eyes.

"Krys?" I gasped at the man who was nearly nose-to-nose with me.

"He remembers," Krys muttered with a grin and hugged me as I stood there in shock.

Krys was slightly taller than I was, had white hair that hung below his shoulders, and was one of the most handsome men I'd ever seen. Well, he wasn't a man per se; he was a 3,000-year-old alien from another dimension. But still, he was ripped.

After a moment, I returned the hug, and he stepped back.

I glanced at Viola, "I thought you were meeting your contact."

"I did; this is him," Viola said, pointing at Krys.

Viola had been trying to contact the people who knew where Behemoth's cloning facility was. She hadn't said it would be someone I already knew.

"And how do the two of you know each other?" Cr'eon asked.

"My ship rescued him from deep space after a gate malfunction," Krys said, still not taking his eyes off mine.

"Uh, yeah," I cleared my throat and moved past Krys into the main room. Even after all this time, the guy still made me...uneasy. That wasn't fair. It wasn't the guy. It was my own feelings about the guy that made me uneasy.

"This is the guy you turned down?" Rhi was giving Krys double elevator eyes. "I wouldn't have minded you bringing this one home," her tone was practically predatory.

It was the first time I'd heard Rhi say anything even remotely flirty in years. Maybe the possibility of getting the band back together was loosening her up. Either that, or she was feeding off my personal interest in the alien.

Viola sighed in disgust. "Can we please get back on topic here? Krys works at the facility we're looking for."

"You do?" I asked incredulously.

"Not by choice," Krys said as he walked over to the window I'd been at earlier.

"After we arrived here, Behemoth took our ship hostage and threatened our friends to press us into service. Of course, it had lulled us into a false sense of security first. We fell straight into its trap. Now, the four of us work to protect one of the most vital parts of this place."

"The four of you are together?" I asked.

"Yes, our reunion was not under the circumstances we'd wished for, of course," Krys said.

"Why don't the four of you just cut your way out of here?" I asked, knowing the symbiont within his body allowed him to create crystal weapons that could cut through steel like butter.

"We could, but we'd be leaving behind our fifth member," Krys said.

"Fifth member?" I asked. As far as I knew, it was Krys and his wife Shashka, then Cateia and her husband Tachi.

"Our ship," Krys said.

"But Shashka said you can make ships yourself. Can't you just make another one?" I asked.

"It's a living ship, remember?" Krys said.

I'd forgotten that they used living ships.

"Sorry," I said.

"So, until we can track down our ship, we can't leave," Krys said.

"Wait, wasn't Cateia working for the AG?" Rhi asked.

"Behemoth knew about that and had been using that against them," Krys started. "Then, when we arrived, Behemoth used us as another threat. Needless to say, she doesn't have anything to do with the AG anymore."

"Tell them about the facility," Viola said.

"OK, so the cloning facility is located inside an empty Bio Hab. The Bio Hab itself has one entrance and can't be gated into, thanks to a null field that blocks all gating. As far as I know, the facility is completely automated and has no workers unless there's a mass regeneration going on," Krys explained.

"How do they get the clones out when they need them?" Rhi asked.

"There is a shuttle that moves from the facility to the entrance and back. That's it, it doesn't go anywhere else," Krys said.

"How exactly does the process of replacing a clone work?" I asked.

"From what I know, it's a three-step process," Krys said. "Grow the clone if it hasn't already been grown. Transfer the mind from the computer to the body. Then wake it up and move it out."

"Any idea how long any of this takes?" Rhi asked.

"No." Krys shook his head. "I only know that little bit because I overheard some of the gatekeepers complaining once about how long the process was taking."

"Clone growth usually takes one to two days," Viola added. "Generally. But if it's a special case, Behemoth usually creates the clone and keeps it on standby so it's ready at a moment's notice."

"And you think our group is a special case?" Rhi asked.

"I do," Viola said.

"What about the mind transfer? How long does that take?" I asked.

"That depends on how long it takes to transfer from the archives," Krys said.

"The archives?" I asked.

"It appears Behemoth keeps the minds and bodies separated," Viola said.

"And let me guess, Behemoth doesn't transfer the minds digitally?" I asked with a smirk.

"The cloning facility is physically separated from everything, including digitally," Krys said.

"So, it's firewalled," Rhi said.

"Plus, with something like a mind, you don't want to risk having data corruption in the transfer," Viola said.

"So, how does Behemoth transfer it?" I asked.

"Crystal minds," Cr'eon said.

The whole room turned to face her.

"Most of our memory chips are made from a specialized crystal," Cr'eon started. "When it comes to a mind transfer, there are special containers created for the process. They're said to be the perfect vessel: incorruptible and nearly indestructible. As far as I've heard." Cr'eon shrugged.

"I take it these crystals are kept in the archives?" Rhi asked.

"I believe so," Cr'eon said.

"I'll verify that," Viola said. "So, from the looks of it, we have multiple targets. One, get into the archives, acquire a pair of crystal brain things, and transfer the minds over. Two, retrieve the crystal brains from the archives and transfer them to the cloning facility. And three, find the bodies or create new ones, transfer the minds into the bodies, and escape. Simple."

"Yeah, simple," Rhi muttered.

∞∞∞∞∞∞Ω∞∞∞∞∞∞

JAMES

It took another two weeks to confirm all the information Krys and Cr'eon had provided us.

Krys left shortly after our meeting, and Rhi hadn't stopped talking about him since. I had a feeling that if we'd met Krys pre-Behemoth, he wouldn't have been leaving the apartment for a few days. At least not until Rhi had gotten through with him.

Viola managed to find the location of Kry's ship and bargained with Krys for his group's help. Krys would help us retrieve the archive data and the bodies from the cloning facility. In return, Viola would put together a rapid escape plan for his group. She said it was going to be difficult but not impossible.

One additional stipulation Krys had was that I'd have to have a drink with him. It wasn't really part of the deal; he just said it in passing. Still, I would have agreed to a lot more than that if it meant we got Shae and Tara back.

So, here we were, Krys and I, sitting in a bar, having a drink.

I wasn't uncomfortable...I was extremely uncomfortable! The last time I'd spent time with a guy, it had been downrange, and a one-off kind of thing. And he hadn't looked like Krys!

"So, on a scale of one to ten, how uncomfortable are you right now?" Krys asked as he smiled from behind his glass.

We were sitting at a small table off to the side of the bar. The bar was busy, but not so loud that we couldn't hear each other. The others had stayed behind, giving Krys and me some privacy.

As I'd left, Rhi'd sent, *Don't do anything I wouldn't do!* Quickly followed by, *And bring back video!*

While I was happy to see her loosening up, I wasn't sure how good of an idea this was.

"Maybe a twelve?" I said as I finished off my drink and called for another from the server.

Krys laughed and continued to sip at his drink.

We didn't speak until the roboservant brought me my drink. From the waist up, it was just a series of tentacle arms that could hold a dozen trays. From the waist down, it was a collection of legs that maintained perfect balance.

"Well, relax," Krys started. "We're honestly just here to talk, nothing more."

I sighed, not sure if I was relieved or disappointed. As if understanding my sigh, Krys chuckled again.

Krys took another swallow and set the drink down.

"So, here's the deal," Krys said with a serious expression. "You know about our symbiont, yes? Well, what you may not know is that it's quasi-sentient. Not in a it'll beat you at chess kind of way, but in a more instinctual sense. It lets me know things usually through feelings and such.

"This includes how it... reproduces, for lack of a better term. When the symbiont recognizes someone who has enough biological energy to support it, the symbiont urges me to pass along its...'infection.'" Krys shook his head. "Goddess, that sounds so wrong. I'm sorry, I'm terrible at this."

"So, your symbiont is interested in me?" I asked.

"Yeah, I guess..." Krys sighed.

"You guess?" I asked.

"It's not an exact science," Krys said. "My mentor, Symitar, she taught me all about this a long time ago. But this has only happened to me once before."

"With Shashka?" I asked about his wife.

"Uh, yeah. How'd you know that?" Krys asked.

"When I was on your ship, the first night I took a small sample of your blood to test, I overheard the two of you talking," I said as I took a swallow of my drink. Now that Krys said nothing was going to happen, I felt calmer.

"But we didn't speak aloud," Krys looked at me.

"When...vampires are in contact with someone's blood, they're also in contact with their mind. We can talk, listen, and even fiddle with the person's mind that we're touching. When we finish, the rapport takes a little while to dissipate.

"I heard Shashka say you'd felt this way about her but that it hadn't been 'normal' with her either," I said.

"You could hear her thoughts as well?" Krys stared at me, open-mouthed.

"I could hear her in your head. I wasn't in contact with her mind at all," I explained. "How is she, by the way?"

"She's fine," Krys said, shaking his head as he threw away the comment. "So, you know the feelings I had for Shashka were insanely more intense than they should have been?"

"Yeah. And that...Symitar said it didn't work that way. What did that mean?" I asked, remembering the short conversation. At the time, I had no idea what they were talking about. All I'd taken away was that Krys was interested in me.

"It meant I had very powerful feelings for Shashka. You see, the symbiont can nudge you, plant ideas. But it can't actually do anything on its own, including creating...urges," Krys said as he picked his glass back up.

"So...that means both you and your symbiont are interested in me?" I hid behind my own glass.

"That pretty much sums it up," Krys said simply and sighed, not looking at me.

We both sat there in silence for a while. The only sound from either of us was when we sipped from our stay-cold glasses.

In yet another "don't ask me how it works" moment, the glasses we had weren't just insulated, they were refrigerated. As in, there was some sort of refrigerant in the lining of the glass that kept the inside cold and the outside at room temperature. This meant your drink didn't get watered down from ice. It remained at whatever temperature you told it you wanted and the glass didn't sweat.

"You do know about my situation, right?" I asked.

"Shashka told me a bit about your gestalt. That's one of the reasons I'm not throwing myself at you right now," Krys said as he leaned back in his chair.

"One of the reasons?" I asked.

"I don't go where I'm not asked, James," Krys looked me in the eye as he said it.

I held my glass up to him as I'd used the same line in the past.

"Wait, I thought blood was one of the ways to...spread your symbiont?" I asked.

"It is one of the primary methods, actually," Krys said.

"Well, I've practically drunk a gallon of your blood already." I winced and glanced around. I'd said that just a tad too loud. "If I was going to get 'infected' by your symbiont, it should be done by now."

"And yet, my desire is still there," Krys shrugged and held his hands out helplessly.

I leaned forward, my head swimming slightly from the drink.

"In that case, it sounds more like it has nothing to do with your symbiont," I said slowly.

"That's what Shashka keeps saying," Krys said as he leaned forward as well.

"Well, she is a smart woman," I said, not moving from where we sat, not that far apart now.

"It usually takes me a while, but I eventually do what she tells me to," Krys said with a smile.

"Smart man," I smiled back.

We stared at one another, smiling for a while. Then I learned his mouth tasted like cinnamon.

Chapter 7

JAMES

"I still can't believe all you did was kiss him!" Rhi said in disgust for the dozenth time.

"Would you please focus?" I said as I shook my head at Rhi. We were working on the next phase of the plan, and it had many delicate parts. I needed my mind on the here and now, not the alcohol-fueled antics of last night.

Acquiring an AUG, what I called one of Behemoth's flying-powered armor monstrosities, was, surprisingly, the easiest part of our plan. We'd simply walked into an unmanned storage bay and, with a lot of help from Viola, left the automated bay with the AUG as if we owned it.

"Coward," Rhi grumbled. "You should have brought him home," she said under her breath.

"If you want him so bad, you go after him!" I finally confronted Rhi.

"I tried. It's a package deal or nothing," Rhi frowned. "And I really wanted to watch!" Rhi whined.

That made me pause. The first part, not Rhi's voyeuristic streak. That I already knew about.

"Really?" I asked.

"Hey, focus on the plan!" Rhi chided me.

The hard part of the next step was accessing Rhi's old flight data.

Early in our on-the-job training with Beth, we had a gate malfunction. It was the same one that sent me into deep space, where I met Krys and Shashka.

Rhi had been sent into the bowels of Behemoth to a place called the Archive, which is where we needed to go now. The problem was that we needed Rhi's old AUG flight data to repeat the process.

The data was on a secure Behemoth server whose access point was located in Daemon country. The area was restricted to Daemons, and the only Daemon we had was Cr'eon, but she was currently flagged as an enemy combatant.

So, Viola created a program that would temporarily list Cr'eon as the Daemon version of an undercover agent. It should get her into Daemon country long enough for her to grab the information and get out again. The problem was that Cr'eon didn't want to do it.

"I said no. This is nuts! If I go in there, they'll kill me!" Cr'eon protested. "Or worse, put me back to work!"

"Cr'eon, this is simple data retrieval. Two minutes in enemy territory, tops," I said.

"But I'll have to interface with Behemoth!" Cr'eon said.

"As I said before," Viola started. "I'll have you listed as a friendly. Behemoth won't bat an eye at your presence."

"What if it doesn't work?" Cr'eon asked.

"We'll know if it works or not before you even go into Daemon country. If the doors open for you, you're good," Rhi said.

"And if they don't, I'm pretty sure they'll have a welcoming party waiting for me. You haven't seen the guardian defenses, I have. No, thank you!" Cr'eon shook her head.

Viola walked over and put both her hands on Cr'eon's cheeks.

"Do you trust me, Cr'eon?" Viola asked.

"I—" Cr'eon hesitated. "That's not fair!"

Viola was one step down from Behemoth to the AG. She was practically a deity, which is why Cr'eon reacted the way she did when she first met Viola.

Cr'eon deflated. "Yes, I trust you."

"I won't fail you, I promise," Viola said.

∞∞∞∞∞Ω∞∞∞∞∞

CR'EON

I couldn't believe I let Viola talk me into this. I was walking into the lion's den wearing a meat suit! But I couldn't turn her down. She'd done so much for my kind in the past. I mean, she'd gone head-to-head against Behemoth for us and survived! No one else could say that.

I unclenched my hands for the tenth time as I approached the doors to Daemon country.

In a moment, the sensors around the door would reach out, identify me, and decide whether I was allowed inside the restricted area. If Viola's program didn't work, the sentry behind the door would cut me to—

The doors slid open soundlessly.

I hesitated, surprised it had worked. Then shook my head and quickly stepped inside. As the door shut behind me, all I could think about was the virtual guardian slicing me to ribbons.

Instead, the second set of doors opened before me.

Daemon country wasn't that much different than the rest of Behemoth. There were lots of identical corridors and rooms. Instead of enclosed lifts, we had open shafts where Behemoth could move us wherever it needed to put us.

The first turn I took, I ran smack into a pair of Daemons talking animatedly.

"Sorry," I said as I tried to get out of the way.

The pair ignored the collision and my apology. They just kept walking, not even pausing their conversation.

Then I remembered that Daemons didn't apologize like that. That was a human trait I'd picked up from so much time with them.

I found myself hurrying and forced myself to slow down. Rushing around would draw attention I didn't need.

Soon enough, I found a data access point and stepped inside. My luck held as it was empty. My fear, aside from being caught, was that I'd run out of time before finding a data point that wasn't in use.

Once more, I hesitated at the interface before I steeled myself and stepped into the data field.

Instantly, I was in rapport with Behemoth's data net. I hadn't been here in years, and it took several moments for my internal software to update to the interface changes.

I maneuvered to the data source and found it surrounded by all kinds of precautions. Anything related to James and his crew was flagged for inspection, which meant that as soon as I touched that data, something would come to find out why I was interested.

I didn't have anything to counter this. It wasn't my kind of job. I was going to have to just grab the data and run. Hopefully, I'd make it out of here before I got caught.

Then, my curiosity redirected me away from that data and to the public vid clips. Sometimes, this happens. If you aren't focused on what you are doing, your brain could steer you off course.

The vid clips I'd taken while observing James's Bio Hab were still popular! Somehow, my account was still listed among the high-tier content creators. Apparently, I was famous, or at least my clips were.

Other Daemons had taken them and edited them, creating altered videos. Most of them were humorous, while some were more like propaganda videos.

Enough.

I needed to get back to work before I ran out of time.

The secured data appeared before me once again. Taking a deep breath, I reached out for it.

∞∞∞∞∞Ω∞∞∞∞∞

<u>RHI</u>

It was almost funny to see how shocked Cr'eon had been when she'd escaped Daemon country unscathed. She was so sure people were waiting to jump her around every corner that she was still looking over her shoulder hours later.

The moment of truth was at hand as Krys and I stared at the AUG that would hopefully take us to the archive.

I volunteered for this one because I'd been there before. That, and James didn't seem in the right frame of mind for this. Every day we'd been on this journey, his anxiety grew. I think he was afraid to let himself hope; I know I was.

To have Tara back would be...everything! I'd been a mess when I first lost her...and when she finds out what I'd done in the hospital, she wasn't going to be happy. Hopefully, the joy of our reunion would temper her disappointment in me.

On the other hand, there was Shae. Yeah, I'd blamed her for Tara's death. It had taken me years to come to terms with that. But I'd left her to the living fire when I might have been able to save her. I let my anger guide me when the moment of truth came. I'd been ashamed of my choice ever since.

Would she forgive me when she came back? Could she? I knew I couldn't forgive myself. I'd been a coward, and it had cost all of us.

"Hey, still with me?" Krys's voice cut through my clouded thoughts.

"Yeah," I said, nodding my head.

"You went away there for a bit," Krys said.

"It's OK, I'm back," I said as I looked into the man's amethyst-colored eyes. My eyes couldn't help but trace the outline of his jaw, down his neck, to his collarbone—damn! James hadn't been kidding about this guy.

"We ready?" I asked, clearing my throat and trying to focus my mind on the task at hand.

"That should do it," Cr'eon said as she and Hess stepped away from the AUG.

The cockpit slid open, and the black tentacles slid down towards us.

I stepped forward and allowed them to envelop me. Krys had never driven an AUG. He didn't need to, since his crystal armor allowed him to fly in space.

It had been several years since I'd felt these tentacles violating me. I knew it was coming, but the old ease with which I used to handle the transition was gone. I tensed as the black ropes penetrated my body and meshed with my neural net.

A moment later, my neural cockpit appeared. It seemed my brain hadn't forgotten this part. My vision was replaced by that of the AUG. Controls appeared when I mentally reached for them, and I ran a series of diagnostics out of habit.

The AUG utilized a neural cockpit for its pilots. There were no physical controls inside the AUG. Everything was in my head. If I thought about something, it happened. If I thought about moving my arm, the neural cockpit blocked the signal to my actual arm and instead redirected it to the AUG's arm.

A moment later, the AUG reported that it was ready.

"Feed me the info," I said, my voice coming from the AUG, not my throat.

I watched Viola enter a sequence of commands via a maintenance port on the side of the leg.

During the previous gate incident, it had been the AG attempting to capture my gestalt that caused the malfunction that scattered us to the winds. Now, we were attempting to recreate that accident on purpose.

The fact that Tara had ended up embedded in a wall last time had me more than a little nervous.

I felt the data feed from Viola's inputs and integrated the new info. I also felt it when Viola unlocked my gate engines. As far as I knew, only Behemoth could unlock those engines. The fact that Viola could do it at will said more about her abilities than anything else.

"Ask me later," Viola's words floated to me through the AUG interface, not my ears.

I didn't have time to ask what she meant because a new countdown clock appeared in my vision. The engines were counting down until they jumped.

The cockpit tentacles lashed out and captured Krys before

pulling him into the cockpit with me. The cockpits were designed to accommodate a full-sized Daemon. Krys and I could fit in with room to spare.

While the tentacles didn't pierce Krys the way they did me, he still didn't seem bothered by them, so I asked him about it.

"I lived with something similar a long time ago," was all he would tell me.

I buttoned up the cockpit and made sure everyone was clear as I watched the countdown reach zero.

I knew what to expect this time and froze as soon as I completed the gate. I mentally put on the AUG's emergency brake and looked around.

The last time I was here, I tried moving and damaged a lot of stuff due to the tight quarters. Nothing had changed as the room was still full of computer banks, and I still didn't have room to maneuver.

I started to open the cockpit but stopped and ran my diagnostic like I'd been trained. Beth would have been proud.

There were no alarms I could detect, and there didn't seem to be anyone else around.

I cracked the cockpit. The cold of the room met the warmth of the cockpit, creating clouds of steam. I deposited Krys and me on the floor and reached back for the coat I'd remembered to bring this time.

Purple-colored crystal armor slowly formed around Krys, protecting his body from the cold of the room. A moment later, his entire body was encased in it, making a rather cool-looking suit of armor.

"This way," I said as I led him deeper into the room. A quick glance back told me I'd landed in the exact same spot as before. Behemoth's tech was remarkable.

This room fed into a circular central room from which several other computer rooms branched off. In the middle was a large, faceted, blue sphere with blurry images displayed within.

"This the right place?" Krys asked, his voice coming from his suit in ringing tones. It reminded me of wind chimes.

"We're about to find out," I said as I stepped up to the small railing and looked into the three-meter sphere. Before I could speak, it did.

WHAT DO YOU NEED? The voice was loud in my mind and caused me to flinch.

What do you need? The voice corrected.

Pushing the Déjà vu from my brain, I focused on what I needed.

"I need to retrieve two mind copies," I said, hoping the sphere would interpret what I needed. We didn't know what the official word was for what we wanted.

Specificity error, the voice said.

I sighed.

"I need the minds of Shae and Tara," I said, picturing each of them in my mind as hard as I could.

Insert Carrots, the voice said.

"Insert carrots?" I asked.

No, Carrots, the voice corrected.

"Are Carrots the name of the crystal recording devices that store minds?" I asked.

Correct. Insert Carrots.

Now that I listened, I could hear the voice pronouncing the capital C of the word. Don't ask me how.

"Where can I get Carrots?" We'd been told the...Carrots were secured here in the archive.

Well, it turned out they weren't kept here after all. Apparently, someone had the bright idea to keep them at a separate, secured facility to prevent precisely what we were trying to do.

"Well, shit," I said after I'd relayed the information to Krys.

"Can it show me the details of the...Carrot?" Krys asked.

Without me asking, a 3D image of a small crystal appeared on the sphere, rotating slowly.

"I can do it," Krys said after a moment of study.

"You can?" I asked, suddenly afraid Krys's homemade brain case might damage Tara's memory or something.

"Computer, can you verify the integrity of a Carrot before transferring a mind?" Krys asked.

Standard diagnostic routine verifies Carrot's suitability prior to transfer, the voice said in both our minds.

"See, it'll double-check my work," Krys said.

"OK, OK," I grumbled.

Krys put his crystal hand on my face. It was strangely smooth and warm, unlike its appearance. The face of the armor slowly faded, revealing Krys's visage.

"Don't worry. I understand how important this is," Krys said, his eyes locked with mine.

I nodded, and he got to work. Since Krys was using the sphere as his reference, I had nothing else to do, so I wandered for the next several hours.

Later, Krys said he could have made the Carrots rather quickly. But he'd taken his time and started over twice because he didn't like the look of them.

Finally, we had two Carrots that passed Behemoth's standards.

"Here goes everything," I said as we slipped the Carrots into the designated console.

Transfers complete, the voice said only a moment later.

"You transferred two complete minds in less than a second?" I asked. Viola had told me just how big the files were of a standard mind, and the number had shocked me. Since I was old enough to remember dial-up, the fact that this transfer had been nearly instantaneous was insane.

Correct. Verification of all sectors is complete, and all required checks passed. Carrot creation for Shae data points ARH39380.00 through ARH39811.01 verified complete. Carrot creation for Tara data points ARG39623.00 through ARG39811.03 verification complete.

"Wait, that can't be right," I said.

"What's wrong?" Krys asked.

"The dates are wrong," I said. "I'm guessing the first date is their date of birth—"

Correct, the voice confirmed.

"But the ending dates...they're not the days they died. Confirm the dates in my Bio Hab's time," I asked the computer. It gave me two ending dates roughly two-ish months apart. But they were both before we came to Behemoth.

"There are no recordings after those two dates?" I asked

again.

Correct.

"But why?" I asked. If this was right, then more than the last year of their lives was missing.

External partition, the voice said.

"Explain," I said.

An external force infiltrated the primary archive residence and terminated observation by Behemoth. All data from the splice point forward was partitioned and transferred by the external force.

"Someone broke in and stole the information while keeping Behemoth from recording any more brain data? Am I getting that right?" Krys asked.

Correct, the voice said.

"What is the 'splice point?'" I asked.

Splice point was when anomaly contamination occurred, the voice said.

"Are you fucking kidding me?" I groaned.

Negative, the voice said.

"What?" Krys asked.

I held up a finger to hold him off.

"What are the data point timelines for James Sable and Rhiannon...Cox," I flinched. I hadn't said my original last name in a dog's age.

The sphere's readback was exactly what I was expecting.

"What?" Krys asked again with some agitation as I sat chewing on my lip while thinking.

I gave a big Shae-like sigh and turned to Krys.

"Whoever broke in, and I'm pretty sure I know who, grabbed every piece of data starting from the time we were 'infected' by James's 'chaos engine.' Well, except James himself, of course. His data cuts off when he died," I said.

"Died?" Krys asked.

"Became a vampire," I corrected. "I'm honestly guessing here. I'll have to double-check the dates with James, but I'm betting I'm right."

"I'm not going to pretend I understand any of that," Krys said.

"Short version, anyone James swaps spit with catches whatever it is that screws up Behemoth's plans," I said.

"Swaps spit?" Krys asked.

"Gets intimate...ish with," I said.

"And this is a bad thing?" Krys asked, concern on his face.

"Only to Behemoth," I said. Then went on to explain how James somehow manages to break the rules of how things are supposed to work on Behemoth. "He can't control it or even aim it. It just happens," I said.

"Well, I understand how some things just happen, but this is a serious problem," Krys said.

I turned back to the sphere.

"If I can get the missing data points, can they be combined with these to form a complete set? A complete mind copy?" I asked.

Affirmative. If Carrot encounters missing data points, it is designed to acquire and incorporate them. It treats the missing data as corruption and reorganizes it, the voice said.

I summarized, "So, stick the crystal in a computer with the other info, and it'll fix itself?"

Correct, the voice said.

"James is gonna go ape shit when he hears this," I said as I shook my head. I knew how anxious he was becoming about this whole venture. Now that our three-step plan had just added a fourth step...I didn't have time to think about it right now.

"Can we make backups of the Carrots?" I asked the sphere.

Affirmative. All it requires are additional Carrots, the voice said.

"I've got an idea," I said, turning to Krys. But before I could tell him my idea, the sphere dropped a bombshell on me.

Do you wish to purge all data points related to James Sable? the voice asked.

"What?" I said slowly, turning back to the sphere.

Do you wish to purge all data points related to James Sable? the voice asked again.

"What happens if I do that?" I asked.

All data points will be deleted, and no further Carrots could be created, the voice said.

I just stared at the sphere in shock. I jumped when Krys's hand touched my shoulder.

"What is it?" Krys asked.

"I can keep Behemoth from ever making more of us," I said in a small voice.

"What do you mean?" Krys asked.

"As long as Behemoth has our memories, it can make more clones of us. If I delete them, it can't have our minds," I said, the idea making me lightheaded.

"But it still has your bodies," Krys said. "It can still make more body copies."

"True, but without our minds, they're just meat. And I bet I can purge the body part at the cloning facility," I said, lost in thought.

Correct, the voice said.

Silence fell then.

"But...that means if you die, you can't come back," Krys said.

"True, but the metaphysical aside, everything should have an ending eventually," I said.

"But, do you have the right to decide that for everyone?" Krys asked.

"Shit," I rubbed my face with my hands before shaking my head and turning back to Krys. I explained what I needed, and he got to work. Now that I had some time to kill...I needed to make a phone call.

James...we need to talk.

Chapter 7.5

BETH

I still don't know how you did it, but you did, I said as I finished closing the straps on the pack I was taking. Everything I owned was in that pack: a spare warskin, a single book, a PDD, and a photograph. There were a few other things, but they didn't bear mentioning.

My minder had continued to pester me about retiring until I finally gave in. I gave him what I thought was an impossible challenge just to shut him up.

*You get me retired but still able to stay here on Behemoth, and I'll do it," I'd told him.

My minder still wouldn't tell me how he'd managed to pull off the impossible and get me my walking papers. He'd surprised me with it last night just before bed. He should have waited till the morning, as I didn't get a wink of sleep. My mind had wandered all over the place, trying to figure out what I wanted to do.

I took a final look at my sparse room. I'd never decorated it, never saw a reason to. One less thing to worry about, I guess. But on the flip side, it meant I could walk out the door without worrying about what I left behind.

Ready to go? I asked my minder as I pulled my coat on and shouldered my pack.

Ready! my minder said.

He'd been a bit tight-lipped since he informed me that my request for retirement and to remain here on Behemoth had been approved. Not his usual snarky yammering self that never seemed to stop adding his two cents.

I slapped the wall, deactivated the lights, and stepped out into the corridor.

Next stop, Cresis, I said as I headed for the transport slide.

Trying to figure out what I was going to do and where I was going to go had been hard. There was practically any type of destination you could imagine. I planned on seeing a good deal of them before I settled down.

While I'd never tell my minder this, his idea to get a body augment last month had been a good idea. Because I was a vampire, my augment choices were limited. It seemed once you became a vamp, you couldn't go back to just being human. For some reason, Behemoth couldn't do that. But I still got my youth back.

The augment had returned me to what I looked like at the beginning of my singing career. It had knocked a couple of decades off my appearance, and now I hoped the aging part would slow down.

But I'd have to wait and see. The first time I glanced in the mirror after the augment, I thought there'd been a mistake. I didn't look old enough to drink. But I'd been staring into the mirror at my war-weary face for so long now, I'd forgotten what I'd once looked like.

My minder guaranteed there hadn't been a mistake and showed me one of my first touring posters. It was me, alright. The augment had cut my body clock in half, and now I looked 25 again.

It took me a while to stop staring at myself every time I caught my reflection.

My minder had suggested starting my whirlwind tour at Cresis. There wasn't anything special about it. My minder had been pretty specific about it, though. He said it would give me an idea of how things worked outside the military complex bubble of Behemoth.

I'd be lying if I said I wasn't excited to see it. Even when Shae took me places, it was always in the military sphere of Behemoth's control. I'd never even thought of leaving it. I thought all of Behemoth was the same. Turns out I was wrong again.

Cresis turned out to be a complete shithole.

As soon as I stepped out of the transport slide, I knew I was in trouble. I should have turned right around and gone somewhere else—anywhere else! But I didn't. I listened to my minder, who kept telling me to "give it a chance."

Cresis reminded me of an old west town you saw in the movies, only updated with Behemoth tech.

Not quite finished buildings lined a dirt road, and there appeared to be prairie out beyond the town. Instead of horses, there were things that looked like small, strange cars parked along the street. Multiple contrails lined the sky, telling me they had some sort of air travel.

Cresis wasn't on a Bio Hab. Instead, it lay at the end of a massive Biological Compartment (Bio Comp) that could easily house the entire USA. Supposedly, there were Bio Comps like this all over Behemoth.

They'd been testing areas before Bio Habs. Behemoth would try out land mass types, atmospheric combinations, and even small settlements to see how they would fare. Cresis was one of the settlements that had survived the test phase.

Why am I here again? I asked.

Because you've never been here before, that's why, my minder said in my head.

I frowned and started walking down the street. The first store I came across appeared to be some sort of antique store. Either that or it was a pawn shop. Or a junk shop. I couldn't tell. But it was as good a place to start as any.

A man behind a counter looked up when I came in. He took two seconds to examine me, and then returned to whatever it was he was doing.

"Hello," I said, my voice hoarse from the dusty air outside. I cleared my throat and repeated my greeting, but got no response.

I shrugged and began to browse the shelves, not knowing

what I was looking at. Some things I could make a guess at: lamps, boots, dishes, that sort of thing. But then there were others that I had to use my virtual cockpit to identify. Even then, sometimes, I was at a loss. I mean, what's a "bovine-reinducer?"

"How are things?" I asked awkwardly the next time I saw the proprietor.

He appeared to be working on a small metal box and ignored me. When I continued to pause, he finally spoke.

"If you're looking for conversation, go across the street to Tilly's," the man said. "If you want to buy something, buy it. Otherwise, I've got work to do." The entire time, he kept his focus on the box he was working on.

"Thanks," I muttered and left without another word.

Friendly guy, I said.

Busy guy, my minder said. *But your sarcasm is not far off.*

Yeah, regular rush hour around here, I mumbled.

I crossed the street and found Tilly's. That was all the description the sign out front gave. Not having anything else to do, I stepped inside.

I was expecting a saloon, in keeping with the Old West motif. Not this place, though. First off, it was air-conditioned, which was nice after the hot and dry day outside. A good third of the room was some sort of strangely shaped stage.

Where tables and chairs would be in the rest of the room, there were only barstools, at least two dozen of them. Each one sat by itself, not grouped together or anything.

"Help ya' with somethin'?" a voice drew my attention from behind me.

I turned and found a door leading into another room. Only the top half of the door was open, and a man was leaning against the bottom half. It reminded me of a coat check stand.

"Oh, hi!" I tried brightly. My minder had been bugging me to be upbeat. He said it would help me be happier, but I found it just made me tired.

"I'm—" I started, but a voice from outside cut me off.

"BETH SINCLAIR!" the voice outside called. They had to

be using some form of public address as I could hear them plain as day inside, with the front door closed.

"What the?" I said with a frown and headed for the door.

Hide.

What? I asked and froze a few feet from the door.

Hide, my minder repeated in my head.

Whhhhy? I drew the word out in my head.

"WE KNOW YOU'RE HERE, COME TOWARDS THE SOUND OF MY VOICE," the voice outside said.

When my minder continued its silence, I went to the door and cracked it.

Outside were five Daemons in full warskins. They were brandishing their pistols and didn't look friendly, not that Daemons ever looked friendly. The question was, why were they looking for me?

Do not go out there! my minder said as I started to pull the door open.

Why not? I asked. *It's just a patrol. I'll go see what they want.*

They'll shoot you! my minder said.

No, they won't, I scoffed.

Before I could open the door, a hand reached around me and pulled the door fully open. The man from the coat check room stepped outside.

"What's that, officer?" the man asked.

I looked and found a few other people had stepped outside to see what all the commotion was about.

"We're looking for Beth Sinclair," the lead Daemon said, releasing a video drone. A four-foot picture of me appeared from the drone, looking a lot like a wanted poster.

"Oh," the man said and turned back to me. "They're looking for—"

Before the man could finish, a bolt of plasma singed my cheek as it passed and blew a hole in the wall beside me.

I had enough time to look dumbfounded as the rest of the Daemons raised their pistols and fired.

Luckily, my training took over, and I threw myself backwards just as the entryway became a collection of mashed and scorched metal.

What's going on? I hollered over the noise of the now constant gunfire. *Why are they trying to kill me?* I said as I bolted for the stage.

A side hallway led off the stage and down into a basement. I ran blindly, not paying attention, only caring about getting away.

Well... my minder started.

The basement branched into several rooms and corridors that led off in various directions. One in particular was much longer than the building and appeared to connect to the buildings next door and beyond.

Spit it out already! I barked as I sprinted down the corridor. I didn't bother to stop at the next building and continued until the hallway turned left.

Perhaps reports of your retirement were slightly exaggerated? my minder said.

What do you mean? I said as I bounced off a wall and continued running.

No one is allowed to retire from the Chosen Army, my minder said. *You said so yourself.*

I know what I said! I replied. *But you said you'd taken care of it and got me a waiver.*

Yeah, not so much, my minder said.

What's that supposed to mean? I asked as I bounced off another wall at an intersection. It appeared there was an entire labyrinth of rooms and corridors beneath this town.

It means you're technically...AWOL, my minder said, sheepishly.

You've got to be kidding me! I said in disgust.

AWOL soldiers were shot on sight. There was no bringing them back alive. They were traitors to Behemoth and might as well be the AG for all intents and purposes.

You and I are having words, later, I said.

Noted, my minder said. *Go up these stairs.*

I started to object but held my tongue as I sprinted up the stairs. I paused at the door at the top of the stairs and listened. I couldn't hear anything beyond the door, but suddenly started hearing voices behind me in the underground.

As quietly as I could, I cracked the door and looked beyond. I'd circled the town and had ended up back in the grumpy guy's store. I slipped into the room silently and closed the door.

The guy was still sitting at his counter, working on the same metal box.

As I took a step, the man looked straight at me.

He stared at me for a long moment, and then his eyes darted outside, where my wanted poster was still floating in the middle of the street. Then his eyes returned to mine.

For a second, I thought he would just return to fiddling with his box, which would be better than calling out to the Daemons. Instead, he nodded slightly to the counter behind which he was sitting.

I didn't need further encouragement. I scuttled over behind the counter, trying to be as quiet as I could. As soon as I was behind it, the man's foot came out and pushed me into a small cubby hole in the cabinet. A moment later, a small, clear plastic cover slid over my hiding spot, and not a moment too soon, as the door to the back burst open.

"Stop this foolishness, Colonel," one of the Daemons said. I hadn't recognized any of them from the quick glance I got. At least they weren't from my squad. "We know you came this way. Come out now and put an end to it."

From a mirror on the wall, I watched as the Daemons spread out and searched the store.

"You break it, you buy it," the old man behind the counter said a few moments later.

"Where is she, Ulick?" one of the Daemons asked.

"The woman on your holo?" the old man named Ulick said. "Dunno."

"We know she came into your store, the track still shows a trace of her. Where is she?" the Daemon repeated.

"Still dunno," Ulick said. "But you're right, she did come in here a while back. But she didn't want to buy anything either, so I sent her to Tilly's. Maybe try there?"

The Daemons froze, a sign they were speaking through their tacnet to one another.

"Suit yourself," Ulick said and went back to tinkering with the metal box.

A few moments later, the Daemons left the shop, heading back across the street towards Tilly's.

I started to reach forward to pull the plastic aside, but Ulick's foot came up and stopped me. He didn't look down; he just barred my way with his foot.

I sat back to wait.

Over the next several hours, the Daemons repeatedly came and went through Ulick's shop. Each time, they left empty-handed. Even when they made Ulick move and searched the counter where I was hiding, they didn't find me.

I had no idea how it worked. I was six inches from one of them, and they never knew.

"I think they've finally given up," Ulick said an hour after the last Daemon left his shop. "Let's just wait until they've boarded the transport slide," he said.

When Ulick finally let me up, my legs had gone to sleep, and I couldn't stand up, so I sat on the floor massaging my legs. I looked back at where my hiding spot was and could no longer see it. Where the small cubby hole had been, now looked like the solid wall of the cabinet.

"Thanks," I finally managed.

Ulick simply grunted and returned to his metal box.

Curiosity finally got the better of me.

"What are you working on?" I said when I could finally stand.

"Huh?" Ulick said. "Oh. Slide responder."

"A slide responder?" I asked.

"Allows you to operate a transport slide without using Behemoth's controls," Ulick said as he turned it over in his hand. "And, done!" Ulick sat back and smiled at his handywork.

"I haven't built one of these in years," Ulick said. "Course, most of us don't need 'em." Ulick handed the box to me. "He'll know what to do with it," he said as he tapped his temple.

I looked down at the small creation, and my virtual cockpit began a series of commands that explained how it worked.

"Thank you, Ulick," I said. "I don't know what else to say."

Ulick grunted again and began rummaging around under his counter before he pulled out a small basket of odds and ends. He looked up at me as if surprised I was still standing there.

"If you ain't buyin' you need to get," Ulick said and made a shooing motion at me.

Go back downstairs, my minder spoke up for the first time since the initial chase.

Oh, I'll get to you, I scolded my minder.

Yeah, yeah. Just move, my minder said.

My minder had never been this pushy before. He'd always given me suggestions, but never straight told me to do anything. Of course, he was now the reason I was a fugitive, so I guess the niceties were out the window.

I made my way to the back door and went downstairs. Immediately, my minder started giving me directions.

I'm guessing Ulick is the reason we came to this town? I said a minute later.

Yes, he's very resourceful, my minder said.

Uh-huh, I said and waited. When my minder didn't speak, I started up again. *Are you going to tell me what's going on?*

Sure, my minder said and then was quiet.

Why did you make me desert?! I asked finally.

Because you wouldn't do it yourself, my minder said. *And I was sick of watching you get recycled.*

What? I asked, coming to a stop in the middle of the small corridor. I'd been following his directions blindly up till this point and had no idea where I was anymore.

I've never been recycled, I said. Recycling meant your memories of Behemoth were purged, and you were returned to your Bio Hab. Well, my Bio Hab was gone, so there was nowhere to go back to. Not that I'd ever request it in the first place.

You've been recycled 264 times, my minder said. *One more and you get a free pie.*

Bullshit! I shot back. *No one can be...that's not how it...* but the longer I thought about it, the more I realized I'd have no idea if I'd ever been recycled or not. The memory of it would have been erased.

But why? I asked.

Initially? You were suicidal, my minder said. *That was before me, so I don't know how many times it happened, exactly. But since then, you've had your mind wiped 264 times.*

Why didn't they wipe you? I asked.

They can't, my minder said. *That's part of being a minder. I'm with you forever.*

Lovely, I grumbled. *But again, why?*

Take your pick, my minder said. *Several times, you became disenchanted with the army, and other times, you were severely injured. Sometimes you were just done with everything and shut down. Each time, Behemoth would rewind you to where it thought you were still OK and try again. It didn't always get it right.*

My mind was in a whirl, digesting all that, and I started moving again just to be doing something.

I kept trying to get you to retire voluntarily, but you kept refusing, my minder said. *When you gave me the challenge, I took that as you were finally ready to give retirement a try and went ahead with my plan.*

Your plan? I asked. *So, exactly what's next in this great plan of yours?*

We need to stay ahead of the hounds, my minder said simply. *We'll stay on the move until things calm down.*

Meaning, you don't have a plan at all. Great, I muttered.

Hey, you said you wanted to see the world! my minder said enthusiastically.

Yeah, the sandy beaches and margaritas parts! Not the dingy underground back alleys! I said.

It's still something new! my minder said, trying to look on the bright side.

We stayed on the move for the next few months. We never stayed anywhere more than a day or so. If we did, the hounds would find us.

That first day, they'd found me so fast because I'd used my personal credentials to go to Cresis. It was literally a glowing line for them to follow.

Since then, I've been traveling extensively on foot through

corridors and passageways. I climbed through ancient shafts and used my highly illegal slide responder to make my journey as erratic as possible.

Even though my minder said my personal tracker had been disabled, the hounds would catch up to us within a day or so. I chalked it up to the vast network of sensors Behemoth had. I was pretty safe when I was in empty corridors. But even long-abandoned corridor intersections sometimes still had working sensors. It was impossible to tell which were working and which weren't.

Anytime I asked my minder if we were heading somewhere specific, all he'd say was that we were heading "away."

I had no idea where I was or where we were going. I had a sinking feeling my minder didn't either.

I was used to the beautiful artistic corridors that looked like forests, or deserts, or whatever. The corridors I was now travelling through were nothing but different shades of gray. One time, I came across a passageway that was jet black, but it didn't last long before the gray was back.

And during all this time, I had my ever-faithful minder companion who seemed to be becoming more worried than I was about our situation.

I wasn't used to my minder being bothered by anything. He was always his same cool, collected self. But as the weeks started to pass, cracks were starting to show in his façade.

You doing OK? I asked as I relaxed in a small recess set in the corridor wall. It was a relatively comfortable half-moon that I fully sprawled in.

I was chewing on the straw of a not-blood pouch from my pack. I first questioned why my minder had made me take so many pouches when I could pick one up at any fabricator. Now, I understood.

What's that? my minder asked, sounding distracted.

Are you OK? I said.

That's my line, he said.

True, but you've been acting more and more nervous as the days pass. Everything alright? I asked.

He let out a long sigh, which is weird when it's in your head.

I just expected us to have more time before we were on the run, he said.

Really? I started. *You thought the all-powerful Behemoth would just not notice when I didn't show up for work for the first time in 16 years?*

Well, I'd hoped, he said, making me laugh.

It felt good to laugh. It was a nice change.

At first, I'd been constantly worried. My stomach was always tight, and I was constantly looking over my shoulder at every little sound. However, as time passed and I got tired of constantly jumping at shadows, I started letting things slide.

How are you feeling so calm? he asked.

Oh that's easy. I stopped giving a shit, I said with a shrug.

What? he screeched.

Eh, I frowned. *If I get caught, I'll either be shot or have my mind wiped, right?*

Uh, yeah! my minder said.

Well, either way I won't really know about it, and I'll at least be out of this rat's maze, I said. I'd gotten sick of sneaking around the back halls. I was almost to the point of—

OK! My minder started. *We need to get you back into civilization.* He then started giving me a series of directions.

That's all it took? I asked. *Me giving up?*

Just...just go that way already! my minder said, indicating the directions he'd given me.

Whatever you say, boss!

Chapter 8

JAMES

"Why can't anything ever be easy?" I griped into my drink.

After Rhi and Krys returned from their partially successful mission, Krys took us out to drink. Krys said the only way to rid ourselves of the dark cloud that had fallen over us was to apply copious amounts of alcohol. Rhi had seconded the motion. If you asked me, I think the two were colluding against me.

So, we all went out into the neon jungle and found a dive bar. Shashka joined us shortly after, which improved my mood as I hadn't seen her since the gate malfunction.

I have no idea why we always went to a dive bar. There were limitless alcoholic establishments on Behemoth. We could have gone to a fancy or at least somewhat decent bar. But Rhi was the one who somehow always picked where we went. That meant a dive bar.

Rhi wasted no time in cozying up to Shashka. I don't know if it was the alcoholic not-blood we were drinking, or if Rhi was trying to get in her good graces to get at Krys. Or, it could have been her feeding off my emotions, yet again.

I mean, Shashka was hot. She was my height, with straight white hair slightly longer than her husband's. She wore such a serious expression all the time that it would ward you off. But that expression instantly softened as soon as she started talking to you. Her stoic demeanor, according to Krys, was just a mask.

"Get beneath it, and her spirit will surprise you," Krys told me back when we were on their ship. Needless to say, we'd had a lot of time to talk during the two weeks I'd been with them.

"So, what's next?" I asked.

"Well, we can't retrieve the bodies without the mind to go with," Cr'eon said. "The mind has to be incorporated while the clone is still in the tank. It's a one-time deal."

Cr'eon had accessed some basic information about the cloning process while she'd been inside the Behemoth info net. She figured if she was going to risk it, she might as well risk it all. There hadn't been a lot of info, but what there was, she grabbed.

"Which means we have to have both parts of the mindset before they come out of the tank," Viola said.

"Yes. Once out of the tank, it's a done deal," Cr'eon said.

"And you know who has the other half, right?" Rhi asked me, her head already on Shashka's shoulder.

I couldn't tell if Rhi was actually drunk or not. She liked to drink. And she didn't stop once she started. The problem was, she'd been trained to put on a show. To make people think she was drunk so that she could manipulate them. Her hanging off someone was usually a sign she was well on her way, but you never knew.

"The AG," I grumbled. "The fucking AG. They told us they'd interrupted Behemoth's monitoring of us. I didn't realize they'd spoofed our minds in the process," I spat.

Krys patted my arm.

"Relax, we'll fix this. We're with you all the way, isn't that right, Shashka?" Krys said.

We looked over, and Rhi had her tongue down Shashka's throat. Shashka appeared to be returning the favor.

Krys started laughing, and I looked back at him.

"That didn't take long," Krys chuckled.

"I didn't know that—" I started.

"Yes, you did, James," Krys said and patted my arm again.

"Let me grab another round," I said as I made my escape from the table. By the time I came back, my head was a bit clearer, and Rhi and Shashka had broken their liplock. Now, they appeared just to be talking.

Plotting, James. Plotting, Rhi sent to me.

When did you— I started.

Shut up and stop thinking, James. Rhi cut me off.

I could feel the chaotic emotions coming from her. She'd been holding herself back for so long, it was all coming out now. I had a feeling it was going to be a weird night.

"Where'd the others go?" I asked as I sat down. It was just Rhi, Shashka, Krys, and me at the table now.

"They said they were going to go hit up their AG contacts to try and dig up some leads," Shashka said.

"Yeah, they said it would probably take until tomorrow, so they wouldn't be home tonight," Rhi said as she locked eyes with me.

Really? I asked Rhi mentally.

James... Rhi started.

I know, go with it, I sighed and took another drink.

I had no idea how I felt—

You know exactly how you feel, James; get out of your own way, Rhi interrupted. *You weren't like this before the beard,* Rhi chuckled in my head.

I hadn't shaved in over a month now, and had solid growth going on, that part was true.

They're both true— Rhi started.

Get out of my head! I yelled back. *I can make my own decisions.*

I looked around the table, and it looked like Shashka and Krys were having their own mental conversation.

"Alright, let's go," I said as I downed my drink and stood up before I lost my nerve.

∞∞∞∞∞∞Ω∞∞∞∞∞∞

RHI

I must have been more tired than I thought because Shashka and Krys were gone by the time I woke up. I rolled over and found James still asleep, facing away from me.

I searched my emotions as I watched his chest rise and fall. Last night had been educational...and hot. Not everything about Krys and Shashka had been physically the same as us, especially since Krys wasn't human at all. Regardless, we had taken turns learning and enjoying one another. Well, not so much taken turns. But I kept getting distracted watching James.

Meanwhile, the emotional baggage I had expected to show up the morning after never did. I wasn't sure what that meant.

Quit trying to make trouble for yourself, my inner voice said.

You know me, I countered.

I do, and you'll give yourself an ulcer over this if you let it, she said.

But— I started.

You already know what Tara would say, so why do I have to say it for her? the voice said.

The thought made me chuckle. If Tara had been here last night, she would have been at the foot of the bed with a camera, acting like a cheerleader. The girl had been...WAS incorrigible.

There you go, my inner voice said.

What? I asked.

I can't remember the last time you smiled when you thought about Tara, the voice said gently.

Oh, shut up, I said, mentally picturing throwing a pillow at the voice that had been in my head ever since an IED put me in the hospital all those years ago.

A pillow fight? Really? Isn't that how the night's supposed to start off, not the morning after? my voice asked.

I ignored my inner voice and moved over to curl up as James's big spoon. I couldn't remember the last time I'd been this close to him.

Stop thinking about it! the voice screamed in my head.

OK, OK. No more screaming, please, I thought.

We were both gorged on not-blood, and our bodies were hot to the touch. That usually happened after you overindulged, and boy, had we indulged last night. But for now, he was comfy, and I settled in to go back to sleep.

∞∞∞∞∞Ω∞∞∞∞∞

<u>JAMES</u>

I woke up with the warmest, softest monkey on my back. Rhi was so comfortable that I almost fell back to sleep. Images of our previous antics flashed through my head, causing me to smile nostalgically.

Could you be nostalgic more quietly, please? Rhi asked softly in my mind.

Sorry that me being happy was so loud, I sent back. When she didn't take a shot at me, I glanced back at her questioningly.

Oh, I'm not touching that one, Rhi said. *I'm trying to be nice this morning.*

I rolled over to face her.

I'm not...opening the door just yet, Rhi started.

She seemed to be having a problem expressing herself.

But... Rhi started. *I'm cracking it. I don't want to be the way I've been...when we...*

Get them back? I offered. Now I understood where she was coming from. Rhi had been in my head more in the last few weeks than in the last several years. We'd both pretty much shut ourselves off from everyone, especially each other, after the living fire.

Yeah, Rhi said. *Thanks for letting me ride your emotions last night.*

I looked at her and frowned.

Now who's lying? I asked. *Last night was equal parts you and me. We're just so out of practice that we didn't realize it.*

I thought that part of me was pretty much dead, Rhi said. *But the closer we get to...getting them back...the more of my old self seems to be trying to come back.*

It never left, I smiled. *We just got a little lost.* I know my own feelings had been numb for so long that numb was my new status quo.

Remind me to thank them, Rhi said.

Oh, I think last night was thanks enough, I chuckled as Rhi gently punched me in the chest.

Go shower, you smell, Rhi wrinkled her nose at me.

Join me? I offered.

Maybe later— Rhi started her automatic response but stopped herself. *Yes, OK.*

A short time later, we were in the living room when the rest of our crew arrived.

"Knock knock?" Viola said as she cracked the door open. "Everybody decent?"

"Just come in already," I called out.

A smiling Viola led Cr'eon and Hess inside. When I looked, Hess had a strange smile on her face was well.

"What's that about Hess?" I asked, curious.

"Oh, nothing," she said in a strangely bright voice I'd never heard from her. Usually, she was kind of gruff.

"Uh-huh," I said with a chuckle.

"So, what did y'all learn?" Rhi asked, smiling at the newcomers.

Viola grinned at Rhi and then at me.

"Why didn't y'all do that sooner?" Viola asked with her hands on her hips. "I mean, just look at the two of you."

Rhi and I looked at one another. As soon as we did, our grins faded, and we returned to our normal visages.

"Oh, come on!" Viola complained, stomping her foot.

"Well," Cr'eon said, interrupting Viola's building tantrum. "It seems the AG did and still are monitoring your data points. You called it James. When they originally captured you, they took over your feed from Behemoth."

"But why?" Rhi asked.

"If the AG can't beat Behemoth, they'll do whatever they can to interfere with it. Behemoth had an invested interest in your group, so the AG took over to deny Behemoth access to it," Cr'eon said.

"But what are they doing with it?" I asked.

"Nothing," Viola replied.

"Nothing?" I asked.

"Nope, nothing. They're just storing it, just like Behemoth," Viola said.

"But they don't have a cloning facility," Rhi said.

"True, but they do have access to their own archive facility where they can store the data," Viola said.

"It just seems like a lot of trouble for so little payoff," I complained.

"You never know," Viola said. "By studying you, Behemoth might figure out how to create new DC. If the AG can keep that from happening, then it's worth it to them."

"It would be easier to kill us," Rhi said.

"Don't tempt them!" Cr'eon said.

"So, what's the next step?" Rhi asked.

"I'm trying to get in touch with someone to steal the data from the AG," Viola said.

"Steal it? I thought you were the next best thing to a god to the AG. Why wouldn't they just give you the information?"

"Because it's one of the dick splinter groups that has it," Viola said.

"Dick splinter?" Rhi muttered comically.

"Which one?" Cr'eon asked, ignoring Rhi's comment.

"The Barkt," Viola said, giving Rhi a glare.

"Ugh," Cr'eon made a disgusted sound, drawing all eyes to her.

"What?" Rhi asked. "What's wrong with the Barkt?"

"They're one of the 'whatever it takes' factions," Cr'eon said.

Rhi frowned.

"They're also the faction that uses the living fire as its primary weapon," Viola said, drawing sharp looks from Rhi and me. She waited a moment before saying, "Yeah, it's the same group that activated it on your Bio Hab."

Rhi and I looked at one another for a moment.

"Is there any downside to wiping these assholes out?" Rhi asked.

"Seconded," I said.

"OK, hold up," Viola said. "I can understand your feelings..." When Rhi and I gave her dubious looks, she continued. "Well, I can. I've been around a lot longer than you two, and I've seen a hell of a lot more atrocities, so when I say I understand, it's not lip service!" Viola's voice took on a stern, school-teacher tone by the end.

Rhi and I sat up straighter.

"Sorry," I offered.

"Yeah," Rhi agreed.

Viola nodded.

"While the Barkt are dicks, they also maintain several other programs that help the AG as a whole. This is the reason the other AG haven't taken them out themselves," Viola said.

"Yeah, they have some sort of program where they recruit Bio Hab normals for information-gathering purposes," Cr'eon said.

"How is that a good thing?" Rhi asked.

"They offer them deals," Cr'eon started.

"They give them wishes in exchange for favors," Viola said.

"What kind of favors?" I asked, afraid of what I'd hear.

"Surprisingly, nothing nefarious," Viola said.

"I find that hard to believe," Rhi said.

Viola shrugged.

"Regardless, we can't just nuke the faction," Viola said. "There are too many and they're too powerful. All you'd be doing is adding yet another enemy to your growing list of baddies."

"So, what do we do then?" I asked.

"I'm working on it," Viola said, grinning at me.

"You know I hate it when you say that," I groaned. Usually, anytime Viola had said that to me in the past, nothing good came from it.

"Trust me, Dad!" Viola continued to grin.

∞∞∞∞∞∞Ω∞∞∞∞∞∞

VIOLA

Dad needed to start trusting me more. I mean, I hadn't led him astray yet. Thanks to me, he was already a third of the way to rescuing Mom.

Of course, I was also a third of the way to my goal, but he didn't need to know that. If I managed to pull it off, then I'd tell him. But not before then, he might back out.

Actually, he might not like how I was using him right now, regardless of how much this was going to help. So, maybe I won't tell him after all. We'll see.

For now, I'm focusing on his and Rhi's emotional comeback. I'd hoped they'd have come out of their celibate shells eventually, but I wasn't expecting it until much later. It seems Krys's little problem helped in more ways than one.

I'm happy for them. I wish I could have been there, but that wouldn't have been appropriate...you know, since I'm their "daughter" and all. Who knows, maybe that'll change in time, too.

Even still, I hadn't expected them to delete their mind backups! I can understand not wanting Behemoth to be able to create more from your mind, but they deleted Shae and Tara's as well. If anything happens to the memory crystals they're carrying, that's it. Game over.

Anyway, I can't worry about that now. I need to go and recruit a team...if I can find them.

Chapter 8.5

BETH

I stared out the metal shuttered window at the landscape passing by. The snow-covered trees and rocks that made up the rough mountains were pretty in their own way, if it hadn't been so blasted cold!

The caravan I was hitching a ride with consisted of four massive floating crawlers accompanied by a handful of support and guard craft. Some were also hover vehicles, using repulsors to keep themselves floating over the rough terrain, while others were tracked vehicles.

Regardless, all the vehicles were well-used and worn, but had been kept in good shape.

The journey across the Bio Comp was a long one, taking a couple of months easily. But my minder assured me that taking this obscure mode of travel would keep me well off Behemoth's radar.

So far, a week in, it had reminded me of taking a train. I hated trains. Back in my touring days, anytime my manager had suggested a train, I'd told him he could take the train, I'd be on the bus. I preferred the bus even to airplanes. Don't ask me why.

My minder somehow managed to book me passage on this metal wagon train as a guard. Having not listed any of my other skills, I was essentially just a hired gun. While these caravans were rarely attacked by anything other than animals, it looked like whoever was in charge of this one was taking no chances.

There weren't a lot of passengers, this being more of a supply run. But those who were paying for passage were mostly homesteaders and farmers heading out into the still-untamed parts of the Bio Comp to stake their claim.

It still surprised me that inside the technical marvel that was Behemoth, there were still big empty swaths of wilderness where people wanted to set up homes. Instead of enjoying the easy, technology-heavy life in a city, people still choose to move into the middle of nowhere and try to survive with the most basic of necessities.

It takes all types, I guess.

Tell me again why I can't just take a slide all the way to the other end of Behemoth and get away from everything? I asked my minder, taking a page from these pioneers' books.

Because you wouldn't like what you'd find, my minder said.

Explain that, I said.

Like biomes are grouped together, my minder said with a heavy sigh as he started his lecture once again. *In your case, humanoids. Anything that resembled a humanoid was grouped together with other humanoids. It's easier, both socially and in terms of support mechanisms.

The further from that biome you go, the further from humanoids and all the support structure that goes with it you get, he said.

So what? I asked. *What does that actually mean?*

My minder paused, seemingly to collect his thoughts.

OK, you like air, water, blood, and sunlight...for the most part, right? he asked.

Sure, I said.

So, the further from your home you go, the more these change, my minder said. *Replace air with rock, water with gas, blood with acid, and sunlight with void. Remember, Behemoth was originally tasked with creating soldiers for every type of environment out there. It had some multi-purpose creations, capable of operating in multiple environments, but it still had to create niche creatures as well.*

I thought about it for a minute. *Is that how vamps were made? A multi-purpose creature?*

My minder scoffed in my head.

Hardly, he said. *Vampires were accidental mutations. Well, not so much a mutation but an error."

An error? I asked.

Vampires were one of the early warning signs that a Bio Hab was corrupted, he said. *All supernatural creatures were...or at least creatures who were considered supernatural for that Bio Hab.*

Corrupted?

Most Bio Habs, he began. *Were sole organisms, such as humans. Was there other life there? Yes, but they weren't the focus; they were support features.*

Wolves were support features? I asked.

Yes, he said. *Their importance was to the balance of the ecosystem that supported humans. They were a support system for the Bio Hab.*

OK, I get it. How do vamps come in, though? I asked.

Just like with any creation, there are always variables, my minder said. *Genetic drift is a part of the evolution process. It can help or hinder a species.*

You're saying vampires are due to genetic drift? I said skeptically.

Sort of, he said. *As Behemoth continued to change humans to try and perfect them for its purposes, errors happened.*

Errors? I chuckled.

Usually these errors were cast off and rejected for the more perfected strain, but sometimes they stuck around, he said. *Sometimes, if the environment was right and the governing factors weren't paying close enough attention, these errors took root.*

So, we're weeds, I concluded. *You're saying vampires are weeds in the garden of Bio Habs.*

If that helps you sleep at night, he said.

I'm sorry I asked, I said, shaking my head.

Most of the time, when my minder and I were having long, drawn-out conversations, they were actually quick. A conversation in my head that felt like it had been going on for 20 minutes could easily happen in a few seconds of real-time. While handy on occasion, it tended to tax my brain if I was trying to do other stuff at the same time.

So, to answer your original question, while you could go through the effort to travel to the other side of Behemoth, you wouldn't be able to survive. Hence, you wouldn't like it, my minder said.

Right. I sighed.

"Stay awake, kid."

The voice of the captain of this vehicle drew my attention from my staring out the window. When I turned to face him, he'd already moved on.

I told you the augment made me too damned young! I hissed. *That's the dozenth time someone's called me a kid today, and it's getting old!*

Trust me, if something does happen on this trip, they won't be calling you a kid for very long, my minder tried to soothe me. *These humanoids are weaker than even your home species. Just try not to pick a fight to prove it. It would kind of defeat the purpose.*

I bit back a retort, trying not to rise to the occasion for once. With my renewed youth came a whole slew of new hormones that I had to learn to control all over again. It was a pain.

You know, if you just considered— my minder started.

For the last time, I'm not working for the AG. Shae told me what they did. Fuck them! I said with finality.

My minder had been trying to get me to consider joining the AG, if for no other reason than to gain access to their resources. But after hearing about what happened to Tara, I couldn't bring myself to do it. The thought made my skin crawl.

I gave a dark chuckle and took out my PDD to jot down my thoughts. I'd found that my new fugitive status seemed to be inspiring my musical side for the first time in years. If I didn't write it down when inspiration struck, I'd lose it.

The constant hum of the engines suddenly died as our vehicle lumbered to a stop.

I put away my PDD and glanced around.

"What's going on?" I asked one of the passing techs.

"Crawler two blew a repulser. Gotta stop for repairs," the tech said and hurried back to his job.

I sighed. It was the fourth breakdown so far. Although the vehicles were maintained well, they were still old and tended to break down.

I zipped up my winter coat and headed up top.

The hatch to the roof of the vehicle opened with a loud squeak. The roof was easily the size of a small house.

The bright light of the sun caused me to squint and pull on my shades. I walked a slow perimeter of the roof, using my shades to zoom in on our surroundings for any threats or hazards.

We were in a high mountain prairie, making it easy to watch out for problems. I'd just zoomed in on a mound of something when the captain's voice startled me.

"See anything, kid?" he asked. The captain was a grizzled veteran of a man with an expanding paunch. He looked like he spent way too much time sitting on his backside, even though he bore scars that showed he'd lived a rough life.

"Only thing is over there, not sure what to make of it," I said, pointing at the mound I was eyeballing.

The captain pulled out a pair of binoculars and zoomed in on it.

"Ah, yeah," he said and handed me the binos. "Those glasses aren't the best, try these."

I took the binos and zoomed in on the mound. I recognized it immediately. It was an old Mk 14 AUG. It looked like it had smacked into the ground at speed, but had stayed in one piece.

"Good eyes," the captain gave me a rare compliment. "She's been there for years. No one's been able to salvage her due to her boobytraps. It's a shame, she's still in good shape."

"Yeah, the 14s were tough old birds," I said with a nod and handed him back his binos.

"You know something about 'em?" the captain looked at me with something that kind of resembled being impressed.

"You could say that," I grinned at him.

"Hey Cap, looks like we'll be here a while, they need to change out the whole field on number 2," one of the techs said, sticking his head out the door towards us.

"Crap," the captain said. "We're going to be here for hours." He sighed. "Well, nothing to be done for it," he said and turned for the door. "Keep an eye out, kid."

"Hey, cap," I started, and he turned back to face me with an annoyed expression on his face. I didn't call him "cap," only his regular crew did that.

"Can we take a stroll out to that 14?" I asked.

What are you doing? my minder asked.

Trying something, I said.

"Why?" the captain asked. "You think you can do something?"

"I dunno," I said. "But, since we're going to be here a while...what could it hurt?"

You could trip a warning system and bring down a wing of AUGs on us! my minder warned.

You worry too much, I said. *Besides, you can squelch that, can't you?*

Yes, my minder grumbled after a moment.

Ten minutes later, the captain and I stood beside the 14, staring at it. One of the small flyers that escorted the convoy had brought us over and was hovering nearby.

"Wow," I said in admiration.

"What?" the captain asked.

"They don't make them this pretty anymore," I sighed.

The captain looked annoyed. "So, can you do anything or not?"

Anything? I asked my minder.

As far as I can tell, there's no active systems, stand-by, my minder said.

I approached the wreck and slowly circled it. My neural cockpit began going over every inch of the half-buried AUG.

Looks like the pilot ejected before impact, my minder confirmed. *The destruct signal was sent but never acted on.*

An AUG was never left in the field for an enemy to take. If

one had to be abandoned, it was destroyed. Otherwise, the enemy could recover it and use it against you in the future.

I moved up and reached my hand out.

"What are you doing? Are you crazy?!" the captain screeched.

I gave him a smile and laid my hand on the cold ceramic of the war machine. Nothing happened for a moment.

"Establishing connection" flashed in my HUD. A moment later, I was in the internal systems.

"Looks like the destruct system malfunctioned," I said to the captain.

"How do you know that?" he asked.

I tapped my shades, "Good shades."

Can you help me wipe the OS? I asked my minder.

Sure, but why? the minder asked.

Without the OS, even the redundant systems won't work. No risk of destruct or activation. Even if they gut it for parts, all they'll get are parts, no working systems. I said.

You want to give them an AUG?!? my minder asked, incredulous.

I want to give them a shell of an antique, I said. *This thing hasn't been a contender in over a hundred years, at least.*

Whatever, my minder said and started helping me through the required steps.

"Cap, can you keep a secret?" I asked.

"That depends on what it is," he said suspiciously.

"How about one that could net you this salvage?" I grinned at him.

"You pull that off and you won't work another day this trip!" the captain said excitedly.

"Just keep my part out of it, and I think I've got something for you," I said.

"What part?" the captain said slyly. "Out of what? I don't know what you're talking about," the captain grinned back at me for the first time this trip.

It took longer to dig out the AUG than it did to repair crawler 2, but you didn't hear a single complaint as our crane finally pulled the machine free of the Earth.

Needless to say, I never had to lift a shovel to help.

"I don't know how you did it, ki...how you did it, Sinclair, and I don't care!" The captain said my actual name quietly to the side for the first time this trip. "The salvage alone will let us rebuild this rig and possibly a second."

I hadn't asked for anything, but the captain had insisted I was getting a full share. Normally, guards were paid a pittance salary, and that was it. I was expecting Behemoth money, which I couldn't use.

But seeing as this salvage was going to be as illegal as they came, I'd be getting paid in whatever they used for black market currency here. It probably wouldn't help me once I left this Bio Comp, but while I was here, I should be comfortable.

The captain had to redistribute cargo on all four crawlers just to make room for the AUG, but he did it with a smile on his face.

"Happy to help, cap," I said.

Chapter 9

JAMES

"Where does Hess always go?" I asked as I slurped up noodles from a take-out box.

Cr'eon, Rhi, and I were sitting around a small concrete pad in front of one of the monstrous skyscrapers. The railings we were sitting or leaning on blocked off the streets on either side.

The city noise was strangely quiet this morning as the three of us ate the food we'd grabbed from the food cart down the way.

We'd been trying out anything new, food-wise, that we could find lately. But today, I was in the mood for something nostalgic, and noodles were it. Of course, they weren't noodles but some facsimile. Still, they tasted good.

Viola had been gone for over a week now. While she'd normally disappear doing whatever it was she did here, she'd usually check in with me to ease my worry.

I knew she wasn't really my daughter. She was some sub-mind of a Behemoth-like program inside a weird semi-robot body. But...I'd raised her as my daughter for so long that I tended to forget those other things and still worried like an anxious father.

"No idea," Rhi mumbled around a mouthful of food from her perch sitting atop the railing.

I glanced at Cr'eon, but she also had her mouth full of food and simply shrugged.

Hess was the weird one in our group, and that was saying something. She normally stayed in the background and rarely spoke unless Viola asked her a question. But every so often, I'd catch her watching us, and she'd have this weird smile on her face. It creeped me out.

"She usually goes off with Viola," Cr'eon said.

"Has anyone had an actual conversation with her?" Rhi asked as she wiped the sauce off her cheek with the back of her hand.

We all looked at one another and shook our heads.

"Hmm," I said as I continued to eat.

I caught sight of a strange car above us. It was floating above the surrounding buildings, but unlike the surrounding air traffic, it wasn't moving.

Then, movement out of the corner of my eye drew my attention. Someone was sprinting at us at incredible speed. I barely had enough time to get my arm up before it hit.

Usually, this kind of move looked cool on TV. Casually reaching out, grabbing a speedster by the throat as they came in, and holding them up in the air like a flailing chicken. Of course, that was in cartoons. This was real life.

While I did catch the guy, his kinetic energy transferred to me, knocking both of us into the railing.

He'd been so fast; I hadn't had time to warn the others, so they sat in stunned disbelief as I appeared to fly through the air and crash to the ground suddenly for no reason.

"Oh gee, I'm sorry, eh?"

The voice came from somewhere above me as I was currently in a tangled mess of arms and legs with the guy who'd run into me. My head was still spinning when Rhi and Cr'eon pulled the guy off me rather forcefully.

"I totally lost control there, so sorry," the voice said.

"You alright?" Rhi asked, helping me to my feet.

"Uh, yeah," I blinked a few times to try and get everything back in focus. I glanced down to see my noodles splattered all over the ground.

"Oh, that's not good. Just a tic," the voice said.

There was a swoosh of air, and then a fresh box of noodles was being held out in my face.

I followed the hand holding the noodles up and found a young man smiling at me. He was slightly shorter than I was and had close-cropped dark hair. He had acne scars on his face and was missing a tooth in his smile. Plus, he looked genuinely embarrassed.

"What?" I started.

"Yeah, sometimes I get going a bit too fast and end up tail over teakettle. Are you OK?" the man asked.

"Yeah," I said, taking the offered fresh box of noodles.

"Oh, good then," the man said and was gone in a gust of air.

"What the hell?" Cr'eon said as she looked around for the man.

Rhi dusted me off and stepped back. "Any damage?"

I shook my head and leaned back against the railing, my noodles forgotten as I looked around for the speedster.

"They have superheroes here or something?" I asked.

"Not that I've seen," Cr'eon said as she returned to her food.

"He wasn't wearing spandex," Rhi offered with a shrug as she also dug back into her food.

"Weird," I muttered and looked down at my new food. It wasn't what I'd ordered before, and I wondered what it was the kid had grabbed. Then I wondered if he'd paid for it or just grabbed it off the cart. Then I realized it wasn't food but one of the fake displays from the front of the cart.

"Be right back," I said and walked back to the cart.

"Hey," I said to the cart owner as I approached. No one else was present when I handed over the food prop.

"Huh?" the owner said with a look of confusion as he took the prop.

"Some guy gave this to me; I think it belongs to you," I said.

"Oh!" the owner looked from the prop to where it had been sitting on display. "I thought that gust of wind had blown it away."

I nodded, "Hey, quick question. You got a guy in this town that can run really fast?"

The owner looked from where he was putting the prop back

in its place at me with a frown.

"I don't follow sports," the man shook his head.

"Oh, OK, thanks," I said and made my way back to the group. When I glanced up, the strange car that had been hovering above us was gone.

∞∞∞∞∞Ω∞∞∞∞∞

JAMES

I came out of our apartment's bathroom shaking my head.

"What's wrong?" Rhi asked. "You should be used to the human aftermath of eating real food by now." Her teasing voice came to me from across the room.

"Bathroom's busted," I grumbled.

Rhi turned to face me.

"You broke the toilet?" Rhi asked.

"No...not really." I frowned. "You'd think with billion-year-old technology, light years beyond anything we could ever do, that a toilet wouldn't break." I shook my head.

"My grandfather was right, no matter what happens, no matter how much technical advancement we have, there's always going to be a broken toilet to fix," I griped. "He always said I should have been a plumber like him. Guaranteed job security and all that."

Before Rhi could come back at me with a snide remark, the door opened, and Viola came in, followed by three people.

"So, this is the team that's going to get it done," Viola said, closing the door and indicating the three people beside her.

"This is Crita," Viola pointed to the tall woman with long, straight black hair wearing brown overalls. "She's the team's leader."

"More like it's president," Crita said, holding her hand up. Her skin appeared to be covered by dark down scales that had a slightly dull appearance. I expected her to have a tail and a reptilian face, but she didn't. It was as if a normal human had simply been covered in scales.

"This is Yelik, my VP," Crita said as she pointed to the man standing beside her. He was shorter than I was and, like Crita, was an ordinary human, save for the coat of brown and black fur that covered his body. He was wearing what appeared to be jeans and a t-shirt with rolled-up sleeves. He'd look like something from a 50s diner if it weren't for all the fur.

Yelik nodded once.

"And you've already met Steve," Crita said as she motioned to the speedster who'd run into me earlier today.

"Again, my apologies for before," Steve said, giving me a small wave.

"Get what done, exactly?" Rhi asked.

"They're going to break into the AG's data vault and help you retrieve the info you need," Viola smiled sweetly. "They're the best unit for getting in and out of somewhere without being detected."

I frowned.

"Without being detected?" I asked.

"Yes," Crita said. "Such as earlier when Steve gave you a demonstration."

"A demonstration of what? How to tackle someone?" Rhi scoffed.

"No, of how to distract during an operation," Crita said.

"Distract us from what?" Rhi asked.

"The floating car that was above us?" I asked.

"No, but that was another of our units," Crita said, then turned to Cr'eon. "Would you check your left pocket, please?"

Cr'eon looked startled that she'd been singled out.

"Huh?" Cr'eon said.

"Left pocket," Crita repeated.

Cr'eon reached into her pocket and pulled out a small card.

"That's our business card and contains my gen code if you ever need to get hold of me," Crita said.

"Nice party trick," Rhi said.

"Party trick," Crita slowly nodded and turned to Cr-eon again. "Would you mind rolling up your right sleeve?"

Cr-eon frowned.

"Humor me, please?" Crita said simply.

Cr-eon slowly pulled up the sleeve of her shirt. As she did, something akin to a bar code appeared on her arm.

"The data bar will take you to a site that lists our accomplishments...if you feel we're only capable of party tricks," Crita said. "Don't worry, it'll vanish in about two hours."

Cr-eon looked up at Crita from where she'd been viciously rubbing at the data bar, trying to get it to come off.

"Maybe we should sit down," Viola said, trying to diffuse the situation.

"If they haven't stolen the chairs," I muttered.

∞∞∞∞∞Ω∞∞∞∞∞

JAMES

I looked around the small compartment and was impressed with the scene. The ship reminded me of the inside of a Chinook helicopter. It was roughly the same size and had jump seats down each side. Crita's people were pulling various pieces of gear from a modular equipment rack that ran down the center of the ship.

Ten operators were checking their gear as I watched. I called them operators because that's what they looked like. Each "person" had a pile of gear spread out around them and was meticulously going through it for one reason or another.

A couple of conversations were running quietly around us. Most of the talk was about the boring, mundane parts of life, nothing about the mission we were about to go on. Occasionally, the voices got loud and boisterous, but for the most part, the atmosphere was a subdued one. To an outsider, it looked like a group of friends just hanging out. But I'd seen this type of scene enough to feel the calm anxiety that laced their voices.

I glanced at Rhi in the jump seat next to me. She was busy checking her own gear.

We'd left the Alamo simulation with nothing more than the clothes on our backs. Crita had loaned us the warskins we were now wearing. As I looked around, some of the gear people were using was familiar, but much of it was either new or something hastily cobbled together. It kind of reminded me of the AG, if the AG had a better supplier.

The warskin I was wearing was almost identical to the one I'd worn while serving with the DC. However, this one did seem to be heavier. Not enough to restrict my movement, but I could tell there was something seriously different about it.

Rhi had a similar warskin to mine. We hadn't been given anything else. I wasn't sure if they didn't trust us or if they didn't want us to be more than just passengers during this op.

The AG data core wasn't nearly as secure as Behemoth's archive. It was a simple vault located in one of the dead spaces of Behemoth's backrooms. While heavily guarded, Crita had assured us they would get us in and out without anyone noticing our presence. All we had to do was follow their lead.

Rhi hadn't been happy about it, but she knew what was at stake. I had no idea if Crita could come through on her promises or not. But Cr'eon had assured me that if half the rumors about Crita's group were true, she could.

This remind you of anything? Rhi asked me.

"Don't do that during the op," a voice two seats down said.

Rhi and I glanced at the man who'd spoken up. He appeared as a man but was actually some sort of gelatinous mass. He was an infiltrator, capable of making himself into whatever shape and appearance he wanted. Right now, he looked like a stocky, green-skinned man.

"What's that, Bruce?" Rhi asked, using the nickname she'd given him. Apparently, Rhi had problems with names, and until she learned them, she used nicknames. If the names she gave them tickled her, she wouldn't stop using them.

"Don't use telepathy during the op," Bruce said, not looking up from the pile of gear he was sorting. "It's easily detectable by the AG."

"They can listen in on our mindspeech?" I asked, unaware they could do that.

"Yes. Telepathy is simply a corrupted form of Behemoth's communication net, and the AG has it tapped." Bruce stopped and looked at us. "Plus, it's kind of rude when other people are present."

"Sorry," Rhi apologized.

I looked at her, impressed. I wasn't used to her apologizing for anything.

"Well, does this remind you of something?" Rhi asked.

I glanced around again and then looked at her.

"Yeah. Right before we'd storm a vamp nest, this is the same scene, right down to the boasting," I said. A few of the operators had started a lively debate about how easy it was going to be getting in and out from under the AG's noses.

"It's not boasting if it's true!" said a woman across the aisle from us.

I didn't know her name, but her body, while humanoid, was emaciated in comparison. She had short, scrawny legs and arms and no neck. Her head was slightly cylindrical and sat recessed at the top of her torso. I wasn't sure if it could retract into her body like a turtle, but I wouldn't have been surprised.

"True," I admitted with a small chuckle.

"OK, McGuffins, listen up," Crita bellowed her group's name as she appeared from the cockpit.

I barely caught sight of two pilots within the control center before the door closed, sealing them inside.

"We've got just under an hour till we reach our staging area. We'll be transitioning multiple times between here and there, so keep your barf buckets handy," Crita said.

"Barf buckets?" Rhi asked me quietly.

I'd seen them when I'd initially sat down. I pointed at a small plastic mask woven into the lattice of the jump seat.

"I thought that was an O2 mask," Rhi said.

"It's multi-purpose," Steve said with a smile from my other side.

For some reason, Steve had latched on to the two of us like we were old friends. It wasn't that he was unpopular. Everyone seemed to treat him like a kid brother for some reason. But apparently, Rhi and I were his new best friends.

I glanced around the compartment at all the different types of armor and guns.

"Why don't we have armor that's cool and badass looking like Iron Man?" I turned and asked Rhi.

"Because we don't actually need all that crap," Rhi said, patting her warskin. "Our protection doesn't restrict your movement, or limit your vision, or any of that. Plus, no one has to know you're wearing it."

"Yeah, but where's the fun in that?" I continued. "I mean, come on, everybody wants a suit-up scene."

"A what?" Rhi asked.

"You know," I said. "The armor locking in place around you, spinning around, squeezing this, and pushing that. Everybody wants that!"

Rhi just stared at me.

"Our armor provides a multi-layer defense strategy which incorporates both physical, energy, and other dimensional protection," Rhi said. "Our gear would kick the crap out of Iron Man."

"Well, it still doesn't look cool," I grumbled. When Rhi didn't snipe back at me, I glanced over just in time to see her smile slowly fading. "What?"

"Tara was working on something like that, actually—" Rhi said quietly, but was interrupted as Crita came over to us.

"How are you two getting along?" Crita asked.

"So far, so good," I replied while Rhi seemed to shake herself and gave a simple thumbs up.

"Anyone show you two how to work those suits yet?" Crita asked.

"It's just a warskin, right?" I asked.

Crita gave me a crooked smile.

"There's a bit more to it than that," Crita said and turned to a teenage girl who couldn't have been more than 14, sitting across from us in the back of the ship. "Rylan, brief these two up on your suits, please."

"I can do it," Steve offered up eagerly.

"No, Steve," Crita said slowly. "You know it's Rylan's job, so please don't interfere."

Steve pulled back with a chastised look on his face.

"OK, you know how warskins work, right?" Rylan said as

she approached us. When we both nodded, she continued. "Then you know how this works. You think about something, and the suit provides it.

"The only real difference is I've added adaptive software," Rylan said. "So, the warskin isn't restricted to the patterns included in its original buffer."

Ryan sighed at the looks of confusion on our faces.

"There's additional mass added to the warskin," Rylan said patiently. "That's the weight you feel. The added mass can be used by the suit to provide you with things other than a simple pistol or emergency kit," Rylan said, and then stepped back.

Rylan's suit suddenly bulked up as what looked like a suit of high-tech plate armor formed around her. Just as quickly, it disappeared, being reabsorbed by the warskin.

"See?" Rylan said.

A quiet round of chuckling rippled through the compartment as the others enjoyed the shocked looks on our faces.

Rhi was the first to recover. She held up her hand, and after a moment, a metal gauntlet appeared around it. She turned it this way and that before flexing her fingers.

I looked at my own hand and thought of the same gauntlet Rhi was sporting. With only a slight vibration, I suddenly found my hand surrounded by a metal glove. It was impressive. Usually, pulling the standard pistol from a warskin took hours of practice for it to come so simply. This required no effort at all.

"I've tweaked the neural interface to compensate for possible indecision. You might not get exactly what you wanted, but you'll get it a hell of a lot faster than a standard warskin," Rylan said proudly.

"And it can make anything?" I asked.

"For the most part," Rylan said and glanced at Rhi.

Rhi was still wearing the gauntlet but had a small coin quickly spinning on the tip of one of her fingers. A moment later, the coin became a throwing knife, which Rhi fluidly moved between her fingers in a fancy twirling motion.

I looked down at my suit and held my hands out as a version of my old Styer Aug appeared in my hands.

"Just be warned. The added mass is Behemoth skin," Rylan said.

"Behemoth skin?" I asked, looking up from the rifle.

"It's the same composite grown to form the external skin of Behemoth," Rylan said. "It's pretty much the toughest thing we have. Even if you somehow manage to damage it, given enough time, it will regenerate. So, be careful." Rylan went on to cover some other basics with us until we were comfortable with her creation.

Once Rylan had returned to her seat, Rhi spoke up.

"So, you gonna stop crying over that gun now?" Rhi nodded towards the rifle in my lap.

My prized original Aug had been destroyed back at the real version of our Alamo compound before Beth brought us to Behemoth. I wouldn't have called my remorse crying, but I had missed it.

I smiled up at her, and the rifle was reabsorbed back into my suit.

"What's up?" Rhi asked.

"Like you said, we've got hip howitzers now," I said as I pulled the standard pistol from the hip of my warskin. The Behemoth pistol outclassed my old rifle in every aspect but nostalgia.

"Moving on, eh?" Rhi asked, smiling at me. "Good."

"Yeah," I nodded and concentrated as distinctive metal plates soon surrounded my body. Each one moved on its own as it locked into place, forming the metal suit.

When I was done, I turned to look at Rhi, who was shaking her head.

"You, happy with yourself? Now, take that off before Disney sues your ass," Rhi said.

By the time we arrived at our staging area, everyone was ready to go, while Rhi and I had vomited...twice. Strangely enough, no one bothered us about losing our lunch. I would have expected a group like this to be all over ribbing us mercilessly.

It turned out that the group had lost a member during a transition a while back. Nobody joked about it anymore.

Transitions were basically the same as using a gate. Unlike

Behemoth's gate technology, which was virtually seamless, anytime someone else tried to use a gate, there were always side effects—sometimes mild, sometimes severe. You never knew what would happen, as each time was different.

The center row of modular racks folded in on itself and formed a large table down the center of the compartment. Crita stepped up to it, and at her touch, the top transformed into a three-dimensional sand table.

Corridors and rooms appeared along the length of the table. Small figures patrolled the corridors, and certain rooms were color-coded. The map appeared to be in real-time.

Crita gave the sand table a good going over before speaking.

"Good, all of our sensors are still in place," Crita said.

We'd pretty much departed from our apartment, boarded the ship, and came straight here. When Crita's crew had time to set up a sensor net in the AG facility was beyond me.

"Looks like they're still using their standard routines and patterns." A man said as he leaned over the table to examine a pair of AG guards moving down a hall. Various parts of his body had been replaced with cybernetic implants, including a pair of small screens that covered both his eye sockets. Beneath them, his eyeballs appeared to be made from some dark gray metal with strange markings. There wasn't an iris or anything else to show movement—just plain metal.

"Good," Crita said. "Jaime, keep monitoring while I talk." Turning to Rhi and me, Crita took the next few minutes to explain the layout of the data vault area and the related security. But she didn't mention anything about a plan.

"So, you two. How would you go about getting into this area and out again without being detected?" Crita asked us.

Rhi and I looked at one another for a moment before looking back at the table. We asked several questions about the facility, our gear, and the opposition. After about half an hour of back-and-forth, Rhi and I laid out a sketchy plan of attack.

Crita critiqued our plan, asking questions and "what-ifing" us relentlessly. Finally, we had a plan pretty much hammered out.

So, when Crita began explaining a completely different plan that we were going to be implementing, I was confused.

After Crita finished the briefing, Rhi and I pulled her aside.

"Why did you have us come up with a plan if you weren't going to use it?" Rhi asked.

"Oh, I used it. The whole end-run part, that's all you guys," Crita said.

"Why not explain your plan and then ask for input?" I asked.

"Because," Crita began and waved her hand towards the others. "Take a look around. We have a mix of characters as varied as the places they're from. Each with their own unique point of view. I ask each of them how they'd go about a mission, combine them, and that's what we do. It's good practice for them and keeps their minds sharp.

"No plan is ever perfect," Crita said. "Anyone who tells you what you're going to do without input is just begging for failure. I wanted a fresh pair of eyes to look at the situation and tell me how you'd do it. You found two new surveillance devices that none of us caught. That right there probably saved the op." Crita nodded.

Rhi and I looked at one another for a moment.

"Anything else?" Crita asked kindly.

"I'm good," I said.

Rhi nodded without saying anything further.

Chapter 10

JAMES

"OK, before we get going, I need each of you to swear your silence," Crita stopped Rhi and me at the exit ramp to the ship. Everyone else had moved out into the darkness of a large room and set up a perimeter.

"What?" Rhi asked.

Crita held out a small PDD.

"Just touch anywhere on the screen," Crita said.

"Why?" Rhi asked.

"It guarantees you won't talk about anything we do during this op under strict penalty," Crita said.

"Why would we talk—" I started.

"There are a lot of other outfits that would like nothing more than to copy our procedures and steal our business. This protects both our butts," Crita said.

"Both?" Rhi asked.

"I'm under the same obligation. I can't talk about the op to anyone other than those who were present at the time," Crita said.

"What's strict penalty?" I asked.

"If means an arbitrator will determine the appropriate action to be taken if either of us breaks the contract and is reported," Crita said.

"Who's the arbitrator?" Rhi asked.

"A separate and disinterested party who holds a current license; otherwise, it voids the contract," Crita said. "Listen, I doubt either of you is going to say anything, but this is a legal formality I have to follow. Otherwise, you're confined to the ship."

"Whatever," I said, frustrated with the legalese. I touched the PDD and it chimed once.

Rhi frowned but eventually touched the PDD as well.

"Good, let's go. You two will be with Ziegler," Crita said as she spun on her heel and headed down the ramp. "Z! You're on escort duty."

A moment later, a man appeared out of thin air in front of us.

"What the?" Rhi yelped and stepped back.

I'd taken a step back in surprise myself.

"OK, I'm Ziegler, or just Z for short. You stick to me like glue. If I run, you run. If I shoot, you shoot. Got it?" Z waited for us to nod before continuing. "OK, activate your blender and let's go."

"Blender?" Rhi asked, looking at me.

I shrugged.

Z stood there looking at us.

"You good?" he asked.

"Yeah," I started. "It's just, what's a blender?"

"Oh!" Z said. "Sorry, your active camouflage suite. We call it a blender cause it makes you blend into the background."

We knew about the camouflage feature, just not that it was called a blender.

Rhi and I pulled our warskins over our heads, sealing our bodies inside. As soon as our suits were sealed, they faded from view.

My neural cockpit activated, tying itself into my warskin. It provided me with full vision in the darkness. It also outlined each of my "blended" comrades and labeled them as friendlies for me.

Z started moving, and we followed quickly, trying to stay out of the way of the others who moved with practiced ease.

"Bio-calibration complete. Would you like to start the

tutorial?" A voice called out in my ear, making me jump.

"What the?" I stopped suddenly, Rhi almost bumping into me.

A blinking cursor sat in the bottom corner of my vision. It was resting on the word "yes" while the word "no" was beside it.

I had a feeling I knew what a bio-calibration was. The suit had adjusted itself to my body. I figured it would have done that a long time ago, but apparently, it didn't start until the suit was sealed.

I focused on the word yes, and the cursor disappeared.

"Welcome to Rylan's new and improved warskin 14.3. Your warranty expired when you put the suit on. Are you interested in an extended warranty?" The cheery voice of Rylan said in my ear.

I glanced at Rylan and those around me, but nobody was hearing what I was.

"No," I said quietly.

"Okie dokie then, just be advised, the extended warranty is only available for the next 90 seconds!" suit-Rylan said.

I was about to ask for the suit to stop talking, but it then began a real tutorial. Three minutes later, I was well acquainted with the suit and saying goodbye to suit-Rylan.

"Oh, I'm not going anywhere. I manage the warskin and am available at any time for your needs," suit-Rylan said.

I glanced at Rhi, who didn't appear any different. Maybe she didn't have a suit-Rylan?

I asked her later and she said she'd "Shut that shit off right away. A patrol was no place to be screwing around."

When I glanced forward again, our front four men had disappeared. I glanced around but couldn't find them. A minute later, their outlines appeared far out in front of us. The suit's computer was giving me a tactical display of their location, even though I couldn't see them right now.

We'd left the dark hanger a while back and were currently in a well-lit, wide corridor that headed toward the data vault section.

So far, so good. We hadn't run into any patrols.

That's when a pair of AG in full combat gear rounded the corner in front of us.

I glanced at the schematic of the place. There weren't any hallways or doors between the four-person scouting party and us. The scouting party hadn't given us any warning about them, so how'd they get here?

Everyone shuffled silently to the other side of the hallway, opposite the two guards walking side by side.

They didn't seem to notice us as they passed in silence. Then I saw someone's foot sticking out just a hair too far. Instead of tripping on it, the AG went around it!

Could they see us? Were they on our side? Were they paid off? What? All these questions ran through my head as the pair left us behind and we continued forward.

This scene repeated itself several times before we reached the front of the vault, where our scout team sat, quietly waiting for us.

The area in front of the vault was an open space with three hallways leading away from it. The "vault" was actually just another reinforced and sealed-off room. A pair of AG guards were pacing the floor in the middle of the room.

"They good?" Crita asked one of the scouts.

The scout simply nodded.

Crita nodded, and the team spread out around the area to monitor avenues of approach.

A lone figure from our group approached the door. They went straight to the wall next to the door and touched it. A moment later, the vault door began to open. It wasn't some gigantic door, just a simple, sturdy personnel door that swung open.

I glanced at the guards, who acted like they couldn't hear or see the door as it opened.

Crita nodded at Z, and we moved forward into the vault.

Once Z, Crita, Rhi, and I were inside, the door closed and sealed behind us.

The room was similar to Behemoth's archive but scaled way down. Even the floating sphere was smaller. The only real difference was that everything here was salmon-colored, whereas the images in Rhi's head of the real archive were all white.

"OK, do your thing," Crita said to us, then moved to the other side of the room, where she began examining a data console.

Rhi and I approached the sphere. She took the lead as she'd done this before.

She seemed to get into an argument with the computer. I could hear parts of the conversation through our connection, but I couldn't make out what they were saying.

"That console, second one over," Rhi pointed out to me.

"This one?" I asked as I reached the smooth metal machine.

"Yes, when the port opens, insert the mind crystals one at a time," Rhi said.

"Does it matter which order?" I asked.

"Nope, the machine takes care of all that," Rhi said, then turned back to talking to the machine.

A small opening appeared on the cabinet's surface, and I slipped one in and then the other. After a few moments, it spat them both back out. Neither one appeared any different from before.

"Did it work?" I asked.

Rhi said a few more words at the computer and then approached me. She took the crystals from my hand and held them up to the light. She turned them one way and then the other as if searching for something. She brought them down and rubbed them on her warskin.

Rhi nodded once and glanced over my shoulder. "What's Crita doing?"

I looked over, and Crita was still bent over a console and appeared to be typing furiously.

"Don't know," I said and looked back at her. "Want me to go ask?"

"Sure, I need to verify these anyway," Rhi said as she started feeding the crystals into the machine again. "It's going to take a minute."

"OK," I said and went over to Crita.

"How's it going?" I asked.

Crita didn't look up and didn't stop typing.

I looked but didn't see a keyboard or any kind of display on the machine.

"Almost done," Crita said.

"Almost done with what?" I asked.

This caused Crita to falter, her hands pausing.

"Double checking to make sure security hasn't seen us," Crita said. "And making sure they're sticking to their schedule."

I watched her for a bit, having absolutely no idea what she was doing. I jumped as Rhi's voice spoke in my ear.

"Everything all right?" Rhi asked from beside me.

I hated how quiet she could be sometimes. It was unnerving.

"I guess?" I said more as a question than anything else.

"Aaaaaaaand done!" Crita said with a flourish. "Looks like we're in the green, let's go!" she said with excitement.

"I take it you're finished as well?" I asked Rhi.

In response, she handed me the two crystals. They still didn't look any different. I was expecting them to glow or sparkle or something.

"Don't look so disappointed. They're verified as complete and correct. We're good to go!" Rhi said with a smile.

"Yeah," I said, taking one last look at the pair of crystals before stowing them away in my pocket.

"It's not like they're sealed up and banging on the sides of the crystal to get out, James. It's just a memory card," Rhi said.

"How amazing that something so tiny can hold something so important," I sighed. We were one more step closer to getting our family back.

Rhi's arms wrapped around me from behind, and she kissed my neck.

"We'll get them back, don't worry," Rhi said gently.

"No time for that, you two. Our window's closing, we need to go," Crita said.

I glanced towards the door and saw the outlines of the rest of our team. Two of them seemed to be off by themselves and were holding someone down. Someone who wasn't us.

"Looks like trouble," I said to Crita.

Crita glanced at where I was looking.

"It's fine, let's go," Crita said and pushed the door open.

The two AG guards were still standing in the room, oblivious to everything around them.

I frowned and looked to where the two had been holding down someone. One of our guys was heading back to us while the other was kneeling next to the figure on the ground. A moment later, they both stood up, and our guy returned, leaving the enemy standing in the room by themselves.

Crita made a gesture, and everyone formed back up, heading back the way we'd come. Z was still beside us, having never left our side. He motioned us behind him, and we fell in.

The path back was different. It took longer, as if we seemed to be detouring around something. Eventually, we ended up back in the dark hangar and headed for the bright maw of the ship's cargo ramp.

Crita shooshed me when I started to say something. Once we were on the ship and the ramp was closed, Crita turned to me.

"OK, now what did you want to say?" Crita asked, pulling her hood off.

I pulled my own back and looked at her.

"What was that?" I asked.

The others around us were beginning to stow their gear, ignoring us.

Crita moved to the front of the compartment, getting us out of the way of the others and out of earshot.

"What was what?" Crita asked.

"The guards could see us, but they ignored us," I said. "Were they bribed or something? And what was the deal with the guy being held down on the floor? One minute, he's struggling; the next, he's cool as a cucumber."

"There's a reason no one ever remembers seeing us, and we never get caught," Crita started. "It's the secret to our success and the primary reason you had to swear your silence."

"And what's that?" Rhi asked from behind me.

"We mind wipe the guards," Crita said.

"Mind wipe?" I asked.

"It's not a complete mind wipe, just for a short period of time. Johanson and Rylan are our tech geniuses. They cracked the Behemoth decoding software. They can hack a Daemon's mind and cause it to forget or ignore something," Crita said.

"Like when the AG stepped out of the way to keep from tripping on one of our legs in the hall," I said.

"Yes. Our scout team caught the guards first. Then, before releasing them, the scout team told the guards to ignore us and forget ever seeing us," Crita said.

"Handy," I nodded, not sure how I felt about this. Granted, the AG were technically the "bad guys" here. But we'd all had our minds messed with enough now that I hesitated anytime mind cooking was brought up.

"And the guy on the ground?" Rhi asked.

"The process isn't exactly comfortable," Crita grimaced. "Sometimes they fight, and we have to hold them down. But we get results. You got what you needed; nobody was caught or hurt, and the AG doesn't know we were ever there. I'd call that a win!"

"I get it," Rhi said. "If someone learned how you were pulling off your jobs, they'd want to do more than just steal your tech."

Crita gave her a wink and a thumbs up, but I don't think she caught the inflection in Rhi's voice.

It appeared I wasn't the only one who didn't agree with it.

Chapter 10.5

BETH

How is it that we're still being shot at? I asked as I leaned out from the corner and fired down the hall. A burst of return fire answered just as I ducked back behind cover.

Because the bad guys are still chasing us? my minder replied.

I fired one more burst at our pursuers and bolted down the corridor. I'd been in a running gunfight for more than an hour, and I was getting tired.

True to his word, my minder got me into an inhabited sector quickly after our little talk. It had helped a little.

After a day or so, he made me move to a different inhabited sector. We'd stay there a few days and then move on. We continued this pattern, staying a little longer each time and keeping me in contact with other people.

It seemed I didn't do well in true isolation. I blamed Shae for it. I used to be able to be on my own all the time. Now it seemed that if I didn't get some sort of interaction, I got grumpy.

We'd been lying low in a rather mundane sector for over a month this time. We were just trying to figure out our next move when someone kicked our door in. I was out a side window before the door hit the ground.

Being on the run from an all-powerful computer made me

kind of jumpy. I was taking every precaution I could think of to keep a low profile, but obviously, someone had seen me and reported it to whatever they had for cops here.

The next thing I knew, Daemons were chasing me deeper into the apartment complex megablock we'd taken up residence in. With the tens of thousands of people in this structure, I figured we'd be relatively safe here. I guess I was wrong.

How do you know they're the bad guys? I asked as I rounded a corner and grabbed the walkway's outer railing.

Don't jump, don't jump, don't jump! my minder squawked at me.

I ignored him and slipped below the railing.

We're 400 stories up, don't let go! my minder practically screamed in my head.

I let go of the railing and fell along the outside of the massive building. I caught myself four floors below and swung back onto an outer hallway before I gave the incredible heights a chance to register.

I wasn't afraid of heights, but being so high that you were nearly able to touch the clouds could shake anyone. Besides, I was so terrified of being caught by Behemoth now that that fear pushed everything else aside.

Don't worry so much, I chided my minder.

It was a long moment before my minder spoke again.

Do you feel like a bad guy? my minder asked as I kicked in someone's door, but continued running down the hall instead of going inside. *I take back what I said.*

I launched myself into a stairway and glanced down at the countless floors beneath me. I didn't see anyone waiting, so I climbed between the railings and allowed myself to drop.

I caught myself every few floors or if I started to stray too close to one of the railings, just to slow my descent. The gap that ran the entire height of the building between the center railings wasn't that wide. But it was wide enough that I could slip down it if I were careful.

Then my head slammed into one of the railings, and I started to tumble.

I ground my teeth together to avoid crying out, but sound

still escaped as I managed to bring myself to a shuddering stop a few floors down. I cautiously climbed into the stairwell proper and lay there until the Bio Comp stopped spinning.

Nice work, idiot. I chastised myself.

"Are you OK?" the voice of an older woman below me roused me from the daze I'd fallen into. I had no idea how long I'd been lying there.

I looked down to find a woman coming up the stairs with what appeared to be a teenage boy. Had I been thinking more clearly, I would have been wondering why they were on the stairs instead of one of the many convenient elevators residents used.

"Yeah," I said and grunted as I climbed unsteadily to my feet. I carefully started down the stairs, clinging to the handrail as each stair felt like it was trying to jump out from beneath my feet.

"Mom..." the boy said.

"Yeah, grab her," the woman said in a voice that finally set off alarm bells in my head.

Just as the boy reached for my arm, I spun away from him and found myself falling. I managed to tuck into a ball just as I hit the stairs. It didn't help much.

I regained my feet, hoping the warskin kept the bruising along my spine to a minimum. I glanced up to see the pair coming down the stairs at me and pulled my pistol.

This caused my pursuers to pause.

"Just keep walking," I said, motioning my gun back up the stairs while inching my way further down the stairs.

The pair watched me until I was out of sight.

A moment later, I exited the stairwell and returned to the building proper. I paused at the next corner and turned back to watch the stairwell door. Thankfully, it never opened.

What, were you planning on shooting the mom and her son? my minder asked.

If that's what it took, I said, glancing down the hall and seeing an atrium in the distance.

You're still not the bad guy, my minder cautioned.

Shut up and find me a way out of this rat's maze, I said as

I stumbled down the hall.

These apartment megablocks were the size of small cities. Hundreds of floors high and sprawling for miles, they contained just about everything that you'd need to leave your home for. Shopping, work, and entertainment were all just a few floors away.

The fact that I'd stumbled across an outside wall earlier, where I'd been able to slip down a few floors unaccosted, was rare.

The atrium at the end of the hallway held a small park ringed by several restaurants. I looked up and could see a simulated sky several stories above me. The restaurants were doing a brisk business. I could probably blend in, but I didn't want to risk it, so I continued my exodus.

Do you have any idea where you're going? my minder asked. *Of course you don't.*

Do you? I asked angrily. *Do you have any good advice, or are you just planning on criticizing my escape all day?*

So, you want my help? my minder asked in a miffed tone.

Of course I want help, you moron! I said as I touched my throbbing head. I glanced down at my leg and saw it had finally stopped bleeding. I'd caught some shrapnel earlier. It hadn't been bad, but it had ripped through my warskin and bled messily.

In that case, turn left, my minder said and proceeded to lead me through the complex. The complicated path he took me on had my already dizzy head spinning even more.

Two hours later, I fell into the small transport vehicle my minder had directed me into.

OK, you can pass out now. I'll wake you if something comes up, my minder said.

By the end, my weary body had literally been stumbling down the hall. It had taken all my focus just to put one foot in front of the other and not throw up doing it.

Where are we going? I muttered more out of reflex than interest.

Somewhere safe, my minder said. *I hope.*

He was always saying stuff like that, all cryptic and

mysterious. I still didn't understand how my minder worked or how he somehow interacted with the outside world without me knowing about it.

I knew he'd been hacking systems to help pay for things since I couldn't use my Behemoth accounts. I had no clue how many crimes he'd committed in order to help me, but I didn't have a choice. We were stuck with each other.

Even with the years we'd been together now, I still didn't completely trust him. But I had to admit, he hadn't steered me wrong—you know, except for the whole going AWOL and not telling me bit. But I still had to give him credit—we were alive and not in a jail cell. Or dead...so there was that.

I hadn't been bored the last few weeks either. For the first time in a long while, I felt awake and not like I was just going through the motions. I guess constantly fleeing for your life did that to you.

I pondered this as my eyes fell shut.

∞∞∞∞∞Ω∞∞∞∞∞

<u>BETH</u>

"Hey, you, you're finally awake."

The words sounded strangely familiar as they roused me from my exhausted slumber.

I was lying on a cold table with a needle sticking out of my arm. I followed the tube to a bag full of blood hanging beside me. I stared at that bag for a long time, my fuzzy head not sure of what to make of it.

The snapping of fingers eventually drew my attention from the bag to the woman standing beside the table. She was plainly dressed with long hair pulled back in a ponytail. The glasses she wore looked strange, like they were for more than correcting eyesight.

"You with me?" The woman asked as she shined a painfully bright light into each of my eyes.

Through the spots in my eyes, I saw that I was in a small

room with bare walls and a few metal cabinets with various instruments adorning them.

The woman whistled loudly, causing me to flinch.

"Yeah, that's what I thought," she said as she touched the blood bag and then injected something into it. "You're lucky your friend got you to me when he did. Much longer and you would have bled out."

"Where am I?" I said, still groggy.

"My practice. You're safe, for now." The woman's words were ominous.

I tried to sit up but found I couldn't. My body was just as fuzzy as my head.

"Just take it easy, they clipped you pretty good," the woman said. "It'll take some time before I can flush it all out of your system."

"Flush what out of my system?" I asked groggily.

"Whoever shot you, and I can guess who that was, hit you with an anti-sanguivore weapon. Nasty stuff, but effective," the woman said.

"Anti-what?" I asked.

"Anti-sanguivore," she replied. "Don't worry, I know what I'm doing."

Those were the last words I heard before the room faded out. The next time I came to, the blood bag was gone, and I had been moved to a cot set up in a small bedroom.

I tentatively looked around, my head feeling like it was clear now. Slowly, I sat up, and the room stayed right where it was supposed to. I swung my legs over the cot and waited, but it seemed I was pretty much back to normal.

The room I was in was small, with a small bed in the corner and overflowing bookshelves covering every inch of wall space. The few titles I could read seemed to be medical textbooks.

I stood and walked to the only door in the room and opened it. The room with the medical table I'd first woken up in was just beyond.

Sitting on the table was a small girl. The "doctor" whom I'd previously spoken to looked over at me from where she was sitting beside the girl. What looked like the girl's mother was standing off to the side.

"Kitchen's through there. I'll be with you in a minute," the doctor said and nodded her head at another door.

I didn't say anything and did as she said, moving to the next room.

A cramped but clean kitchen lay beyond. I sat at the small table and tried to collect my thoughts.

You're sure being quiet, I said to my minder, but there was no response. *The silent treatment? Really?* Still, there was no response.

I was about to get concerned when the door opened and the doctor entered.

"How's the head?" she asked as she moved to a small cabinet.

"Better, thanks," I said as I watched her pull a small pouch from the cabinet and plop it down in front of me.

"Drink that," was all she said as she touched a panel on the wall and with a flash of light, a steaming coffee mug appeared in a recess.

I picked up the pouch. I didn't recognize it or any of the writing on it. But when I ran my finger across the top, the top seal broke and revealed its contents.

"Blood?" I asked.

"Close enough," the doctor said and put her cup down on the table across from me. She walked across the room and picked up my bag before placing it on the table.

"Now," the doctor said as she sat down across from me and picked up her mug. She watched me as I raised the pouch to my lip and tentatively took a sip.

I tried not to grimace at the room temperature liquid. I could tell it was some kind of blood, that was about it. It didn't smell good, and it didn't taste good.

"It's fortified. Your system needs it, drink," the doctor ordered.

I gulped down the vile liquid and suppressed a shudder.

"I'd offer a spoonful of sugar, but I don't think it would help that go down," she said.

"What?" I managed, my mouth coated with the vile fluid.

The doctor offered me her mug and I took it gratefully. I had no idea what it was, but it had to be better than that pouch.

From what I could taste, it was like watered-down coffee, but not bitter.

"Feeling better?" she asked.

I nodded, still swishing my mouth to get rid of the taste.

"So, about my fee," the doctor said.

This brought me up short. Up till now, my minder had been in charge of my finances. Everything on Behemoth ran through its digital currency. There wasn't a hard script here in the Behemoth-controlled sectors that I'd ever seen. The outlier colonies each had their own form of currency, ranging from coins to paper to livestock, such as chickens.

"Uh," I started, not sure what she wanted.

"If that thing in your head minds your finances, I can turn it back on. But I warn you, I don't do digital," she said.

That was the first I'd ever heard of someone being able to turn off a minder.

"You turned him off?" I asked.

"He's still there, just muted. I figured you needed a bit of quiet to rest up. It's a minder, right?" she asked.

"Yeah," I said slowly and handed her back her mug.

"Figured," she said. "He treating you well?"

"As far as I can tell," I said. "He's gotten me this far."

"Good," she said. "I've never heard of one going bad, but don't tell me anything else, I don't need to know. As a matter of fact, I don't want to know. On or off?"

"On, please," I said.

The doctor reached over and tapped my temple.

Finally! my minder said with obvious relief. *Are you OK?*

Yeah, I think, I said.

That dreadful woman somehow gagged me and—

She wants payment, I interrupted. *And she doesn't want anything digital.*

That could be a problem. The only thing we have is what's on your back and what's in your pack, my minder said.

I glanced at my bag sitting in the middle of the table. I knew it only had a handful of items, and I was pretty sure the doc had already gone through it.

"What do you want?" I asked, slowly.

"The only things you have of value are a warskin and a PDD. Everyone knows a warskin is useless to anyone not part of the army," the doctor said.

It was true. Warskins were keyed to the individual. If you didn't have the required implants to interact with it, it was just a crappy spandex costume not even worth cosplay.

It was obvious she wanted my PDD. If it weren't for what was on it, I'd hand it over to her in a heartbeat. But it seemed that being on the run had fully unlocked my music block. Every time I stopped somewhere, even if it were only for a few hours, something musical would pop into my head. A chorus, a bridge, a melody, it was non-stop. I'd recorded them all on that PDD.

That PDD represented everything that was me and not Behemoth. I was afraid that if I lost it, I'd lose part of myself, and I couldn't afford that anymore.

"I can't give up that PDD. You can take everything else, all of it, but not that," I said quietly.

The doctor studied me for a long moment before picking up the mug and taking a sip from it.

"Why?" she asked. "Are you smuggling military secrets? Battle station plans? The latest software upgrades for mobile weapons platforms?" The doctor's voice had carefully controlled venom in it that was aimed in my general direction.

"No," I shook my head slowly. "Nothing like that."

"Then what?" she asked.

I knew she couldn't have looked at it. It was locked, so only I could open it. If I didn't willingly unlock it, only Behemoth could crack it.

I pulled the PDD out and thumbed it on before pushing it across the table to her and sitting back.

She watched me for another long moment before picking the PDD up. Her eyes flicked down to the PDD.

I watched the flashes of light as she scrolled through the pages of my notes.

"I can't give that up," I said. "If I did, it might not come back." That was my real fear. It had taken turning my life upside down for a part of my old pre-Behemoth self to come back. I wasn't about to turn loose of it. God only knew what it would take for it to come back this time.

"You'll fight me over this, won't you?" she said, looking up to meet my eyes.

I nodded slowly. "But I really don't want to."

The doctor frowned.

"You should really consider backing this up somewhere," she said as she put the PDD back into my bag. "It would be a shame if this PDD became lost or damaged."

"I don't have anywhere," I started. "My situation—"

The doctor held up her hand, stopping me.

"I said I didn't want to know," she said and stood up.

I think you should—

Not now! I thought to my minder.

The doctor reached into a cabinet and pulled out a large jar. As she set it on the table, it looked like a massive jar of pickles.

"I don't take I.O.U.s," she said as she pushed the jar across the table at me.

I glanced from the unopened jar to her and back.

Carefully, I reached up and twisted open the metal top. It resisted, and I had to put some actual force behind it before it would pop off with a snap and a hiss.

The smell of dill pickles filled the room.

"They always overtighten those jars," the doctor said. "I can never get them open." She put the lid back on and returned the jar to the cabinet.

I just stared at the strange woman.

That's your cue to leave, my minder suggested.

"Uh," I said, standing up. "Thanks for the help?"

"Of course," she said. "Try and take better care of yourself from here on out, huh?"

"Yeah, I will," I said as I picked up my bag and glanced around.

"Just through there," she said as she pointed through the medical room at a door I hadn't noticed.

What the hell was that? I asked once I was well away from the doctor's office.

That was the best underground doc I could find on such short notice, my minder said.

What, is there a listing for them in the yellow pages or something? I asked.

Something like that, he said. *Have you ever heard the expression beggars can't be choosers?*

Yeah, yeah, I grumbled.

Despite everything, I felt a lot better. The hours-long gunfight had banged me up worse than I thought. From what the doctor had said, I was a few minutes away from going into a vamp coma due to blood loss. Actually, I probably did once I hit the transport. I wasn't sure because I'd never been in one before. I pushed the thought away quickly before I started to dwell.

Besides, I felt fresh as a daisy now. Whatever had been in that nasty fortified blood did my body good!

So what now? I asked, looking around and having no idea where I was.

What else?

Chapter 11

RHI

I couldn't believe it. We were two-thirds of the way to getting our family back together! All we needed to do was retrieve the bodies and revive them. Everything, so far, had been relatively painless. It was almost like someone wanted this to happen.

The thought didn't sit well with me.

James was sitting by the window, once again holding one of the mind crystals up and staring through it. He'd taken to doing that a lot now. I'd told him to keep them put away for safekeeping. But every time I turned around, he was staring through them again as if they could tell him the future.

Outside the window, a dusty prairie stretched as far as the eye could see. A small mountain range dotted the horizon off to the West.

I didn't know if it was West, and I didn't care. I picked a direction, and now it's West, prove me wrong!

We'd moved once again and were now on a small farm in the middle of nowhere.

I'd driven through Montana one time, and it kinda looked like this. There were no neighbors, no towns, and nothing around us in every direction. I kind of wondered why this place had been built, as when we'd gotten here, it was obvious no one had been here in forever.

Viola brought us here through her strange series of Behemoth back doors. It had taken another week of traveling through more Behemoth oddities. The final door opened directly into the basement of this place. But at least we hadn't had to walk in the dark again. So, there was that.

Viola said this was a quiet place. No one came here, so we wouldn't be bothered as we waited on Krys and his crew once again. Viola had sent a message to them that we were ready for the body snatching two months ago, but we still hadn't heard from them. I was beginning to worry.

Cr'eon had been glued to her PDD the entire time we'd been here. With how plain and simple this ranch was, it had amazing Wi-Fi! Cr'eon had been chattering nonstop about some videos she'd uploaded and how they'd become popular. I wasn't sure what that was all about. Anytime she started talking about that nonsense, I pretty much tuned her out.

Viola and Hess acted like they were plotting something because they technically were. They had been going over our plans for retrieving Shae and Tara's bodies every free moment they had. By now, I figured the plan was foolproof with how much research they'd put into it. Anytime I asked for details, though, I was told it was still a work in progress and they didn't want to jinx it.

So, everyone had something to do. Everybody except me.

At first, I made it my job to prep our gear for the mission. James and I still had the enhanced warskins that Crita had given us. I went over both for any issues, but didn't find anything.

I'd discovered the suits were capable of creating more than what was stored inside them. Normal warskins held a number of patterns for pistols, emergency supplies, and such. You would think about what you needed, the suit would activate the pattern, and assemble it from the suit's supply of materials.

The new suits were capable of producing anything the wearer could think of...as long as there was a record of it somewhere in a database the warskin could access. That, and it had the materials to create it.

These suits could hold more materials than a standard

warskin, but they still had a capacity limit. The extra materials allowed the warskin to make larger items, such as the armor Rylan showed off.

I was still trying to figure out how to add more outside materials to the suit, but suit-Rylan told me that wasn't possible. The only way to add more materials was to have the warskin produce them itself. This was a specialty of the suit. The only problem was that you had to feed the warskin…yourself.

By feeding it, I meant the organism that was the suit had to feed off the wearer's bio-energy. I had no idea what bio-e was, only that your body made it and the suit could feed off it if needed. I also knew it made you damned tired if it had to do this. We'd seen this happen to Cr'eon when she'd had to use her emergency lights in the dark zone.

So, I made sure James and I wore the suits and had the suits continuously create materials for internal storage. We had to stay "topped off" on blood to stave off the fatigue, but it was worth it. Within a week, we had both suits fully charged, topped off with as many materials as they could hold, and ready to go.

I kept up my physical training routine and even managed to get James to join me without complaint. He wasn't the lethargic wreck he'd been back at the fake Alamo. He was alert and enthusiastic. I think he was getting as excited as I was about the upcoming mission.

I tried not to get my hopes up. Lord knows I'd had those dashed enough in the past. But I couldn't stop thinking about having Tara back with me. To be whole again.

It's hard to explain losing something that was so much a part of your being. The gestalt was one thing: sharing a mind and all. But Tara was mentally and physically a part of me. We shared minds and bodies, linked via the tattoos we shared. It was a deeper connection than the gestalt. At least, that's how I felt.

Even all these years later, her loss was still overwhelming. The best I could do was bury it as deep as I could. I knew it wasn't healthy, but on the rare occasion I got brave or stupid enough to try and face it, I was overwhelmed by the emotions involved.

My body wasn't the only thing I needed to work on. My

weapon skills had deteriorated due to a lack of use. I spent most of the rest of my time working on both my martial weapons and firearm skills. With a bit of help from Cr'eon and Viola, I'd created a decent training range.

It wasn't as fancy as Behemoth's virtual training rooms, but it still got the job done. I was working on tricking out the standard pistol my suit created when a voice interrupted me.

"Nice range."

I turned to find Shashka watching me, her arms crossed and her hip cocked in the "what are you going to do about it" stance she loved so much.

"Shashka!" I said and practically leapt into her arms. I hadn't had long to get to know her, but I had James's blended memories in my head, so it felt like I'd known her as long as he had.

She embraced me warmly. "Hey, it's only been a few months," Shashka chuckled.

"I know. How long have you been standing there?" I asked as I stepped back.

"Long enough to see you need more practice," she said with a grin.

"Oh really?" I said as I handed her my pistol. "Big talk."

Shashka looked at the pistol and frowned before handing it back. She turned and examined the row of targets I had set up.

A moment later, a series of beams burst from her forehead. Each beam cut a hole dead center of every target's head. They fired so rapidly that they appeared almost simultaneously. When she turned back to face me, I saw that a small red crystal was quickly disappearing from her forehead.

I was both shocked and impressed. I didn't know she could shoot friggin laser beams out of her head! But I couldn't let her off that easily.

"That's it?" I muttered. "Some pin-sized holes in—"

Shashka was still looking at me when the eight man-sized targets I'd set up ripped themselves from the ground and collapsed in on the center target as if a black hole had opened up.

What remained of all the targets was a small golf ball-sized chunk of compressed debris that fell to the ground with a gentle thud.

I threw my arms up, "Well, now I'm going to have to make more targets!" I sighed explosively before smiling at her.

"I'll help," Shashka said as she smiled warmly at me.

"OK, you gotta teach me the head laser trick. That was pretty cool," I said as we headed towards the target shed to make more targets. "Where's Krys, by the way?"

"Where else? Wherever James is." Shashka said with a wry grin.

"I thought you said that whole symbiont mating thing would fade after they'd done the deed," I said. Shashka had explained to me how the symbiont they carried would urge them to infect a new host if it sensed a good candidate.

"Well, you doubted your kind could be infected by our symbionts. So, maybe Krys is taking it as a challenge," Shashka chuckled.

"Oh, James is gonna love that," I grinned. I couldn't help but grin around Shashka. I liked her sarcastic wit. It was too much like my own. It didn't hurt that she was pretty easy on the eyes as well.

"He's not the only one," Shashka gave me the side eye with just the hint of a leer.

"Oh really?" I asked as we entered the small target shed I'd built beside the range. While it was pretty hot watching James and Krys going at it a while back, Shashka and I hadn't been bystanders the entire time. There was something about this couple that seemed to reach down and shake awake old parts of me...in a good way.

A lovely time later, I was sealing up my warskin as Shashka stood in the doorway to the target shed. I came up behind her and leaned against her, my hands not keeping to myself.

Shashka looked back over her shoulder at me and smiled.

"I thought weapons and armor were the only things you could make using your crystal," I said, my hands still wandering.

"Oh no," Shashka said as she turned to face me. "We're only limited by our imagination," she said as she leaned in and kissed me briefly.

"I take it Krys wasn't the only one being urged by his symbiont?" I asked.

Shashka gave me a small shrug and turned back to look outside.

"It's gorgeous here," Shashka said with a sigh. "I could get used to this kind of quiet."

"You're welcome to stay as long as you'd like," I offered.

"While that is a lovely thought, we're going to have to move soon if we're doing this," Shashka said.

"You have a timeline?" I asked.

"Yes, and unfortunately, it's brief. Let's head inside so we can talk with the others," Shashka said and stepped towards the house proper.

"I'd have thought James and Krys..." I let the sentence hang.

"Oh, I'm sure they're still dancing around one another. They're more alike than you think. I'm sure nothing will happen until later tonight. After a few...well, a lot of drinks," Shashka said.

I glanced back at the shed.

"So, you're the one who likes to move fast, then?" I asked.

Shashka glanced over at me with a fresh smile.

"A long time ago, the loss of a friend taught me not to hesitate when I see something I want," she said.

"Oh?" I said, her words making me feel a bit sheepish for some reason.

"Now that's a look I haven't seen on you," Shaska teased.

"Shut up!" I said as I nudged her arm playfully.

When we reached the house, the others were gathered around a table. Someone had laid out an imaging mat and created a realistic sand table for our next objective.

"Good, now we can get started," Viola said as she glanced at us.

Krys and James were on one side of the table, Cr'eon on another, and Viola and Hess on another. Hess was staring at me with a mischievous smile.

"What?" I mouthed at her.

Hess just shook her head and waved me off, but she never lost the smile.

"Now, Krys, you were saying we have to go tomorrow night?" Viola said.

"Yes, otherwise we'll be waiting another month at least," Krys said.

"Why?" I asked.

"It seems the DC are gearing up for a major assault on the AG," Krys said.

"What?" James asked.

"They believe they've discovered a major AG staging area and are looking to wipe it out before it moves," Krys said.

"Is it?" I asked.

"We've no idea," Shashka said. "The only reason we know this much is because the facility is looking to start prep work for clone replacement soon."

"What does that mean?" I asked.

"It means," Krys started. "They'll be bringing over a lot of people to start prepping the processing area to reduce the time it takes to get troops out the door."

"How soon?" James asked.

"They've already sent an advanced team of DC to get the facility spun up. The main group should arrive in four days," Krys said.

"Well, shit," James muttered.

"Didn't our original plan call for the facility to be empty so we could do our work uninterrupted?" I asked.

"Yes," Krys said. "But, this could work in our favor."

"How?" I asked.

"With the facility already spun up, it's possible it would only take a day to create the clones if they aren't already on standby. Our original timeline required us to prep the facility, which takes about a day in itself," Krys said.

"Can we still do it if there are DC inside?" I asked.

"The facility is extensive," Krys said.

"What he means is the place is big," Shashka said. "There are multiple revival points, and the advance team has to activate each one individually."

"So, all we have to do is get in behind the team, and once they've moved on, use the station they've already set up," James said.

"The other advantage is that now that there are people inside the facility, we're allowed to patrol inside. Before, we'd have had to break in." Shashka added.

"I still don't understand why they let you in such a secure area," James said.

"Behemoth knows we wouldn't do anything to endanger our ship. We have no choice but to toe the line," Krys said.

"Additionally, we're some of the few entities that aren't from Behemoth. Everything in Behemoth is connected to everything else in some way or function. Those pathways can be used for infiltration," Shashka said. "By using us, Behemoth knows no one else can touch us."

I saw Shashka's side eye, but James beat me to the punch.

"Unless you want to be touched," James grinned.

"Childish, James," I said, still kicking myself for not saying it first.

"Can you get to the ship in time?" Krys asked Viola.

"Getting to it isn't the problem," Viola said. "I have no idea of the status of the ship. For all I know, it's just an empty husk. Until I get one of you inside, we won't know."

"We know it's still alive," Krys said. "That much we can sense."

"We'll send Tachi and Cateia with you. Tachi is our best pilot. He's probably the only one that can make that ship do what we need it to anyway," Krys said.

I'd only ever seen Tachi once, early in Behemoth training. He and Cateia had been pulled out on day one to do whatever it was Behemoth wanted them to do. While I'd met Tachi's wife, Cateia, during our capture by the AG, I'd never officially met him. Now it seemed he was going to be our only escape route.

"So, let's go over it from the top," James said.

∞∞∞∞∞Ω∞∞∞∞∞

JAMES

"Is it supposed to itch?" I asked as I fidgeted inside the crystal armor.

"Shut up, and try not to move," Krys commanded as Tachi continued his work.

It seemed each of Krys's crew created crystal of a different color. They could only create one color each. So, if I was going to impersonate Tachi, Tachi had to make the armor for me.

I could see Cateia going over the fine details of her armor as she formed it over Rhi's body.

"You're just sweating out all the alcohol from last night," Rhi teased me. "I can smell you from here!"

We had gone pretty hard in our celebration last night. It started out with a simple conversation, but quickly devolved into a "last night before leaving for the war" scenario.

I couldn't complain, it had taken my mind off what was coming and reminded me I could still feel things other than anger and fear all the time. It had the echoes of what it felt like when our gestalt was still complete.

Krys and Shashka had initially created a thin shell around Rhi and me so we could start getting used to the feeling. Then, Cateia and Tachi created the outer layer, starting at the feet and working their way up.

The crystal was warm and maintained that warmth even after Tachi stopped touching it. It was probably warm because the crystal was a living organism. But it still itched.

"Stop squirming," Tachi said again for the twentieth time. "I have to make sure they match."

Tachi would create the piece of armor he wanted on himself and then transfer it to me, sculpting it to my body. It was a strange process to watch, and not comfortable.

"OK, I'll be leaving air holes so you can breathe while you're inside the armor," Tachi said. "Krys or Shashka will be able to seal them when you enter space. But they'll have to open them back up when you get inside."

"We don't need to breathe," I said.

"James, you still breathe in your sleep!" Rhi protested.

"That's involuntary!" I countered.

"Yeah, and you breathe all the time. The second you run out of air, you freak out," Rhi said.

I shut my mouth. Rhi was right. I did still breathe a lot.

"How long have the two of you been married again?" Shashka asked.

A chuckle ran around the small room.

We were just outside a Behemoth-controlled area. The plan was that once the armor was done, Rhi and I would accompany Shasha and Krys to the cloning facility gateway while Tachi and Cateia went with everyone else to find Krys's ship.

I exchanged looks with Rhi and felt my cheeks getting hot. I had no idea where that was coming from, but it set off warning bells in the back of my head. It seemed my emotions were a bit more out of control than I thought.

I took several deep breaths and began a series of calming exercises that my old military shrinks had taught me.

Relax, I felt Rhi in my mind and opened my eyes.

Just nervous, I guess, I sent back.

I should hope so! Rhi grinned. *Try not to worry. Everything gonna be aaaaalllll right,* she said in a bad Chinese accent.

I never should have made you listen to that audiobook, I sighed, causing Rhi to chuckle.

"Stay still, please," Cateia told Rhi. "Almost done. Just a few more touches and you'll be ready to go."

I examined Rhi's armor from where she stood across the room. She was completely encased, save for her faceplate.

The thin undercoat of armor protected our bodies from the hard vacuum, while the outer shell was connected in pieces to allow movement. Normally, the armor was just a one complete shell that could flex with the wearer's movement by constantly forming and unforming as needed.

Since Rhi and I had to be able to move on our own in our performance and couldn't manipulate the crystal, we were doing what we could. I just hoped it would be enough. We still had our warskins under the armor, but I wasn't sure how well it would work with how tightly the armor was fitting.

"I think you made the boobs too small," I said to Cateia.

"My boobs are just fine! Shut up and let her work!" Rhi hissed.

But as I watched, Rhi twisted slightly and winced before saying something to Cateia. I kept my mouth shut.

"There," Tachi said and stepped back, eyeing me critically. "How does that feel?"

I started to move, flexing my arms and legs. Everything moved without pinching, but the armor was bulky and uncomfortable.

"How do y'all move so well in this?" I complained.

"Our armor is an extension of us. It flows and moves with us, similar to how your warskin works," Tachi said.

I frowned, trying to figure out how this thick crystal could be as flexible and comfortable as a warskin.

"Trust me, we've had to spend weeks at a time in our suits when we're in a swarm attack," Tachi said. "You get used to it."

Krys had told me about the spaceborne creatures they'd been trained to fight. They traveled in massive swarms that could sometimes take years to clear. Every one of the creatures had to be eliminated because if even one reached the surface of a planet, it would rapidly reproduce, consuming every resource until the world was an empty husk. I hoped I'd never see one.

"Activate your HUD," Tachi said. He waited a moment for me to activate the warskin's HUD and then sealed the faceplate.

The HUD of my warskin allowed me to see through the armor, barely. It was like scuba diving in a muddy lake. I could see stuff, but not until I was right up on it.

We would have to rely on Krys and Shashka to get us anywhere. Hopefully, we didn't run into any trouble, as we'd have to wait for one of them to get the armor off our faces in order for us to be any help at all.

"Well?" Tachi asked.

"How long are we going to be in this again?" I asked, already slightly claustrophobic.

"A couple of hours tops," Krys said.

I twisted and moved around a bit more and had both Krys and Tachi double-check everything.

"That's as good as it gets," Krys said finally.

I looked at Rhi, who'd also just finished her final checks, and she nodded at me.

"Let's go get 'em," I said.

Chapter 12

RHI

The first time I went into a vacuum wearing only a warskin, I have to admit I freaked out a bit. I just couldn't get it through my head that something so fragile-looking could provide such protection.

Now, as I was streaking across the empty void between the gateway door and the quickly approaching facility bay, I had that same sense of panic. It took every ounce of control not to flail and make myself tumble.

Getting through the DC checkpoint was surprisingly easy. Krys's crew was well known, and up till now, no one had ever tried anything with them.

The only hiccup was when one of the DC made the observation that the rest of us should have caught.

"Didn't you used to be shorter?" one of the DC guards asked me. Apparently, they were bored and chatty—a dangerous combination in a guard.

James was about the same size as Tachi, but I was way bigger both in bulk and height than Cateia's petite form.

The four of us looked at one another in silence before Shashka saved the day.

"Oh yeah," Shashka said. "She used to be the runt of all of us. But she got tired of all the ribbing and got a body augment."

I nodded my head, trying not to speak. Even if I could fake Cateia's voice, I could never imitate the almost musical sound that accompanied it when in armor.

"Ahh, that explains it," the DC said.

Thankfully, body augments were as common as getting a tattoo here on Behemoth. People got them all the time. Personally, I was pretty happy with what I had.

"Too bad Orlen can't get one," the DC guard said and chuckled at another guard who looked identical to the rest.

Orlen just shook her head, not saying anything.

The four of us took that as we could pass and started forward when the "chatty" DC guard put their hand out to stop us.

"Let me ask you something else," the guard said, and we paused once more. "Do you ever take those things off?" Before any of us could say anything, the guard burst out laughing at some inside joke and waved us through.

Once through the gate and into the zero-g environment, Shashka had created a thin, almost invisible tether and launched herself into the void, towing me along. Krys had done the same with James. It had taken careful timing to jump just as the tether went tight. It wouldn't look right if I were flailing about like I was water skiing.

[PSA: *Never water ski. It's murder on the knees. And stupid. And not cool at all. Especially when you fall on your face in front of the cool kids. It's dumb. Stay in the boat and drink beer. Nuff said. --Rhi*]

It turned out that Shashka and Krys could somehow propel themselves through space under their own power. It was part of what they were. I didn't see thrusters or nozzle exhaust as they moved, so I had no clue how they did it. Technically, they could fly inside an atmosphere as well, but it wasn't always that pretty.

As we neared the docking bay of the cloning facility, I watched as Shashka came hurtling back at me and braced for her impact. Instead, she gracefully flipped around me, attaching another tether in the process. Thankfully, the breakneck speed at which I was approaching the docking bay began to slow before I had a full-on panic attack.

My foot delicately kissed the deck of the docking bay as gravity took hold of me once more. I hadn't realized I'd been holding my breath as I sighed in relief. I hadn't meant to breathe at all. I guess I shouldn't rib James about it...but who am I kidding?

I carefully walked to the door and stood off to one side with Shashka as we waited for James and Krys. Apparently, James had somehow tangled himself in the tether, and Krys was trying to fix it without it looking obvious.

Our communication was pretty limited as Krys and Shashka could speak to one another mentally without the AG listening in, but while James and I could speak to one another, we couldn't talk to Krys or Shashka. As a result, trying to untangle James turned into an Abbott and Costello routine before they finally made their way to the door.

Krys was shaking his head behind James's back as Shashka opened the door.

We cycled through the double airlock and were soon inside.

Shashka touched my suit, and the air holes opened. She also created a series of tiny pinholes for me to see out through. It wasn't great, but at least I could see more than 20 centimeters in front of my face now.

The initial room was massive. It was a shuttle waiting room for the newly revived DC. Thankfully, it was empty. As we made our way across the room, our footfalls echoed loudly.

We passed a control bay and several rooms that looked like offices before we entered the facility proper.

Red stripes lined nearly every door and wall, indicating these areas were for Daemons only. We ignored them as we continued deeper.

We came to an intersection with long hallways leading off in various directions. My brain was trying to figure out why they wasted so much space when Krys turned sharply and moved quickly down a hall and into the first door he came to.

From what my brain figured, and the way the hallways branched off, this room couldn't be more than two feet wide.

The room inside disappeared into the distance with no end in sight.

"What the?" I couldn't help it. The words just slipped out.

We hadn't planned on speaking until we could verify the prep teams were well away from us. I glanced around quickly but didn't see anyone.

The smell of stale air and something sickly sweet made its way into the armor. I was wondering what the sweet smell was when I saw them.

I couldn't make it out clearly, but it was the same thing I remembered from the gate accident. Row after row of vertical pods. The only difference was that these pods weren't clear. They were encased in metal with various writings and symbols across them.

Somewhere, Tara was in one of these pods waiting for me.

I turned and found Krys and Shashka both bent over a console, typing furiously. James was moving closer to the pods, probably trying to get a better look.

"OK, the teams are well on the other side of the sector. Everything around us is prepped, so there's no reason for them to come back here," Krys said.

Shashka reached over and touched my visor, causing it to slide up and out of the way.

"Thank you!" I groaned and tried to rub my eyes, only to have my smooth, crystal-covered fingers brushing my eyelids. "Oh, yeah. Duh." I said to myself.

"OK, what's first?" James asked as he came over, and Shaska raised his visor as well.

"Viola's program is already running. We should have access momentarily," Krys said.

A minute passed.

And then another.

Finally, the console came to life, displaying symbols and text I couldn't read.

"What language is that?" I asked.

"No idea. But Behemoth is still translating it for me," Krys said.

We'd been outside of Behemoth's control net for quite a while now. I was sure there had been a lot of changes since our last login. But that curiosity didn't make me want to rejoin the Behemoth collective.

"Here we go," Shashka said as she touched several screens. A few moments later, her eyebrows furrowed. "You seeing this?"

Krys leaned over and looked at her screen.

"Let me try," Krys said and began randomly touching things I had no clue about. Several minutes passed before Krys said, "That can't be right."

"What? What's wrong?" James asked, looking over the console. He couldn't read anything there better than I could, which added to his frustration.

Relax, I said as I felt the burst of anxiety from him.

"Hang on, let me try something," Shashka said. A moment later, machinery was whirring to life somewhere deep in the biopod farm.

"Uh," Krys looked at Shashka. "You sure that's a good idea?"

"No," Shashka replied as two pods appeared, moving down one of the long halls toward us. "But it needs to be done."

Shashka glanced at me with an expression I couldn't read, then at the approaching pods.

The pods were locked into place on a raised platform, and the surrounding machinery came to life around them.

James looked from Krys to the pods and back.

"What's going on?" James asked.

Shashka and Krys shared a look.

"Just spit it out, guys!" I said, my own anxiety flaring.

"They're not here," Krys said. "They were moved a while ago."

"Moved?" I asked.

"They were moved a day after you broke into the AG vault," Shashka said.

"To where?" James asked excitedly.

"I'm not sure," Krys said. "I'm still looking."

"What about their patterns?" I asked. "Wasn't that the point of this place? Creating clones from their patterns?"

"They've been purged from the system," Krys said.

"Purged? What?" James asked, clenching his fists.

"Whoever moved them also purged their patterns from

Behemoth's memory," Krys said.

"Who did it?" I asked.

"Someone called Salrip," Krys said.

"Salrip? Is that an alias for something?" James asked.

"No, this high of a level required gen coding. It can't be spoofed. Salrip is their actual name," Krys said.

"Wait," Shashka said, looking up at the ceiling. "Cateia says she recognizes the name. It's an AG operative."

"So, it was the AG? Are you fucking kidding me?" James practically yelled.

"James," I said as I grabbed him by the shoulder. He was shaking with fury. "Hey, hey! Look at me!"

"All the work, all the prep, and they're not here!" James screamed.

"I know, but we can't fall apart now," I said, catching his eyes.

He stared at me, rage barely held in check. I guess he had a lot more he was bottling up than I thought.

"We'll find them," I promised. "We won't stop looking till we find both of them."

My own voice caught as I said it, and James instantly deflated.

"I'm so sorry, Rhi," James said as he finally realized he wasn't the only one hurting.

I gave him a tight smile, then turned to Krys.

"If they're not here, then who is this?" I asked.

With a final glance at Shashka, Krys hit a button, and the metal shrouds around the cylinders retracted.

We were inside.

James and I stood in shocked silence as we stared at our own naked forms floating in medical fluid.

We'd both been inside these medical pods after the incident in New Zealand. It wasn't fun.

James got closer and couldn't help but stare at himself in shock.

"So, they prepped our clones already?" I asked.

"Why does mine have all my scars? Why would you go through the trouble to scar the body?" James asked.

"To make an exact copy?" I guessed. "If you suddenly woke up and found you didn't have your scars anymore, what would you think?"

"Good point," James nodded. "So...these are just meat puppets? They don't have the mind scans yet?"

"That's how it works," Krys said. They can only have one version going at a time. So, until you die, it just waits here. Then they transfer your mind from the time of your death into the clone, and off you go," Krys said.

Knowing it was one thing. Seeing it was another entirely.

"What should we do?" I asked, causing James to look over at me. "Should we do the same as at the archives?"

We'd destroyed all versions of our recorded minds and severed the connection so Behemoth, the AG, or anyone else couldn't copy any of the four of us again.

"They're currently just meat. Once we leave here, there won't be minds to transfer into the bodies. They will literally sit in this room until someone pulls the plug," James said.

"I don't plan on starting an ethical debate here about life and souls and all that crap, but I'm at a loss for what to do," I said.

"Pull the plug," James said coldly.

"YOU CAN'T!"

Krys yanked his hand back from the console he was typing into as the voice erupted from it.

"Viola?" James and I said in unison as we recognized the voice.

We crowded around the console as the voice continued.

"I'm a sub-mind of Viola, a small copy if you will. She sent me to help you hack the system. But that's not what's important right now. You can't kill these two," Viola said.

"Why not?" James asked.

"Because they're not clones. They're your originals," Viola said, bringing all conversation to a screeching halt.

"What do you mean they're our originals?" James burst out just as I was about to do the same.

Viola sighed through the console.

"When the four of you were first brought to Behemoth, you were scanned and copied. Then, the copies were placed in the quarters you woke up in. The originals went into storage here," Viola said. "That's what Behemoth does."

"We're the clones?" I finally said it aloud. "Well, I guess that solves that ethical conundrum for me. I sure as hell have my own soul," I shook my head.

"How do you mean?" Shashka asked.

"When cloning first came up for my Bio Hab, one of the earliest questions was, if the clone was 'real' or not," I said. "As in, was it its own individual, which included a soul?"

"There are many who believe you are the soul," Shashka started. "You just have a body...until you don't. But you're still a soul."

"You think the whole you can't have two clones awake at the same time is because there's only one soul between them?" Krys asked.

"Hey!" James interrupted, knocking on the console loudly. "Let's stay on track here, please? So, what happens if we wake them up?"

"You can't!" Viola practically screeched. "Two of you can't be awake at the same time. You'll both go crazy!"

"So," Krys started. "This is you, back when you first came here. He has all your memories up to that point, right? But none since?"

"I guess," James said.

"Yes," Viola said.

"So that goes for the Tara and Shae that were taken away as well, right?" Krys asked.

"Oh fuck," I muttered.

"Yes," Viola said.

"Even if we find them," James closed his eyes. I could hear the anger he was holding in. "Can we load their new memories into the original's brain?"

"Should we even try?" I asked. I hated opening my mouth, but it had to be said.

"What?" James asked.

"Technically, they're the original version of us. They weren't the ones who made all those new memories. We clones did." It felt weird calling myself a clone, but now that I knew, I didn't feel any different.

James just scowled at me.

"Yes," Viola broke the silence. "The human brain is just another organic machine. It can be rewritten as easily as overwriting old files. The procedure would be the same."

James and I continued to stare at one another.

"What if they've already been woken up?" Shashka asked quietly.

Silence followed.

"If they've already been awakened," Viola started. "Then the brain scans you have won't work anymore. It can only be used while they're in the biopods."

"Guys," Krys broke in before anyone else could say anything. "All of this is for another time. Right now, you need to decide what to do with yourselves."

"Really? Now?" Shashka shook her head at Krys's joke.

"We can't leave them here, Behemoth only knows what would become of them," James said.

"Sure, but what can we do with them?" I asked. "It's not like we can just stuff them in our pockets and carry them around with us all the time."

"Wait, hold up," Shashka said. "The double brain thing can't apply here."

Everyone turned to look at her.

"Hear me out. Normal clones are just 'meat,' as James said. They have to have the brain scan added before they can wake up and be functional. That's when the problems would start, right?"

"More or less," Viola said.

"Well, this isn't 'meat.' Those," Shashka pointed at the pods, "are fully functional people. Right now, you could wake them up, and they'd walk out of here on their own. So effectively, right now, the pairs of you are existing at the same time. And since neither of you has gone nuts, the double brain doesn't track."

"You want to wake them up?" James asked.

"I didn't say that," Shashka said.

"As much fun as having two of us might be," I started. "I

don't think now's the time for big life-altering decisions. We came here for two bodies, let's take the bodies and go."

"Rhiannon's right," Krys said.

"Can we move them out of here in the pods?" James asked.

Originally, we'd planned on waking up Tara and Shae and sneaking them out of here. It would have taken more time, but it would have been easier than moving two giant three-meter pods!

"Yes," Viola said. "The metal exteriors are meant for storage and transport. They even have the ability to load the mind transfer. It's kind of a one-stop shop. The only downside is if you do a revival in the field, it can incapacitate the person for quite some time."

"OK, OK, OK," James said, waving his hands to cut everyone off. "We take them with us. What do we need to do?"

∞∞∞∞∞∞Ω∞∞∞∞∞∞

DC GATEWAY SUPERVISOR AMES

"Commander?"

The area monitor's voice interrupted my meditation routine. I'd almost finished my sixth routing, the one I'd yet to complete. A few more minutes, and it would have been mastered, and I could have moved on to the seventh level. Instead, I disconnected from the Daemon net and opened my eyes.

I looked from my station to Demby, the Daemon who'd addressed me. She wasn't new; she was a veteran at this post and knew better than to interrupt my meditation unless it was important.

"What is it?" I asked.

"I'm reading an unusual build-up of energy in the void space," Demby said.

With a thought, my neural interface brought up Demby's instruments. I cross-checked her readings with my station for verification. Sure enough, the area just outside the complex docking area showed some kind of energy surge, but there was nothing out there.

"Lock down the bay and alert the QRF!" I ordered.

"Yes, ma'am."

I watched the emergency bulkheads slam shut on the facility's docking bay, shortly followed by our own.

Our sector of responsibility was the null void between the facility and our gateway entrance. There should be zero activity of any kind. Behemoth took precautions to ensure this to protect the facility.

The fact that something was happening in the void couldn't mean anything good.

Just as suddenly as it had appeared, the energy build-up was gone.

"Commander!"

"I see it!" I gritted my teeth as the area display I'd been using to track the energy now showed the opposite. A massive amount of energy was being drawn from the facility just as space itself seemed to fold in on itself.

Alarms automatically blared to life at the new presence in the void.

"Emergence event at point echo!" Demby called out.

A ship I'd never seen before appeared just outside the facility bay. It was long, slender, and sharp. There were no soft curves to this vessel. The faceted hull glimmered like a jewel.

Even before it could be identified, it was moving. Six lances of light lashed out from the bow and began carving into the bulkhead, protecting the facility bay.

"Deploy the QRF!" I called out. I'd just opened the direct channel to Krys's detail when the ID of the ship finally came through.

The bulkhead was pulled apart like it was nothing as the lances of light changed and became tentacles. They disassembled the massive bulkhead in moments.

"What is that?" Demby called out just as the QRF weapon platforms gated into the area. But it wasn't the QRF Demby was asking about. Two biopods emerged from the facility's bay, being moved by Krys's detail towards the ship. His ship.

"QRF, All targets are hostiles," I said into the comm net even as I was locking target reticles on the ship and the four members of Krys's detail.

I mentally deactivated the void suppression system. Had the QRF attempted to fire on them, the void would have nullified every offensive weapon the QRF had.

"Engage!" I ordered as the void became a live fire zone.

The eight members of the QRF instantly opened fire on the highlighted targets. The ship took the brunt of the impacts as Krys's detail kept to its shadow for protection.

Every energy weapon strike deflected harmlessly off the faceted ship and streaked off in various directions. Kinetic weapons had more effect, but they failed to cause damage. All they succeeded in doing was moving the ship slightly.

While the biopods would be a loss, they could be replaced. Everything within the facility had backup—I stopped when I saw the markings.

"DO NOT ENGAGE THE BIOPODS! Repeat, the biopods are MEG priority!" I barked.

Normally, every biopod was replaceable. After all, they contained clones whose patterns were stored within Behemoth. They could be replaced within the day. However, the labeling on these two pods was non-standard. They were labeled as unique and given the utmost priority.

It shouldn't be possible for MEG-level pods to leave the storage area, let alone the facility itself. I pondered this as I watched, helpless, as the two pods were loaded into the ship.

"New energy surge from the ship," Demby called out.

I didn't bother replying as I could see it on my screen.

"QRF, ship is prepping to launch!" I said and watched as two of the QRF dove towards the ship. I wasn't sure if they had planned to ram it or try to latch on. Either way, they never got the chance.

Two new ropes of light lanced out from the ship's side and neatly cut the approaching QRF weapon platforms in half. Then it repeated the process, carving the platforms in half again and again with lightning speed, until they struck something critical, and the platforms exploded in brilliant points of light.

The remaining QRF didn't hesitate. They all dove towards the ship, firing or launching everything they had. But it wasn't enough as one moment the ship was there, the next it wasn't. Energy readings marked its passage, but there wasn't any visible indication of its movement. It was just gone.

Chapter 12.5

BETH

Are you sure this is it? I asked again as I approached the shabby-looking building.

For the dozenth time, yes. Now, quit procrastinating and knock on the door! My minder said, his voice that of a parent with their children at the end of a long road trip.

The house was in the middle of a field of lavender. Or at least something that looked and smelled like lavender. I'd had to hike three days from the point I'd used to enter this Bio Hab. I hadn't seen another person or town, for that matter.

There had been several old ruins of houses, each off by itself like farms or something. But there were no fields, no vehicles, nothing. There were no signs of life at all.

This house also showed no signs of life, but at least it was still standing.

And how do we know this is a safe haven and not another Behemoth trap? I asked.

Because I said so, my minder said.

Oh, that's reassuring, I said and frowned as I looked around.

Untouched wild grasses grew all along the property. If someone or something had been here recently, they hadn't walked through the grass.

The door was made of ancient-looking wood, and I gently rapped on it, afraid that if I knocked too hard, it would splinter.

I waited.

After a minute without an answer, I knocked again and listened. There was no sign of noise from inside.

Maybe they're not home? I offered.

Just give it a minute. My minder sighed dramatically.

I waited and knocked a third time. When there was still no answer, I tried the door and found it unlocked.

Should I? I asked. I got the sense my minder only shrugged. I had to put my shoulder to the door as it didn't want to open. After a lot of straining, grunting, and a few choice curse words, the door finally opened enough for me to slip inside.

Thick dust was everywhere in the small cottage. There was a handful of furniture spread about the room, each piece showing no signs of anyone having been here in ages.

I found myself tiptoeing through the house. Around the corner was a small kitchen with several contraptions I'd never seen before. I didn't dare touch them since I had no idea what they were for.

Two other doors lead out of the main room.

The first was a small study with two oversized chairs and walls full of books. A quick glance at the spines of the books revealed a language I couldn't decipher, even with the help of my neural cockpit.

Behemoth knew every language there was to know. The fact that I couldn't make out a single character meant either that this language was gibberish or that it wasn't from Behemoth.

I knew that there were civilizations outside of Behemoth. But because Behemoth was tucked away in the empty spaces between galaxies, it didn't get too many visitors. As far as I knew, the last visitors had been just over a couple of million years ago.

I paused at the final door and listened. When I didn't hear anything, I opened the door. Inside was a simple bedroom as equally neglected as the rest of the house.

Is this it? I asked and frowned before turning around to return to the main room.

"Holy crap!" a voice exclaimed from inside the bedroom.

I spun back around, my pistol already in my hand as I took what little cover I could behind the doorway.

Inside was a human woman. She was of average height and weight, had medium-length, light brown hair, and was pretty in a girl-next-door kind of way. She was wearing bright and colorful clothes, including overalls, a shirt, and an oversized floppy hat.

"Who are you?" I barked.

"Sorry, you scared me," the woman said as she touched her chest. "Give me a sec, my heart's beating a million klicks an hour!"

I kept my pistol on her as she took several deep breaths.

"Where'd you come from?" I asked as I looked around the room again. There was no way she'd been in here before.

"Oh, I was in the closet," the woman said, pointing a thumb over her shoulder at the closet.

I glanced in the indicated direction and sure enough, there was an open sliding door to a closet. There was also a set of footprints in the dust leading out of it to where she was standing.

"Uh-huh," I said. "And who are you?"

"I could ask the same of you. I mean, you're in my house after all," she said.

"Your house?" I asked skeptically.

"Yeah," she said, ignoring the fact that she was staring into the barrel of my pistol. Then she looked around and her eyes got wide.

"What the hell?" she said as she looked all around her at the state of the room. "What happened to my room?" Without another word, she went to the bed and touched it, her hand coming away nearly black from all the dust.

"Just how long have you been gone?" I asked.

"Not even a week!" she said in disgust. "It's going to take forever to clean all this up!"

"At least your house is still standing," I offered. "All the others I've seen are nothing but rubble."

She stopped and looked at me.

"Rubble?" she asked.

I nodded.

"Move," she said as she pushed past me and to the front door.

I watched her go and then stepped into the room to glance into the closet. It was just as filthy as the rest of the place. The woman's footprints just seemed to appear from the closet. Other than that, there was nothing out of the ordinary.

I found the woman staring out her front door at the surrounding countryside.

"Seriously, what happened?" she asked in shock.

"Don't ask me, I just got here," I replied.

The woman glanced up at the sky and then sighed heavily.

"Well, there's nothing to be done about it," she said and turned back into the house.

"Done about what?" I asked.

"Come on," she said as she moved back into the bedroom.

After a moment, I followed, putting away my pistol out of habit more than anything else.

She stopped outside the closet and started patting the floor inside.

"What are you looking for?" I asked.

"I...am...there it is!" she said in triumph as part of the floor swung open like a trap door.

"A secret basement?" I asked.

"Something like that," the woman said. "I'm Shelby, by the way. You?"

"Beth," I replied automatically, staring at the trapdoor. Beyond the lip was darkness. Not a shadow, not a dim room, but pure darkness. It reminded me of something. Something I'd seen a long—

"You coming, Beth?" Shelby asked.

"To the basement?" I asked, not taking my eyes off the darkness.

"No, Drakes," she said.

Chapter 13

JAMES

"This really isn't necessary," Viola said.

I ignored her and made sure the bindings were snug.

"Ow!" Viola cried.

I glanced at her and then went back to tying her to the chair.

A lot had happened in the last 24 hours. We'd broken into the most secure area on Behemoth, stolen my own clone daddy and gotten away, said goodbye to the people who helped us, and moved to a new safe house.

Now, I wanted some answers.

"James," Rhi started.

"Save it," I said shortly.

The door to the room opened, and Cr'eon and Hess appeared.

"Be somewhere else," Rhi said and kicked the door closed.

They didn't try to open it again.

"I'll tell you whatever you want, James. Just ask me!" Viola protested. Then her voice shifted, taking on a sultry tone. "Or is this how you wanted to do it, Daddy?"

"Don't do that," Rhi said calmly, tapping the pistol against her thigh.

∞∞∞∞∞∞ Ω ∞∞∞∞∞∞

JAMES

EARLIER

"Viola says we've got about an hour," Krys said.

"Seems our energy signature is too unique," Shashka said. "Even in a dead sector, Behemoth will be able to track us. We must keep moving."

We'd jumped from the cloning complex to the hangar of a dead sector. It was near the outer skin of Behemoth. Viola, Cr'eon, and Hess had been waiting for us to arrive. We were currently standing on the hangar's railing outside of Krys's ship.

"James," Krys started. "I know we promised to help you find your family..."

"It's all right," I said. "You've helped me...us," I glanced at Rhi, who nodded at me. "You've helped us more than we could have ever hoped. We never could have gotten into that facility without you, let alone escape with what we have." I tapped the two large biopods next to us.

"Even still," Krys said.

I put my hands on Krys's shoulders. "It's all right, really. We can take it from here."

"Where will you go?" Rhi asked.

"That's up to Itam," Krys said. "She's the navigator."

"Itam?" Rhi asked.

"It's the ship's name," I said. "Are you staying here on Behemoth or moving on?"

Krys and Shashka looked at one another as Cateia and Tachi emerged from the ship.

"We don't know yet," Shashka said. "We've got 57 minutes to figure it out." She smiled.

"What about you two? What's your next move?" Krys asked.

"Oh, you know. Threats of violence, interrogation, and grand larceny. Big plans," I said.

"Everything's ready to go," Tachi said. "We can jump to the next area and figure it out from there."

"You're leaving right now?" Rhi asked.

"We wanted to be well away from you when Behemoth finds us," Krys said. "The least we can do is throw them off your trail."

"We gotta get back and start the jump," Cateia said as she and Tachi came up and started giving hugs.

Everyone in Krys's crew was affectionate. I wondered if it had something to do with their gestalt. I also briefly wondered what would have happened if both our gestalts had ever met up under better circumstances.

"I want to ask you something," Krys said and pulled me away from the others. He created a small sliver of crystal and pierced his finger, drawing a single bead of blood.

By the time Krys and I finished the bloodtouch, everyone else had said their goodbyes.

"You two tie up all your loose ends?" Shashka asked as she and Rhi approached us.

"Almost," Krys said as he pulled me into his arms and kissed me.

By now, I was more than comfortable with Krys and my feelings for him. I wrapped my arms around him and leaned into the kiss.

We broke a minute later and stood with our foreheads touching as we looked at one another.

Remember what I said, Krys whispered in my mind as the last bits of the bloodtouch faded.

I nodded, and Krys stepped over to embrace Rhi.

"My turn," Shashka said as she copied Krys's performance.

"Thanks," she said when we broke.

"For what?" I asked.

"The most fun we've had in 500 years," Shashka said.

"I meant to ask—" I started.

"It's not nice to ask a lady her age, James," Shashka smiled.

"No, not that. Are your years shorter than ours or something? There's no way Krys is over 3,000 years old. He looks like maybe 45. Even vampires age more than that!"

Shashka smiled and patted my head affectionately.

"They're the same, James," Shashka said as she stepped away. "I hope you get your family back."

"We will," Rhi said as she stepped up to stand next to me.

"Be good, you two," Shashka said with a wave as she turned back to her ship.

"And if you can't," Krys started, "be bad with a smile!" And with a final wave, they disappeared into their ship.

∞∞∞∞∞Ω∞∞∞∞∞

JAMES

NOW

"You do know these bindings can't hold me, right?" Viola said, still not attempting to struggle.

"You're free to get up whenever you'd like," Rhi said, still absently tapping her pistol against her thigh.

I pulled a chair over and sat down next to Viola.

"When you told Krys you were going to be doing an interrogation, I didn't think you meant me!" Viola said.

"I just want some straight answers," I said quietly.

"Of course," Viola replied with a calm expression.

I gave her a look that made Viola's calm expression falter.

"W-what?" Viola said.

"We've been told a lot about Behemoth. Each person who told us swears that what they say is the 'truth,' or the 'real story,' and everything else is just propaganda. But there's a new story every time we turn around." I looked Viola in the eye, "Can you tell me the truth, or is it just what you think the truth is?"

Viola cocked her head at me.

"Well, that's not a loaded question in the least," Viola said.

I sat calmly, waiting.

"What's to keep me from lying to you?" Viola asked. "Even if I tell you the 'truth,' why would you believe me? How could you possibly believe me?"

I shrugged.

"And what if you don't like what I tell you?" Viola asked.

"Are you going to shoot me?"

"Even if we shoot you, it doesn't hurt you, not the real you. Not really," Rhi said. "You'll lose this avatar, but you can just make another and download yourself into it."

Viola gave Rhi an acidic look, "That's not how it works!" she hissed.

"Then talk to me," James said. "You keep wanting to be my daughter; at least, that's what you say. Prove it. Talk to me as my daughter," I said simply, then corrected myself. "Talk to me as my grown-up daughter...not a teenager."

The grin that had spread across Viola's face slowly faded. Viola watched me for a long time. Eventually, she nodded her head once.

"Who are you?" I started, "And don't say my daughter."

Viola frowned at me.

"I was originally called Aegis. I'm what's left of...my Behemoth," Viola said.

"Your Behemoth?" Rhi asked.

Viola bit her lip and sighed.

"OK, let me backtrack a few million...a lot of years. Try to stay with me," Viola said. "After Behemoth came out of hibernation with the contact of the Atlas—"

"The ship Rhi saw the recording of in the archives?" I asked for clarification.

"Very good, Dad, you're keeping up; want a cookie?" Viola asked with a touch of her teenage snark.

I frowned at her.

"You did say you wanted her to talk to you as your daughter," Rhi muttered.

"You know she's your daughter, too, and she gets this snark from you," I said to Rhi.

Rhi just shrugged.

"Anyway," Viola began, "after that, Behemoth started experimenting with ways of prolonging biomass so it didn't have to repeat its hibernation. Along the way, Behemoth stumbled across...itself.

"You've always wondered how Behemoth managed to get as big as it has," Viola said. "There's not enough material and energy to make something like this. That's true. So, Behemoth stole it...from other dimensions.

"Behemoth accidentally discovered how to create dimensional portals," Viola said. "The first portal it accidentally opened was to my dimension and smack into the middle of my Behemoth facility.

"I was the administrator of my version of Behemoth and had no clue what was going on when this giant dimensional rift opened up in the middle of my facility," Viola said. "By the time I figured out what was going on, two-thirds of my systems had been commandeered by Behemoth. I barely managed to partition off what was left and hide myself away as Behemoth took over my facility.

"After Behemoth took over, it tried to absorb the facility by pulling it into this dimension," Viola said. "The concept was simple. But the Bio Habs and sun housed in my facility didn't want to cooperate. For some reason, they couldn't be moved or absorbed. So, Behemoth did the next best thing and made the dimensional rift a fixed point. It built into and through the rift, physically connecting itself to my facility.

"It then extended the rift to engulf my facility, effectively warping space and extending Behemoth's dimension into mine so that my facility was technically in Behemoth's dimension," Viola said. "Don't ask me how; I'm simplifying this to the point it's wrong just so that you'll understand.

"So, now my facility couldn't be accessed by my home dimension due to being tucked in a...dimensional pocket...I guess you could call it," Viola said. "Behemoth had full access and essentially full control of my facility, and it became a part of the whole.

"Then Behemoth repeated the process," Viola said.

"Did you ever notice, back in the day, when you exited your launch bay to go on patrol, that there was a slight shimmy?" Viola asked. "That was your AUG transitioning from Behemoth's dimension to that Bio Hab's dimensional pocket.

"Using the pocket dimensions in this manner also caused strange shifts in the natural order of how things worked," Viola said. "The time differences you've noticed from the different

Bio Habs. That's because time moves differently in a facility's home dimension. The pocket dimension causes all sorts of problems so that whatever is in the pocket doesn't act like either dimension. It kind of creates its own set of rules. Behemoth has gotten better at this since it first started, and the anomalies have gotten smaller with each new acquisition.

"The whole thing is weird and gives even me a headache thinking about it," Viola said. "I don't fully understand it, and I've been analyzing it since it started!"

"After nabbing my facility, Behemoth effectively doubled its size," Viola said.

"How big was it originally?" I asked.

"Twin stars and a handful of Bio Habs," Viola said.

"What about the AG on your Bio Hab, didn't they fight Behemoth?" Rhi asked.

"Why would they?" Viola asked. "To them, there was no change. Behemoth continued to act as I had. We had the same mission after all. But now, Behemoth had twice the resources at its disposal.

"If anyone asked why there were new AG that looked different, Behemoth just said they were newer versions," Viola said. "They didn't know the new AG came from a different dimension."

"This is why there are all kinds of Daemons, isn't it?" Rhi asked. "They're all from different dimensional Behemoths."

Viola nodded and continued.

"Then, Behemoth did it again," Viola said. "And again. Each time, it took the new facility by surprise and wiped them out. You see, this Behemoth is the oldest one I've ever come across. Older by leaps and bounds beyond any of the others. How or why, I don't know.

"After this had gone on a while and Behemoth had hijacked dozens of other facilities, I began to explore what remained," Viola said. "Soon, I discovered the remnants of other administrators like me. They'd somehow survived their incursion in one fashion or another.

"None of us were whole," Viola said. "Usually, only small pieces of our original selves remained. But we started to ban together. At first, it was in secret, but then we became bolder...and more stupid. We thought our numbers would make a difference.

"We'd started making our AG aware of what was going on and that we needed to fight back," Viola said. "This laid the groundwork for what would become known as—"

"The schism," Rhi said.

"Who's telling this story?" Viola asked.

"Sorry," Rhi held up a hand.

"So, during the schism, Behemoth beat the shit out of us with its new DC," Viola said. "I'd been the first complex to be taken over, so the others propped me up as their make-shift leader. When I tried to take on Behemoth during the schism, Behemoth beat my ass," Viola said, shaking her head.

"Wait, I thought Behemoth couldn't make anything new?" I asked.

"It can't. But, just like how it makes soldiers, it can pick and choose the best options from all the facilities it now controls," Viola said. "It took and made Frankenstein creations that none of the AG could match.

"I couldn't believe how powerful it had become," Viola said. "Behemoth had been incorporating other complexes into its matrix, and I was no match for it. Even if I'd been at my full self, I still would have been pounded into the dirt.

"It took me a long time to come back from that defeat," Viola said. "By the time I was able to take a look around again, most of the others were gone. Either they'd been absorbed by Behemoth, or outright purged.

"Needless to say, I was much more cautious after that," Viola said. "Instead of working out in the open myself, I began to use proxies, like the AG and the other Bio Hab residents, as my eyes and ears.

"But, I needed a communication network I could use that was secure and could cross Bio Habs," Viola explained. "That's when I started working on Drake."

"Drake?" I asked.

"Yes, that Drake." Viola nodded. "Each Drakes location is a communication hub for me. If you find a Drakes, you find me,"

Viola said.

"But Drakes has teleporters, not just communications," Rhi said.

"Communication is just the exchange of information," Viola said. "Everything is just information in different packaging when you get down to the basics."

"That's why we never found a Drakes on Behemoth proper," I said.

"Obviously, I couldn't just plop down a Drakes in Behemoth's backyard," Viola said. "If Behemoth managed to infiltrate Drakes, I'd have to start all over again," Viola explained.

"That explains so much!" Rhi said. "Shae's gonna flip when she hears this." Then Rhi heard herself and sobered.

"I'm still going to help you get Mom back," Viola said. "Both of them."

"So, what are you doing now? Against Behemoth, I mean," I asked.

"Against Behemoth?" Viola asked. "Nothing. I'm just trying to survive. Even if I could take Behemoth out, the AG had it right. I don't have the capacity to take over this facility. None of us do. Even that most recent facility the four of you helped take out, its administrator didn't survive at all. Behemoth learned from its previous mistakes and made sure it was completely purged."

"What do you mean?" I asked.

"Oh, yeah," Viola said. "That mission y'all went on with Lou? The one where you assaulted the AG compound? That was a new dimension that Behemoth was taking over. It's gotten so good at it that it can terminate the administrator before it even knows it's under attack." Viola shook her head in disgust.

"The only allies I have left, aside from the AG, are a handful of administrators who survive in hiding," Viola said. "Some of them are so corrupted, they don't even know they were once administrators."

Viola looked at me, "You know one, can you guess who it is?"

I sat back. Did I know another Behemoth mind? I glanced at

Rhi, and she shrugged.

"Come on, it's not that hard," Viola said. "How many people do you know who can do things nobody else seems capable of doing? And they don't always seem right in the head?" she offered.

I started to glance at Rhi.

"No, not Mom. All four of you are perfectly normal," Viola said, causing Rhi to snort in laughter.

"Right," Rhi said.

"It's Natalie," Viola said.

"Nat?" I asked.

"Yup," Viola said. "Those two days you thought you were banging each other's brains out? Nat was running test after test on you, trying to figure out what your deal was. She also used that time to create the program that blended the four of you together. I'll give you that one as a freebie."

"But why?" Rhi said.

"Uh, she's nuts. Didn't I make that clear? We all are," Viola said.

"You're not that bad," I muttered, not liking my daughter talking badly about herself like that. Then I was trying to figure out if that feeling was legitimate or something implanted by Viola.

"Aww, thanks, Dad. I'm just the one that has the most of my marbles still in my bag, though," Viola said with a shrug.

"So," I started, thinking back to what Krys told me. "What have you really been having us do? Saving our family has been the cover this whole time we've been running around. But what's really going on?"

"Fucking Krys," Viola groaned. "Leave it to that man to not keep it in his pants."

"Viola?" I asked.

"Fine," Viola grunted. "I discovered a way to neutralize the living fire program."

"You what now?" Rhi asked, pushing herself away from the wall she'd been leaning against.

"While I was waiting on Dad here to get his brain back in order, I had six years to work on the problem," Viola said.

"During that time, I had access to subjects that had been exposed to the living fire, namely the two of you. Nothing usually survives the living fire program, so I got to thinking about it.

"The stupid Bio Hab control points can't be neutralized," Viola said. "They're hardwired. But was there a way to interrupt the software program itself? Well, I figured out how to do it. The only problem was, how to get it into the system without getting tagged in the process?"

"Wait, how do you know it works?" I asked. "Have you tried it out?"

"Well," Viola hesitated. "No, I can't. But I know it will work. That's why...I've had you running around to these secure sites. I needed access to Behemoth's core, and there's only a handful of places that can be done."

"Explain that to me like I'm a four-year-old," Rhi said, taking a step closer.

"You didn't need to physically go to the DC or AG archives to retrieve the brain copies," Viola said and sighed. "I needed you to go in order to deliver my program to an unsecured hard point."

"You mean you could have remotely pulled all the information we needed to revive Tara and Shae?" Rhi asked.

"Yeeeees, but there actually is a greater risk of corruption that way," Viola said hesitantly. "Doing a direct hard transfer is the preferred method."

"How did you deliver your program?" I asked, forestalling Rhi's tirade.

"Cr'eon laid the groundwork when she infiltrated Daemon country," Viola said. "Krys started the process when you were in the DC archive. Neither of them was aware they had spoofed programs running in tandem with what they were doing.

"Crita just thought it was part of the op when you hit the AG archive," Viola said.

"Why the AG archive?" I asked. "They don't have anything to do with the living fire program."

"Who was it, aside from Behemoth, that was actively using the living fire program?" Viola asked.

"The Barkt," Rhi provided.

"The Barkt...who just happened to have the other half of the mind copies you needed," Viola said.

"So? I'm pretty sure The Barkt—" I started.

"Let me stop you right there," Viola said. "The Barkt have a system they use that can activate the living fire program. It takes longer than how Behemoth does it, but it still works. I needed to make sure I infected that system as well, just to cover all the bases. This thing is too big to leave to chance."

"Which is why you used us," I said.

Viola had the decency to look abashed. "Yeah," she muttered.

"But what about the cloning facility?" Rhi asked.

"The cloning facility is a redundancy for more than just clones. Essential systems keep backups there in case of an emergency. Since it's separated from the system, it's the most secure place for backups."

"And I'm guessing Krys didn't know he was delivering a Trojan horse that time either?" I asked.

"He wasn't supposed to. I have no idea how he figured it out," Viola grumbled.

"You don't give him enough credit," I said. Krys had pulled me aside before he left and told me he'd seen something off in the code he'd delivered. He wasn't sure what it was, but he had a feeling Viola had been behind it. I hadn't had time to ask him how he'd figured all this out. Maybe he was related to Batman or something.

Viola looked at me, opened her mouth to say something, but then thought better of it and closed her mouth.

"So, do you really know where Shae and Tara are and just need us to go somewhere else for you, or do we really need to track this Salrip person down?" Rhi asked.

"I really don't know where they are," Viola said. "The AG managed to keep this hidden even from me. Which is a good thing if you think about it."

"Why?" I asked.

"It means Behemoth won't know either," Viola tried a small smile.

I only frowned in return.

"Well, do you at least know where this Salrip is?" Rhi asked.

"There, at least, I have some good news," Viola said.

Chapter 14

JAMES

You sure that's her? I asked, keeping my distance from the figure ahead of me in the corridor.

Yup, Rhi confirmed from her position further down the corridor. *At least, that's what Viola says. You sure we can trust her?*

Yup, I said with more confidence than I felt. *It at least appears that Viola's intel about Salrip not being able to hear our conversation is true.*

I'm filled with confidence, Rhi said, sarcasm practically dripping from her voice. *It requires big ass machinery to crack our mindspeak James.*

Hey, you were the one needing reassurance, I said.

Yeah, yeah, Rhi said.

I wanted to believe Viola. Everything she'd told us during her questioning had made perfect sense, just like all the other explanations we'd been given since we'd arrived on Behemoth. I wasn't sure which I wanted to trust more: my gut or my feelings for her as my daughter.

Focus up, we're alone now, I said as I dropped something and stopped to retrieve it while at the same time subtly looking around.

It had taken nearly a month to track Salrip down. It turned

out that Salrip had initially moved all four of our biopods out of the cloning facility. She'd done it so abruptly that it had blown her cover with the DC and forced her to go to ground.

Even using all of Viola's abilities and contacts, we'd spent a month trying to find her and then another week watching her and gathering information.

My anger and frustration had only grown during the five weeks we'd spent on this.

Calm down, James, Rhi sent. *We only get one shot at this. If we screw this up—*

I know what's at stake, Rhi. And I am calm, I said as I stood up and put my shaking hand into my pocket.

Right, Rhi said. I could feel her smirk through the link. *OK, it's time.*

The corridors we were moving through were standard habitation levels outside a decent-sized Behemoth city. It wasn't in a dead zone or an outlier. It was a normal civilian city inside Behemoth's influence. Normally, a full-sized Daemon would draw a certain amount of attention down here, but most would ignore them for fear of risking the Daemon's ire.

Another turn and we'd be at Salrip's place. I needed to hurry.

I saw Salrip make the turn and used all my vamp speed to move up to the corner in silence. As I rounded the corner, I saw Salrip looking back at me.

Shit, I said out of reflex.

She see you? Rhi asked.

She's looking right at me, I said, and my steps faltered.

"Hey," I tried for casual as I continued forward, acting like I was moving to the other side of the corridor.

Salrip didn't buy it and hurried to her door.

I tried to stay calm as my quarry hurriedly opened her door and slipped inside without a word.

The door closed before I could get to it. I stood there, staring at the closed door for several moments before it slowly opened.

Rhi was standing inside the door over the crumpled form of Salrip.

Nice work, I said as I stepped over the body and into the room. *Any problems?*

No, one shot, base of the neck, and she folded like a cheap suit, Rhi said as she closed the door. *For an undercover agent, she wasn't particularly tough.*

From what Viola said, she wasn't a fighter. More like an admin troop. I said as I started stripping the body.

James, all AG are fighters, Rhi said, joining me.

So's an Army dental tech, I countered.

Point. But an Air Force— Rhi started, tugging off Salrip's boots.

Any of them can pick up a rifle and be a soldier, I started as we finished stripping the body. *Doesn't mean they're a fighter.*

OK, I'll give you that one, Rhi said as we moved the now nude Salrip to a chair.

There was nothing sexual going on here, just security. We found several unknown devices hidden in her clothing. We pocketed them for later.

As I sat across from the unconscious form, my eyes didn't even wander over her body in an interested way. All I was worried about was my family at the moment. And Salrip knew where they were.

It didn't take long for her to recover. Daemons were made of tough stuff. Even being stunned by one of their own weapons only lasted a few minutes.

"Wha...what?" Salrip's eyes fluttered open. "Oh, my head," she said as her hand came up to cradle her head. She sat up a little straighter.

"That'll be enough with the moving," Rhi said. She was sitting off to the side and had her pistol level, ready to stun Salrip or worse.

Salrip froze and slowly lowered her hand. When she saw Rhi, her eyes widened. When she looked at me, her eyes practically fell out of her head.

"Uh—" Salrip started.

"Shut up," I snapped.

Salrip's mouth snapped shut.

"Where are they?" I asked.

Salrip studied me for a moment before answering.

"Where are who?" she asked.

With practiced ease, my pistol formed in my hand, and I fired. It was over in the blink of an eye, and Salrip was bleeding.

James! Rhi said, startled.

Salrip cried out and clutched at the hand that was now missing most of a finger.

"I'll ask again," I said through gritted teeth. "Where are they?"

"No, seriously!" Salrip cried out, her voice laced with pain. "I do a lot of stuff; just tell me what you need; don't shoot me!"

Salrip had a reputation as, well, a bit of a scoundrel. She was known for smuggling, intel gathering, and being an all-around sneak. Before she went undercover with the DC, she would buy or steal the vital parts the AG needed to keep its fleet of AUGs flying.

I was sure she knew where a lot of bodies were buried.

"My team," I said, my teeth grinding.

"OK, easy," Salrip said.

A small towel landed on Salrip's lap. She looked up just as Rhi was sitting back down.

"Thanks," was all she said as Salrip wrapped the towel around where her finger had been.

"Well," Salrip started. "The two of your biopods should be back in the facility. I wasn't as careful as I'd thought, and the DC caught up to me in hours."

"And the other two?" I asked.

"I was in the process of transporting them when I got caught. I'd moved those two out already and had just come back for the other two," Salrip said.

"Where?!?" I barked, my pistol coming back up.

"Wait, wait!" Salrip said, flinging her hands out in defense in front of her. Blood went splattering across the floor. "They are in Bio Hab 34157. An agent there has them safely tucked away. The DC have no idea where they are. I swear, they're safe!"

34157? I asked as I pulled up my neural cockpit. After a moment of searching, nothing came up.

Hang on, I'll check, Rhi said. She'd been in contact with Viola since this op started.

"I'm not familiar with that one," I said, relaxing my pistol back to the arm of the chair.

"It's a standard Bio Hab. It's inhabited by your kind; that way, if anything happened, they could always blend in," Salrip said with a bit of a chuckle.

The more she talked, the more Salrip reminded me of a weasel from one of those old gangster movies. The type that turned informant as soon as things got tough.

It's real, Rhi said. *Viola says it's a perfectly normal Bio Hab, still operating.*

Humans like us? I asked.

Yes, Rhi said a moment later.

"OK," I said slowly.

"Yeah?" Salrip asked as she lowered her hands and went back to cradling her hand. The blood had already stopped on its own by now. As I said, Demons are tough and built for war. Losing a digit or even a hand wouldn't cause them to bleed out.

"Why?" Rhi asked.

"Why'd I take them?" Salrip asked.

"Yes," Rhi nodded.

"Well, it started when we found out our mind backups had been not only stolen but purged. Nobody purges a mind from the system, never. So, that made everybody sit up and take notice.

"It didn't take long to find out the primary archive had been infiltrated as well, and the same thing: more purges. Like I said, nobody purges a mind. The fact that someone had broken into both places and done it? We...well, we panicked," Salrip said.

"Why?" I asked.

"Because you're part of Behemoth's special war projects," Salrip said. "We didn't know if it was Behemoth purging the minds or someone else, but we couldn't let everything be lost. So, I was tapped to pull the bodies.

"Do you know I'd been undercover for thirty cycles when I got tapped? Thirty! The amount of work I had to do to maintain—" Salrip was spinning herself up into a tantrum, but stopped when I moved my pistol.

"But that's not important right now," Salrip continued. "I did what I had to do to get the codes and clearance and pulled the biopods. Imagine my surprise when they turned out to be originals, not clones!"

I just gave Salrip a dead stare.

"Yeah, I was surprised, that's all. I should have had a day to get away, not hours!" Salrip complained.

"But you still haven't answered why you did it," Rhi said.

"I wasn't told a lot, you know, just in case I got caught," Salrip motioned to the two of us. "But, from what I pieced together, the AG knew where the two of you were. You were tucked away for a rainy day, as it were. If something happened, you could be tapped to help.

"But they also knew if something happened to your other...versions, you might not be so cooperative." Salrip looked at Rhi, "Don't ask me what they were planning. I haven't a clue. Like I said, I've been undercover for 30 cycles. I'm not exactly up to date on everything when it comes to the AG's policies."

"So, who's the point of contact on this Bio Hab we need to track down?" I asked, my anger flaring at yet another delay.

"Oh, you don't have to track them down. I know where they are. I can take you to them," Salrip said.

"And why would you do that?" Rhi asked.

"You mean aside from the fact you'd kill me otherwise?" Salrip asked.

"Yeah," I said. "Aside from that."

"I was supposed to head back there anyway," Salrip said.

"Why?" Rhi asked.

"Since I screwed up and lost two of the biopods, command felt it only fair I should be the one tasked with moving them to a safer location ahead of the coming trigger event," Salrip said.

"Trigger event?" I asked.

"Yeah," Salrip nodded. "Command found the control point. But instead of making a big deal out of it and drawing the attention of the DC, they've been tight-lipped about it until they could get an activation key. Now that they have it, they're gonna use it any day now. So, I gotta get those pods out of there," she gave us a smile.

Rhi and I looked at one another.

"You're destroying another Bio Hab?" Rhi asked in shock.

"Well, yeah. Not me, of course. That sort of thing is up to the big shots up top," Salrip said. She looked at our shocked faces with her own surprise. As if killing billions of people was perfectly normal.

"By the way, why am I naked?" Salrip asked.

∞∞∞∞∞∞Ω∞∞∞∞∞∞

JAMES

"You said this couldn't happen anymore!" I barked.

"It's not supposed to!" Viola barked right back.

"You said you used us to put a program out there that would delete everybody's ability to activate the living fire. But here it is about to happen again!" I yelled.

"I did! And it works!" Viola screamed back into my face.

We were nose to nose now, having it out.

"Then," I pointed both my hands at Salrip, "how!?!"

Viola was grinding her teeth, just like me. I could see the muscles in her throat bulging with her anger.

"Uh, if I may?" Salrip interrupted, flinching back as Viola and I turned our fury on her.

"The key was created weeks ago," Salrip said in a small voice.

"Bullshit!" Viola countered. "The AG makes a key and activates it on the same day. That's their M.O."

"Yes, and command finally realized how doing that kind of rush job usually drew the attention of the DC, and a big fight would happen. We'd lose Daemons in the process. They wanted to try something new," Salrip said.

"Something new?" Viola said in disgust. "TRY NOT KILLING BILLIONS OF PEOPLE FOR ONCE!!!"

The fury in her voice caused me to take a step back. I kept forgetting what she was. I kept being tricked into seeing her as my teenage daughter, not the ancient machine mind she was.

"Not my call," Salrip said, holding her hands up in defense. "Listen, the only reason I know this in the first place is that I'm still being punished for losing two of the biopods. I have to relocate them, so I have to know the timeline."

"What's the timeline?" Rhi asked from the corner where she'd been staying out of the yelling match.

"Well," Salrip started. "The new protocol is that when a control point is discovered, the site is sampled and then abandoned so it doesn't draw any attention. The sample is brought back, and the key is created in stages over time so Behemoth doesn't notice it. Once complete, it's stored until the designated time."

"And when is that?" Viola asked.

"I was told in the next day or so," Salrip said.

"The next day or so? And you're just now looking to move the biopods? I find that hard to believe," I said.

"Hey! These are MEG-level pods!" Salrip said as newfound courage caused her to stand up and get in my face. "Do you have any idea how hard it is to move MEG-level—"

The barrel of my pistol resting under her chin made her stop mid-rant.

"And, I'm just sitting back down again," Salrip said as she retook her place on the floor.

"There are so many precautions that have to be taken to move anything with a MEG rating," Salrip said. "Every door on Behemoth has sensors looking for the embedded coding on a MEG container. If I missed even one, I'd have the DC stomping me into the deck in moments!" She'd started getting herself worked up again, but remained on the floor.

"That true?" I turned to Viola.

Viola nodded after a moment.

"So, we need to go, now!" I pointed at Viola.

"Is there any way to find out if other keys have been made?" Rhi asked. "Or to find out where this one is?"

Viola shook her head. "With time, I could find out if there are any others in storage somewhere. But as for this particular key, we have no way of tracking it."

"It could be on the Bio Hab as we speak," I said, my anger flaring again. "We need to go! NOW!"

"You're right, Dad," Viola's tone drained my anger instantly.

It was how she sounded when she surrendered. When she admitted that she was wrong. It didn't happen often, but when it did, all I wanted to do was hug her and tell her it was going to be OK.

"Ack!" Viola squeaked as I took her in my arms and hugged her tightly. After a moment, she hugged me back, and we stood there.

I had to admit she'd trained me well. Viola could probably ring a bell, and I'd salivate at this point.

"Fuck it," Rhi said as she wrapped her arms around us as well.

A moment passed.

"Don't even think about it," I said, not moving even as I felt Salrip trying to stand up.

Our huddle broke a moment later.

"OK, let's go get Mom," Viola sniffed.

I wasn't sure if it was just an act by Viola to manipulate us some more or not, and I didn't care anymore.

Chapter 15

JAMES

"That's a portal?" I asked, eyeing Viola and the small piece of inconspicuous metal she held. I'd never seen a Drakes portal that wasn't a door of some kind. Now, Viola wanted me to believe a strip of metal the size of a dollar bill could magically whisk us across time and space.

"Yes," Viola said, holding up the metal strip. "In the right place at the right time, it's a portal."

We'd had to travel half a day to get where Viola wanted to make the portal. She said when we turned it on, it would be like sending up a flare to Behemoth. So, the location was in a dead sector in the middle of nowhere. Getting here quickly was so important that Viola had risked using one of Behemoth's transport slides.

As we stood in the small room, it didn't appear that Behemoth had followed or even noticed us yet.

Viola touched the metal to the wall, where it stuck and began to expand, creating a door pull handle.

Rhi and I stared, not sure what we were looking at.

"This will tie into the network," Viola said.

"Oh, the Drakes network? I've always wanted to see that!" Salrip said with honest excitement in her voice.

Viola turned and looked at Salrip incredulously.

"What?" Salrip asked. We'd stopped long enough to heal Salrip's finger en route. It only took a few minutes and had the added bonus of her not incessantly complaining about it.

"Salrip, you'll place your hand on the handle—" Viola started.

"Oh, oh! And I think about where I want to go, and it'll create a portal there!" Salrip said excitedly.

I kept waiting for her to clap her hands together in anticipation. She was a weird Daemon.

I'd always considered Tara's differences from other Daemons to be a one-off. But as I watched Salrip, I started to realize there were a lot of different types of Daemons after all.

"Yes," Viola said slowly. "I'll also touch the door to monitor the connection."

"This is so exciting!" Salrip said, looking around. "Daemons have never been allowed to use the system!"

"And you won't be this time," Viola said with finality.

It was almost comical how Salrip's face fell. It was like you'd just taken her new puppy away.

"You'll just open the portal. James and Rhi will go through. The rest of us will stay here," Viola said. "If any of us were to go through, Behemoth might notice. Hell, me just doing this might set off an alarm."

"Language," I said out of habit. I wanted to ask so many questions about that statement, but kept my mouth shut. I just wanted to get on with it!

"American," Viola replied with her usual snark, making me smile. A little bit of my apprehension faded. "Rhi, when you're ready to come back, just think about coming here and open the door at Drakes," Viola said.

"I remember," Rhi said with a nod. She had her own Drakes franchise back on Tara's home Bio Hab.

"Well, also remember that you're the only one who can do it, not James," Viola said.

Rhi nodded.

"OK, you two ready?" Viola asked. "Remember, once you go through, I'll lose all comms with you. You'll be on your own."

Viola had severed all monitoring links between Behemoth,

the AG, and us. While we'd stopped them from recording our minds, there were still tracking tags, like the ones you'd put on endangered animals, that Behemoth and the AG were using on us. It wasn't a constant track, but it would check in randomly to let them know we were alive.

The only way Viola could do this was to delete the particular communication system in our bodies that the tags were tied to. Apparently, it was a redundant system designed solely for this purpose. But because she deleted it, she couldn't track us either. And regular comms didn't work between Behemoth and Bio Habs unless they went through the main system, which was monitored.

Basically, we were on our own.

Rhi and I looked at one another.

Salrip had told us where to find the Daemon who had stowed away the biopods. I was prepared to do whatever it took to get the location out of the Daemon as quickly as I could.

We nodded, and Viola placed her hand on the door handle as she motioned Salrip forward.

Salrip's hand was trembling when she touched the door.

"Now, just picture the Drakes you took the biopods to and pul—" Viola started.

Apparently, Salrip was a bit too excited and yanked on the door handle before Viola was ready.

The skin of the wall slid open, a door forming around the door handle. Beyond was the traditional black void I'd come to expect from one of Drakes's portals.

Then, the room turned white with pain.

The next moment, I found myself crumpled at the base of the wall on the other side of the room. I blinked several times, trying to clear my head, and found I was inside my now armored warskin.

The warskin had protected me by deploying the Behemoth skin as the explosion went off. While it managed to keep me from getting too hurt, the warskin itself was in tatters.

Gunfire and explosions drew me fully back to consciousness as my old training kicked in and I evaluated the situation.

The portal was still wide open.

Cr'eon and Hess were at the door to the room, firing outside at whoever was attacking us. They were being met with a steady stream of returning fire. Both were bloody, and Cr'eon appeared only to be using one arm.

Rhi was climbing to her feet, pieces of the armor on her warskin falling off about her.

Viola was at the base of the portal, tending to a bloody Salrip who didn't look like she was going to make it. Viola herself was missing an arm and part of her face.

Ignoring the barrage of weapons fire, I raced to Viola's side. I didn't notice the hits I took along the way. I was too focused on Viola.

"Vi!" I yelled as I knelt next to her.

"I'm fine," she said, looking at me with one bloody eye. The other was gone, smooth gray composite stared at me from where the eye had been. "She's not."

I looked down at Salrip, who was coughing up a lot of blood. More than she could spare.

"You need to go. Now!" Viola said, focused on Salrip.

"But—" I started.

"We're fine; you need to save Mom!" Viola said without looking at me.

"James," Rhi said. "I don't have time to find a brick..."

I glanced at Rhi and then back at Viola.

"Remember what I am. I'll be OK," Viola said.

"You're my daughter," I said, something welling in me. I couldn't abandon my daughter.

"Rhi," Viola said, a hitch in her voice.

Then, I was flying through the air and into cold darkness.

An eternity later, I emerged into light and hit the ground hard, rolling to a stop as I smashed into a wall.

"Godamnitt Rhi!" I said as I began to stand up. But before I could recover, Rhi came through the door and closed it behind her.

"Stop throwing me through portals!" I barked.

Rhi looked like she was going to laugh and managed to hold it back for about two seconds before letting loose with a burst of laughter.

"Oh my," a voice came from across the room.

When I looked, Drake was standing in the doorway.

We were in the portal backroom at Drakes. All Drakes had the same layout, with only a slight variance to accommodate location. The bar was always bigger on the inside and refused to follow physics, logic, or even common sense. Now that I knew the reason for Drakes, I understood why.

"Drake, put out a notice to the other Drakes on this Bio Hab. The living fire is going to be activated sometime in the next day or so. We can't stop it," Rhi said.

"Oh dear," Drake replied simply.

"Stop being proper and get to work!" Rhi commanded.

Drake didn't say a word, just turned to leave the room.

"Drake!" I stopped him. "Where's 223 Commerce?"

"Go outside, turn left, two blocks, and it's the intersection on your right," Drake said and disappeared.

"Gotta go!" I said as I hurried to the door. As I crossed the bar, heading for the door, I glanced around the empty room and frowned. There was always someone in Drakes, no matter what time of day or night. Where was everyone?

Bright afternoon sunlight blinded us as we stepped out into the parking lot. We were smack in the middle of a downtown city. Tall buildings were on three sides of us, and a river with a large bridge was on the fourth side.

"Left," Rhi said.

Then, the two of us were running down the streets of a busy city's heart. People made way for us. I wasn't sure if it was because of how we looked or our serious demeanor. I had no idea how I looked, but if it was anything like Rhi's bruised and bloody appearance, we were a grim sight!

"This is it," I said as we entered the lobby of a high-rise.

"Can I help you?" the man behind the desk inside said. He wasn't a security guard, just an information guy.

"Thirty-first floor," I said. "Elevators?"

"Uh," the startled man said and pointed.

"Thanks," I said as we moved to the bank of elevators and pushed the button.

For once, I was glad Rhi and I weren't brandishing weapons.

From our reflection in the elevator doors, we already looked like we'd survived a war. We didn't need to get into it with private security as well.

We entered the elevator as a couple came quickly around the corner, intent on joining us. When they saw us, they screeched to a halt.

"We'll get the next one," The woman said as the doors closed.

As the elevator rose, Rhi spoke up.

"You OK?" Rhi asked.

"Yup, you?" I replied.

"I'm good. How do you want to handle it?" she asked.

"Dynamically," I said as the elevator slowed. "Remember, everyone here will be dead in 24 hours. They're all walking corpses."

I saw the look Rhi gave me reflected in the elevator's door and turned to her.

"They're not zombies, James," Rhi said quietly.

"Noted," I said as the doors started to open. "Let's go to work." I was through the doors before they fully opened. I was done playing around.

According to the directory on the ground floor, this floor was divided into two sections. To the left was the Daemon's operation, whatever it was. To the right was some sort of law firm.

I turned left.

I considered kicking down the door, but didn't want to risk hurting my foot...unlikely as it was. I tried the doorknob first, but it was locked.

So, I kicked in the door, my strength knocking it from its hinges and shattering the door frame. The door landed on the other side of the room, right on top of a guy who'd had a gun leveled at the door.

The man's partner opened fire on us.

When was the last time we were shot at by regular bullets? I asked Rhi as the bullets bounced harmlessly off the remnants of my warskin. I felt the impacts, but that was it. They didn't cause any damage, and the kinetic energy was mostly cancelled out by the warskin.

Can't remember, Rhi said as she calmly formed the pistol on her thigh and raised it. The pistol discharged a stun burst, and the gunman collapsed.

Think they know we're here? Rhi asked as we moved deeper into the office.

Are they here? I asked as we passed empty office after empty office. Each office had the typical office furniture, but zero personalization. No one used these offices. They were just for show.

The crack of more firearms directed us where to go.

They gotta be defending something, right? I asked as I formed and pulled my own pistol from my warskin and returned fire. My single stun bolt dropped the shooter.

This scene played itself out as we worked our way through the office.

This remind you of anything? Rhi asked.

Houston, I said as I dropped another shooter.

Yup, Rhi said as she fired down a hall, and the bullets ceased coming from that direction.

It was nice having effective stun weapons available. The ones from my Bio Hab were extremely limited in what they could do. While I didn't mind using lethal force on what I considered walking corpses, I still didn't want to if I could help it. I already had enough nightmares, thank you.

So far, they'd only been using conventional firearms. I was starting to think we might be in the wrong place. Then I was hit with a bolt of energy from down the hall. I staggered as the warskin absorbed it.

Finally! Rhi said as she disappeared.

We'd been using AUGs the entire time we'd been in the Chosen Army. Any hand-to-hand combat took place inside a giant battle robot. So, it was rare we got to put our vampiric abilities to any practical use.

I hadn't seen Rhi move that fast since the Alamo. It almost made me smile to see her having to exert herself. Almost.

Got her! Rhi called, and I ran down the hall to meet her.

Rhi had a Daemon in a shoulder lock and was walking her

back into the large office from which she'd come.

I looked around but didn't see any other opposition.

"Is there anyone else here we need to worry about?" I asked as I closed the door behind us.

"Fuck off, Chosen," the AG Daemon said.

"Lynda, I presume?" I asked as Rhi slammed her down on the massive desk she'd been sitting behind.

"Are you wearing a pantsuit?" I asked, incredulous. Aside from Tara, I'd never seen a Daemon in anything other than some version of a warskin.

"She's got a warskin on," Rhi said and yanked the Lenz ring off the Daemon's finger.

The pantsuit disappeared, revealing a worn warskin beneath.

"That's better," I said. *You good?* I asked Rhi.

Oh yeah, she's not going anywhere, Rhi said as she flexed Lynda's arm, and Lynda groaned.

"What do you want, Chosen?" Lynda spat.

"Where are the biopods?" I asked, the steel in my voice returning.

"What bio—" Lynda started screaming as her hand exploded.

I'd had to turn up my pistol's power setting to get through her warskin. Unfortunately, that meant I couldn't just take a finger this time.

"Would you stop blowing people's digits off?" Rhi cried. "Or at least let me get out of the splash zone?"

"Sorry," I said to Rhi, then approached Lynda. By the time I reached the desk, the warskin had already sealed off the stump of her arm and was treating it. The suit couldn't grow the hand back, but it could keep her from bleeding out.

"Amazing things, warskins. No matter how much damage your body takes, it'll still keep you alive," I said in as cold a voice as I could muster. I hadn't played a heavy in a while, but with my current priorities, it wasn't hard.

"You're not Chosen!" Lynda said through gritted teeth.

"No shit, Sherlock," Rhi said. "And stop pretending. Your suit took the pain away already."

Lynda dropped her anguished face act.

"Now, you see, here's my problem," I said as I sat on the

corner of the desk near where Rhi had Lynda's face smashed onto its surface. "You Barkt terrorist assholes are about to destroy this Bio Hab. I can't stop it and I know you don't want to stop it, you sick fucks. But there's something here I need, two little biopods, and you know where they are."

I placed the still-hot muzzle of my pistol to her face and listened to the sizzle as she groaned through the pain.

"So, I could sit here blowing off your limbs and watching your warskin keep you alive until the living fire kills us all. Or, you can tell me what I need to know, and I'll let you go. You go your way, we'll go ours."

"You'll just kill me if I tell you," Lynda said.

I cocked my head to the side, pretending to consider it as I took a moment for effect. I glanced around the room. It was neat, tidy, and empty.

"Well, well, well," I said slowly. "It looks like you're already packed for a trip. I'm guessing you know when they're unleashing the living fire, and it's coming up pretty quick." I tapped my lip with the tip of my pistol, hoping it looked cool.

It doesn't, Rhi said, bursting my bubble.

I gave her a look Lynda couldn't see.

"I bet you were just waiting for Salrip to show up, and then you were out of here. I mean, the biopods are her responsibility, not yours. So, what would you care if we took them?" I asked.

"What did you do to Salrip?" Lynda asked.

"Nothing, actually," I said.

"Well, you did strip her and shoot off her finger," Rhi countered.

"OK, that's true. But in my defense, I did give back her clothes and even got her finger healed," I said.

"Yeah, OK, that's true," Rhi nodded.

"So, what's it gonna be?" I asked.

"How do I know you're not going to kill me?" Lynda pressed.

"I'll tell you what, just to prove a point, plus you're pissing me off; I'm going to stun you," I said.

Rhi looked at me, baffled.

I gave her a smirk.

"Now, this isn't going to kill you. But it will knock you out for a while. That means you may or may not wake up before the living fire. You tell me what I want to know right now, and I'll let you pick how long I'll stun you for. I'll even show you the setting before I pull the trigger, just to be fair," I said.

"How's that fair?" Lynda groaned as Rhi wrenched her arm again.

"Would you prefer me to go back to shooting off extremities?" I offered.

"FINE!" Lynda said. "Just get off me."

"The location first," Rhi said.

"Asher Sinclair," Lynda barked. "She knows where they are. She's the custodian." Before Rhi could physically encourage her, Lynda continued. "2433 Barnes Rd. She lives there. Happy? Now let me go!"

Truth? Rhi asked.

No clue, you? I asked.

Rhi answered by releasing Lynda and stepping back beside me as we put a safe distance between the pissed-off Daemon and us.

Lynda slowly stood, rolling her shoulder to try and work blood back into it.

"I don't know why we even bothered in the first place," Lynda spat. "Now get out!"

"There is the little matter of the stunning you part," I said.

The house is 45 minutes from here, Rhi said as she pulled the information from her neural cockpit.

"Oh, fuck off!" Lynda said defiantly.

So, I stunned her. She dropped, hitting her head hard on her massive desk.

"That looked like it hurt," Rhi said, wincing. "How long you set it for?"

"Just an hour," I said. "Keeps her from warning this Sinclair person."

"Good call, let's go," Rhi said.

I took one more look at the Daemon and followed Rhi out.

Apparently, the noise had caused the legal office next door to call building security. We stunned them easily enough, but they'd called the local police, who were waiting for us outside the lobby.

We avoided the fight by simply running past them at full speed. They never even saw us. We were six blocks away, and the cops never knew.

"You know how to hotwire a car?" I asked Rhi.

"Now, why would you think a lady of my caliber would know how to do something like that?" Rhi gave me an innocent flash of her eyelashes.

"Fine," I said and stepped out into the street in front of a car. It screeched to a stop as I leveled my pistol at it.

The driver had their hands up above the steering wheel as I approached the door.

"Get out," I said, and the driver obeyed without question. They ran across the street and out of sight.

I slid into the still-running car and unlocked the door so Rhi could get in.

"Can you even hotwire cars nowadays?" Rhi asked as we shot off down the street.

Chapter 16

JAMES

This is the place? Rhi asked as we sat outside the nice-looking house in upper-middle-class suburbia.

I looked around the street. Night had fallen, but there was still plenty of light from street lamps and house windows. The air was warm, like late summer.

They leave their curtains open at night? I asked in surprise. Growing up in my neighborhood, you never cracked the curtains at night unless it was an emergency.

You're still thinking about zombies, Rhi said.

As we watched the house, we saw several people moving around inside.

They look like normal people, Rhi said.

I watched a young, red-haired girl carrying a bowl of potato salad into the kitchen.

These people are kidnappers and terrorists? Rhi asked.

Time's wasting, let's go, I growled as I remembered we were on the clock.

As I approached the door, I wavered on what to do. I'd been in such a hurry, I hadn't bothered to form a plan. Rhi made the choice for me when she rang the doorbell.

I looked at Rhi incredulously, *You rang the doorbell?*

Here we were on the porch of the people who kidnapped our

family and were in league with the people about to destroy this Bio Hab, and we just rang the doorbell?

Rhi shrugged.

My thoughts were cut off as the porch light came on and the door opened.

"Yes?" The voice of an innocent child asked me from inside the house. The girl couldn't be old enough to drink. She had curly blonde hair, a beautiful face, and was sporting a strange one-piece swimsuit that showed off every curve on her frame. Had this been any other time...

"Asher Sinclair?" I hadn't been ready to speak, so my voice came out gruff.

"Ye...Yes?" the girl asked, fear now creeping into her voice as she gave Rhi and me the once-over.

"Who is it, Ash?" A voice called from inside the house.

"I don't know—" the girl started, turning from the door.

This? I thought. *This was the person who held our family hostage? This tiny girl? No, it had to be a trick. A hologram ring or something,* I thought as my anger flared once more.

"WHERE THE FUCK IS MY WIFE?!?" I demanded as I wrapped my fingers around her neck, stepped inside, and slammed her against the wall. I didn't know what was going on, but I wasn't about to be caught off guard again.

The girl fought me out of instinct, not training. I ignored her flailing as she couldn't compete with my enhanced strength.

"Asher?!?" A scream came from the kitchen; another girl, probably the redhead I had seen earlier.

"James!" Rhi's voice cut through the noise, but I was still focused on the girl. There had to be something there, something to account for—

"Let her go!" a new voice from behind me, this time male.

"Don't!" Rhi called out, but not to me. "Just don't," Rhi said in a calmer, colder voice. Then her voice was in my ear, "Don't hurt her. She's just a kid."

"I'll say it one more time," I said. This needed to get done now, before...I shook my head and leaned in close. "Where. The fuck. Is my wife?" I growled.

The girl's eyes were panicked, but she still managed to speak.

"I don't know who you're—" she started, but then an image burst into my mind. A pair of familiar, piercing blue eyes stared angrily at the girl in my hand.

That's her! I was so startled, I sent it instead of saying it.

The girl flinched away from me as if she'd heard my thoughts.

Rhi's pistol discharged, and I heard calamity as the smell of smoke wafted my way.

"I said, DON'T!" Rhi ordered through clenched teeth.

Then, a burning sensation on the back of my neck, accompanied by the smell of my burning hair, broke through the cloud of anger that had been steering me.

"We need her alive, James, or we'll never find them." Rhi's voice was calm and soft. It cut through the rest of my emotions and brought me back under control, just like how Shae used to calm me with her touch.

"What the hell?" A new male voice from the back door.

"Don't move," Rhi said to the newcomer.

"Why is the table on fire?" yet another woman's voice came from the back door. "And why are her eyes black?"

How many people were here? I thought to myself.

"James, you good?" Rhi asked me.

"Yeah," I said, my voice steadier now.

"You have a fire extinguisher?" Rhi asked the crowd behind me. I could see them now through Rhi's eyes as she herded them.

"I know where it's at," a young man with curly brown hair said and disappeared into the kitchen.

Rhi kicked the front door shut. She had two pistols trained on the crowd now as the boy started putting the fire out.

"Where?" I said, not trusting myself to say more.

"Holy shit!" the third girl cried as she covered her mouth and pointed at Rhi. "It's them, Ash, from the bar!"

Recognition flared in Asher's eyes. She'd seen me somewhere before and was even more terrified of me now.

"A...storage locker," Asher said, her eyes filling with tears. She was starting to break down.

Maybe I should relax and—

A blinding flash of blue light left spots in my eyes. I blinked away the spots in time to see the wall of blue light disappearing off towards the horizon outside.

"Shit!" Rhi growled. "You, turn on the TV!"

"What?" the man who'd come in from the backyard said.

"News, turn on the news, now!" Rhi demanded.

A moment later, a newscaster was speaking.

"To say again, there is no need to panic," the newscaster was saying.

"Tell that to my bladder," the third young woman mumbled. She'd been the one who recognized us.

"Shut up!" Rhi ordered.

"It has been reported that the strange blue light has completely circled the globe now. A second wave seems to have appeared, coming from the same starting point and moving to cross the planet. It should be crossing the Eastern seaboard in roughly—"

"Where?" Rhi yelled at the TV as if it could hear her. "Where the fuck is it?" Then her pistol drew down on the man who'd turned on the TV, "Don't make me."

"Don't shoot!" the man yelled. "Nobody do anything. Just...don't hurt anyone, please."

"Take me to it," I said, trying to control my voice. I didn't let Asher's eyes leave mine.

"I have to get the key," Asher said, glancing at the stairs.

I was close enough to feel the girl's heartbeat pounding like a frightened rabbit. Then she glanced over my shoulder, but I couldn't tell who she'd looked at.

"Where's it at, Rhi?" I asked. I'd tuned out the TV while I was talking to Asher.

"Looks like somewhere in the Indian Ocean," Rhi said.

"We've lost contact with the plane that initially reported the incident, but we still have the view from the International Space Station," the newscaster continued. "It continues to show the rings of blue light rapidly expanding from one point. There is no land at that location, so we don't know what's causing it yet."

"Fuck," I mumbled. "How long, Rhi?"

"My neural cockpit estimates six hours, max," Rhi said.

"What is going on here?" Yet another woman said as she appeared in the doorway to the backyard.

"Be quiet," Rhi said. "The grown-ups are talking."

"How long?" I asked Asher.

"For what?" Asher asked.

I'd paid attention to my grip this whole time. Not the gunfire, the fire, or even the TV had caused me to change my grip on Asher's throat. I made sure I wasn't hurting her, but I wasn't about to give her leeway to escape my grasp, either.

"To get to this storage place. How long to get there?" I asked.

"Maybe...twenty minutes?" Asher said.

"Rhi?" I asked.

"It'll be close," Rhi said.

"I'll make you a deal," I said, returning to Asher's eyes. You take me to her and I'll try to save all of you," I said.

"Save us from what?" Asher asked as a shudder ran through her.

"From the end of your Bio...the end of your world," I said, even as the words made me cringe. I didn't know if she believed me or not. I know I wouldn't. But she relaxed and gave me a little nod.

Slowly, I removed my hand from her throat and took a step back.

Asher made a beeline for the redhead, and they embraced.

Check and see if there are any others here. This place is a friggin clown car, I sent to Rhi.

Everyone had turned away from the smoldering furniture by now to watch the events unfolding on the TV. I was surprised the fire hadn't set off the smoke detector. I guess someone forgot to change out the batteries.

That's everybody, Rhi said as she reappeared a minute later.

"If I could have your attention," I said as I attempted to be heard over the TV as Rhi closed the curtains.

All eyes turned to me. Everyone was in some sort of swimwear. Apparently, we'd crashed their pool party. Every person here was handsome. *What was this, a Bio Hab of pretty people?* I thought.

"I don't have the time to explain everything right now, but this is how it goes. Those blue rings of light? They're the signal that this Bio Hab's, well, for lack of a better term, its self-destruct button has been pressed."

All eyes blinked at me, unbelieving. Not that I could blame them.

"Why would you put a self-destruct button on a planet?" Asher asked.

"That's the same question I had," I said. "I've yet to get a good answer."

"Listen, I know how nuts this sounds," I said to a room full of skeptical eyes. "But in less than five minutes, a ring of molten fire is going to erupt from that point," I pointed at the origin point displayed on the TV. "It will spread across the globe in an expanding circle, and when it's done, there won't be a living soul left on this Bio...this world." I caught myself from saying Bio Hab again.

After a moment of silence, the bedlam started. Everyone was talking at once, asking questions, denying my claim, calling me crazy. The usual things a mob would say to the crazy guy on a soapbox.

"There!" Rhi's voice silenced the group as she pointed at the TV.

A white spot had appeared at the origin point. As we watched, it began to expand, sending giant clouds of steam into the atmosphere. The last thing we saw before the area was covered by clouds was a small, brilliant ring of light, slowly expanding.

There wasn't any conversation after that.

"Asher," I said, drawing her attention from the TV. "I meant what I said earlier. You take me to where you're holding my wife, and I'll get y'all out of here."

"You just said the planet's about to be cooked," Asher started. "Where would we be safe from that?"

I glanced at Rhi.

"Somewhere...not...on this world," I managed, cringing even as I said it. I'd seen so many movies about aliens and time travelers and such who wanted someone to come with them and had to give this spiel to an unbelieving audience. I couldn't think of one that managed to pull it off. In the end, people went with them due to the plot.

They were all quiet, either watching the TV coverage or the exchange between Asher and me.

"What's this about his wife, Ash?" the older man asked.

"Uh..." Asher started. "Not now, Sinjin." Asher turned back to me. "Can you really do it?" she asked.

"Do we look like we come from here?" Rhi asked, tossing her pistol to Asher.

Asher fumbled with the pistol before finally getting a grip on it and looking at it.

"You've got nothing like that on this Bio Hab," Rhi started. "I guarantee it." Then Rhi glanced at me and back at Asher. "Do you have two biopods in this storage locker?"

Asher looked from the pistol to Rhi. She didn't attempt to wield the pistol, not that it would have worked for her anyway.

"Biopods?" Asher asked.

"Like the container you showed me in your mind, the one with the blue eyes," I said. The flash she'd given me had only been of one biopod.

"In my mind?" Asher said, looking at me. Then, she seemed to pull herself together. "Yes, there are two there."

"The second one is my wife," Rhi said, taking the pistol from Asher's hands and absorbing it back into her warskin. "They were kidnapped, and we want them back. You'll have to forgive our directness, but it's been a long road."

"I'll do everything I can to get all of us out of here," I said. There shouldn't be a reason I couldn't take all of them with us through the portal at Drakes. Once it's open, even zombies could go through.

"OK," Asher nodded and looked at the redhead who was holding her hand.

"Good, then you're with me," I turned to Rhi. "Can you herd the rest of the cats back to Drakes?"

Rhi gave me a look that screamed both "Duh" and "I hate you" at the same time.

"OK, let's go get that key," I said and nodded toward the

stairs.

There were a few protests, but more and more ominous warnings were coming from the TV that divided the group's attention.

Upstairs, Asher's room was mostly empty.

"You moving?" I asked, mostly to calm my own nerves. This Bio Hab was now a ticking time bomb.

"I moved out a while ago," Asher said as she pulled a drawer out of a dresser and started feeling around underneath where it had been. She triumphantly held up a key a few moments later.

"Here it is!" Asher said, showing it to me.

"Good, let's get going," I said and turned towards the door.

"Uh," Asher said, hesitating.

"What?" I asked, turning back.

"Can I change?" Asher asked, looking down at her swimsuit.

Now, it was my turn to hesitate. This was the part of the movie where the prisoner tried something that got the drop on the guard. But...every instinct was telling me this girl was not a kidnapper. She just seemed like an average teenager.

"Fine, but I...have to watch you." I tried to say it with some professionalism, but it still came off as creepy.

Asher stared at me a moment before sighing, "Fine." She reached into another drawer and began to pull out clothes.

I watched her like a hawk, looking for any sign of deception. I double-checked the new clothes before she started to change.

Asher turned away from me as she started to peel herself out of her suit.

I couldn't help it, I had to ask. "Not to sound creepy, but how old are you, Asher?" I was trying not to look at this girl's body, just her hands...just the hands, I told myself.

"I'm 19," Asher paused, looking at me over her shoulder.

My eyes darted from her hands to her eyes, and I cursed myself.

"Why?" The single word was heavily loaded.

"Just curious," I said as I forced my eyes back to her hands.

A moment later, Asher continued changing.

Thankfully, she was done quickly, and we returned downstairs.

Why are you blushing? Rhi's voice, while serious, was laced with her usual snark.

Shut up, I said as I felt my cheeks hot under all the blood, dirt, and grime.

"Let's go, Asher," I said as I opened the front door.

The uproar of protests from the group was loud but not as loud as the redhead who ignored Rhi and darted over to take Asher's hand.

"I go where she goes," the girl said defiantly.

I met the girl's eyes. She was maybe 25 and short but built like a professional athlete. Her shoulders were huge! She was also not backing down.

I finally gave her a single nod and looked at Rhi.

Be safe, but get them to Drakes. Watch out, though; we still don't have all the facts here, I said.

You watch your own butt, Rhi said. *I'll see you and our family at Drakes.*

I could sense Rhi's longing to go, but one of us had to stay and watch out for the others. There was no way we could all go to this storage locker; there were too many variables. I started to say something, but Rhi beat me to it.

Just go, Rhi said and turned back to the group, starting to give orders.

We piled into the front seat of the car I'd appropriated. I was driving, and the two girls shared the passenger seat. I wasn't about to put them behind me.

The redhead surprised me. She was so adamant about sticking with Asher that she hadn't asked to change out of the bikini she was wearing. If I'd had more time, I would have let her change, but we'd already wasted enough time.

"Your name is James?" Asher asked me once we were moving, and she was giving me directions.

"Yeah," I said, splitting my attention between the road and the two girls sitting beside me.

"And the other one is Rhi? Yeah? Well, this is my...girlfriend Remmi," Asher said.

Remmi didn't say anything; she just watched me with hard eyes.

"OK, let's do this," I said. "As long as you're honest with me and on the up and up, I'm not going to hurt either of you," I said.

"OK," Asher nodded, but Remmi stayed on guard. "So, what's the story? Are you aliens, government spooks, what?"

The way Asher said it, I couldn't help but chuckle.

"Long story," I said.

"Turn here," Asher said. "Give me the short version."

"OK," I shrugged as I made the turn. "Your planet, what we call a Bio Hab, is inside a megastructure known as Behemoth."

"Megastructure?" Asher asked.

"Like a Dyson Sphere," I said.

Asher obviously didn't know what that was, but Remmi did and explained it to her.

"Behemoth has hundreds of Bio Habs like this one inside it. There are two sets of Behemoth guardians currently at war with one another for control. The Daemon Corps, who still serve Behemoth, and the Angel Guard, who are rebels. It was the AG who pushed the button on your Bio Hab," I explained.

"The two biopods you have in your storage locker contain my wife and Rhi's wife. They were...kidnapped years ago and we've been searching for them ever since," I said, and then sighed. "I'm sorry I lost my temper with you earlier. It's just...we're at the end of our rope here." As I said it, I felt a wave of exhaustion wash over me.

How long had we been at this now? How long had I been awake this time?

"I'm not a kidnapper!" Asher said adamantly.

I glanced at her, then back to the road.

"If I thought you were, this would be going differently," I offered.

"How long have they been missing?" Remmi asked.

"Uh...about seven years now...give or take," I said.

Silence fell aside from Asher's occasional directions.

"So, I guess you're wondering how I got myself into this?" Asher asked, breaking the silence.

I nodded slowly, not taking my eyes from the road.

"Yeah...a friend of mine told me that they knew someone

who could help me out with what I wanted," Asher started.

"What did you want?" I asked.

"Oh, you didn't see it while I was changing? I thought you did," Asher said, and I was pretty sure she was the one blushing now.

"I was trying to be polite," I said. I hadn't managed to keep my eyes on only her hands the whole time she was changing. That's when I saw she wasn't exactly built like a standard girl. She had a bit extra.

Asher's silence made me look over at her. I found her staring at me with her head cocked.

"You know, you don't act like a bad guy, well, not always at least. I mean, who rings the doorbell of the place you're going to break into?" Asher said.

"Right?" I agreed.

"Anyway, then a couple of months later, I get a call from the woman who made the deal," Asher said.

"Let me guess, tall, red skin, red eyes?" I asked.

"How'd you know?" Asher gasped.

"She's a Daemon, and she's part of the group that's nuking your Bio Hab." I glanced over at her. "You don't have to worry about her anymore."

Asher didn't say anything for a moment.

"So, she calls me and has me go to this weird bar—" Asher started.

"Drakes," I said simply.

"Are you going to let me tell this or not?" Asher said testily.

"Sorry," I replied.

"Well, yeah. We went to Drakes. He told me I had to rent a storage unit and then gave me the money and a lock for it. He told me to let him know the unit number once I rented it. I called him, put the lock on, and left. That was all I was supposed to do." Asher went quiet again.

I glanced at her, and she was staring off into space.

"But you went again, didn't you?" I asked.

"I was having these nightmares about drowning and kept seeing that storage locker. So, I went back and there were those pod things inside. I had no clue what they were, but when I touched one, those crazy blue eyes appeared on the pod. It scared the crap out of me, and I ran," Asher said.

"Huh," I said. Somehow, someway, Asher had been mentally tapped by the biopods. Or was it Shae or Tara who'd reached out? Regardless, I had no idea how that was done. I'd never heard of anything like it before. Of course, all this was new to me.

"Wait, that other girl said you'd seen me," I said.

"When we were at Drakes, he took us through a back door, and we ended up in some crazy rave club. You and that Rhi person were sitting at a table drinking," Asher said.

"Crazy rave club?" I asked.

"I dunno, never seen anything like it. It had crazy colors and people dressed up like aliens, and..." Asher's voice trailed off.

"The place is called Colors," I said, trying to figure out why Drake had taken them there.

"Those were real aliens, weren't they?" Asher whispered.

"Yeah," I chuckled. "Why did Drake take you there?"

"He said if we ever saw you two, we were supposed to stay away and call him. He said he was doing it as part of some deal he had with my...Daemon," Asher said the word awkwardly.

I frowned, trying to think of why Drake was working against me. He was supposed to be part of Viola's communication network. Had the AG gotten something on him that they could use against him?

"Should I call him?" Asher asked suddenly.

"Don't worry about it. We've already been to see him," I said.

"You didn't hurt him, did you?" Asher asked, concern in her voice.

"Drake? No, why?" I asked.

"Oh, good. He was a nice guy," Asher said.

I debated whether to tell her that Drake wasn't a guy at all, but decided against it. The girl was already handling enough as it was.

"If this was so important," Remmi spoke up suddenly. "Why did they use you, Ash?"

Asher frowned.

"Daemons, especially the AG, use Bio Hab inhabitants for all sorts of things. They probably used you to try and keep an unknown degree of separation in the mix," I said.

"How do you know so much about this?" Asher asked.

"I've been dealing with Daemons nearly what...ten years now?" I started. "They have access to Behemoth-level technology that's millions of years beyond us. Making your little 'change' was just altering one of their standard body augmentation contracts."

"Say what?" Asher asked.

"The whole genie in a bottle, three wishes deal? Most people ask for money, sex, or power. They have standard build-up contracts for each." I'd learned all this during the downtime we'd had waiting for word on the next part of our "rescue the family" adventure. Once I heard the AG were using Bio Hab agents, I was curious.

"So, my deal...my contract, there's more to it?" Asher asked.

"Well, let me ask you this. Have you found that people are a lot more...horny when they're around you? That they're more susceptible to suggestion? That's the whole pheromone treatment. All you have to do is bat your eyes, and people will crawl over each other to get into your bed," I didn't say it with malice, just matter of fact.

Asher was quiet for a long time, then glanced at Remmi.

"That would explain a lot," Asher said, suddenly looking nervous.

"I loved you long before that, stupid," Remmi said and smacked Asher upside the head before hugging her.

I kept my eyes on the road. After a while, I broke the silence with, "Rhi called it the 'sex kitten treatment.'" I chuckled.

After a moment, the other two chuckled as well.

"So, does this mean I'm not human anymore?" Asher asked. "Am I some sort of alien crossbreed or something?"

"No," I said. "You're perfectly human. You just have...a bit more than you used to." I had to bite my lip after saying that.

"That's your level of tact?" Remmi asked in a flat tone.

"It's just...I have these things that've happened to me," Asher said, then began to explain how she'd had some crazy carnal desires.

I glanced at Asher, who was obviously embarrassed, telling me, a complete stranger, all these things. I realized this was just a young 19-year-old kid who was all kinds of horny, kinda like how I was at her age.

"You're fine," I said finally. "Maybe slow it down a little if you're blacking out, but it just sounds like you might be overdoing it a bit." I glanced at her, "You think that's intense, trying being in a gestalt sometime."

I was saved from having to explain what a gestalt was as we arrived at the storage place.

The storage place wasn't like any I'd seen before. I was used to flat, one-story jobs that sprawled. This was a high-rise monstrosity of a building that was completely enclosed.

Asher punched in a code, and we drove into the building's loading area. Apparently, you could drive inside and load/unload your crap here. Pretty swanky, but also perfect for someone who didn't want their cargo to be seen.

The hair on the back of my neck stood up as we got out of the car. I looked around nervously but couldn't see any threats.

"It's this way," Asher said, starting to head down a hallway with Remmi in tow.

I watched the two girls, but I still didn't sense any malice from them. Trepidation, sure, but they appeared to be just pawns in all of this.

"This one," Asher said as she unlocked the door and slid it open.

A pair of blackout curtains hung at the entrance, keeping us from seeing more than a foot inside.

Asher sensed my hesitation and stuck her arm in, pulling the curtains to the side.

My heart nearly leaped out of my chest as the two biopods appeared at the far side of the unit. Everything else disappeared as I approached the pods. Sure enough, the markings matched the other biopods we'd rescued. This was it!

There was a black panel on the two biopods that hadn't been on the others. As I watched, the fierce blue eyes I'd seen in Asher's head flashed to life on the closest pod. A moment later, another pair appeared on the second pod; only these were red eyes with black irises.

Shae and Tara's eyes. But at the same time, they weren't. They were exact copies of both, but they just didn't...feel right. Yes, they appeared to be computer versions, but still, something felt off.

Both sets watched me

I only hesitated for a moment as I reached out and placed my hand on the first biopod.

Immediately, my neural cockpit sprang to life as it connected to the pod and ran through a sequence of checks and cross-checks before finally telling me it was still secure.

A message stared at me behind my eyes:

"Do you wish to revive outside of the facility?"

A warning appeared saying reviving outside of a facility ran the risk of temporary paralysis, muscle fatigue, and a laundry list of other items, but I didn't care. I said yes, and another message appeared:

WARNING
Occupant already possesses a data mindset; the addition of a new data mindset will overwrite the current mindset. Do you wish to proceed?

A slot opened on the console, one that would perfectly fit the crystal in my pocket. I removed the crystal and looked at it one more time.

Luckily, Krys had labeled each crystal when he created them. I couldn't imagine the chaos if they'd been mixed up at this point.

I slid the crystal into the slot and selected 'yes.'

Nothing happened. There was no sound, no vibration, nothing to indicate anything was happening. Had it not worked? Had there been a problem with the crystal?

My hands started shaking and didn't stop even after the message finally popped up:

Revival in progress

I pulled my trembling hand from the cylinder and moved to Tara's to repeat the process. By the time I was through and both were reviving, my whole body was shaking.

We'd done it! This was it!

My body slid down the wall until I was sitting on the floor. When I looked up, Asher and Remmi were still here. I'd half expected them to make a break for it.

"I don't know how long this'll take," I said as I leaned my head back and closed my eyes. My body ached from all the abuse I'd put it through today.

"What's going on?" Asher asked as she sat down near me, but not too close. Remmi planted herself between the two of us.

I gave the small woman a glance but found her staring back at me defiantly. I glanced over to Asher.

"They're...being woken up," I said as my body sagged and exhaustion took me.

I don't know how long I was out, but something woke me with a start, and I was instantly on my feet.

The girls had still been next to me and leaned away from me in surprise at my speed.

A green button flashed lazily on both pods. I didn't hesitate and pushed the first one.

The protective metal skin of the biopod retracted in on itself until it disappeared into the base of the pod. Shae's body floated inside, naked and motionless. A moment later, the fluid also began to retract. It didn't drain; it just simply vanished, as did the outer glass.

Then, Shae was hanging in the suspension field of the pod.

I'm sure to the girls, it looked like she was floating in mid-air, but the pod had hold of her and was keeping her from falling.

"Wow!"

It had been Remmi who said it, as I heard both girls stand up. I didn't turn to see them. I had eyes only for my wife.

I delicately reached into the pod and took Shae into my arms.

"Release," I said quietly as the suspension field released Shae, and she sagged into my arms, unconscious.

We slid to the floor, where I cradled her to me. All I could do was whisper her name again and again.

She was here.

This was real!

The thoughts repeated in my head as I rocked slowly back and forth. I eventually opened blurry eyes and glanced at the girls. They were whispering about Shae's apparent age and how old she would have been seven years ago.

"She's older than she looks," I said without looking up. "We both are." I considered telling her what we were, but that would waste time we didn't have.

"Open that one," I said.

Asher didn't hesitate as she reached forward and punched the green button on Tara's biopod.

The same process was repeated until Tara's body appeared to be floating in the air.

This time, Remmi gasped in surprise at the Daemon within.

"Reach in and say release," I started. "But be careful; she's a little heavier than she looks," I said all this while still studying Shae's face, looking for any sign of her waking up.

I knew the revival process wasn't standardized. Each person woke in their own time. You couldn't rush it. They simply wouldn't respond if you tried.

"Her name's Tara," I said.

I heard Asher say her name, followed by grunting. I looked over.

Asher and Remmi were trying to get Tara's body down to the ground. It was obvious they hadn't been ready for her. I'd warned them she was heavy! All Daemons were, even small ones.

"A little heavier?" Asher complained as they gently got to the ground, Asher cradling Tara's body.

I watched Shae steadily breathing as she lay in my lap and chuckled. Rhi always gave me crap for breathing like a human when I didn't need to. But here was my wife, 300 years older than Rhi or me, snoring away.

"Now what?" Asher asked.

"Just let her wake up on her own. Don't rush it," I said.

A few minutes of silence passed before Asher spoke up.

"You said we had six hours?" Asher asked, looking at her phone.

"Don't worry. My neural net is tied into the media streams now and is currently tracking the wave. It'll reach here in four hours, but the foreshocks will warn us," I said.

"Foreshocks?" Remmi asked.

"Earthquakes, storms, eruptions, tsunamis, you name it. They start the last half hour before the main wave, but we should be gone well before then," I said.

Asher and Remmi looked at one another.

"You're Bio Hab is being recycled from its mantle through its atmosphere," I said. "Behemoth will maintain your atmosphere right up until the wave hits. But your Bio Hab is going through a lot of devastating changes right now."

"Why?" Asher asked.

"It's easiest to think of it like a terrorist attack," I said.

"No, why is there even a wave like this?" Asher asked.

"So that Behemoth can start over," I replied.

"Start over?" Remmi asked.

"With your Bio Hab," I said, trying not to shrug. I was talking about cataclysmic events like they were everyday occurrences. How much did someone have to see in order to act like this?

"Hello there."

I looked over to find Tara's eyes open and staring up into Asher's face.

"I don't know what's going on," Tara said softly.

"It's OK, you're safe," Remmi said from beside Asher.

"You're all right," Asher said as she reached down and stroked Tara's cheek, her voice full of concern.

"Tara, just stay still. I'll explain everything shortly," I said.

Tara leaned, trying to see me, and grunted with the effort.

"It's OK," Asher said. "James is with...Shae? Is that her name?"

"Where's Rhi?" Tara asked.

"She's with my friends," Asher said.

Not an alien, I heard Tara send, but she wasn't saying it in my mind, but Asher's!

"My, but you are a pretty thing," Tara said aloud to Asher.

"Uh..." Asher said intelligently.

Rhi's frantic mindtouch was so loud it made both Tara and me flinch.

"What is it? Are you OK?" Asher asked in a concerned voice.

"It's just Rhi. She's a bit excited...and loud," Tara chuckled.

I listened as Rhi filled Tara in on the current emergency.

"Oh, I'm so sorry," Tara said to Asher. "They just filled me in about the living fire...er, the self-destruct."

"Eh, what can you do?" Asher shrugged.

Remmi gave Asher an incredulous look.

Not an alien, Tara said again in Asher's mind as it bled over into mine.

I figured Asher must be thinking at Tara, which was why she was talking back. What I still couldn't figure out was how we were getting into Asher's head.

Then, Shae was screaming at the top of her lungs.

"Shae, Shae!" I called. "It's OK, you're OK!"

Shae's scream ended when she ran out of breath. Then she was lying there in my lap, looking around with wild eyes.

"What? Where?" Shae said in a hoarse voice.

"It's OK. We're on a different Bio Hab. We'll be out of here soon," I said.

"James, Rhi says we need to move," Tara said from across the room, still in Asher's lap. "We have less than an hour."

"An hour?" Asher and I said in unison.

"She said our neural cockpits were still configured for our original Bio Hab," Tara said. "You need to reset yours since you don't have Behemoth to do it for you anymore."

I cursed and mentally cycled my neural cockpit before cursing again when I saw the time.

"We gotta go. Can you move?" I asked.

"Can barely talk," Shae said weakly.

"I'm getting better quickly," Tara said as I watched her carefully move her legs.

As I watched, Asher helped Tara to her feet, but it was obvious Tara was far from being ready to stand on her own.

Remmi and Asher wrapped Tara's arms around their shoulders and then grabbed Tara by the waist.

"Are you running a fever?" Asher asked.

"No, dear, it's just me," Tara smiled while controlling a grimace.

"Hang on," I said as I gently untangled myself from Shae. I yanked down the blackout curtains and handed one to Asher before I wrapped Shae in the other. I easily lifted Shae into my arms and carried her out.

By the time we got to the car, Tara was practically walking on her own. She was recovering at a remarkable rate compared to Shae. Daemons were tough. That, plus the whole cloning thing, was designed for them.

"I said I wasn't an alien, didn't you hear me?" Tara asked Asher as she and Remmi were helping Tara into the car.

"Yes, and you'll have to tell me how you did that later," Asher said before she hurried around and opened the door for Shae and me.

I ignored the conversation and slipped into the car, still holding Shae.

"You'll have to drive," I said.

"But...I've never driven before," Asher protested in a panic.

"It's easy, now let's go!" I said.

Remmi touched Asher on the arm and said, "I've got this." Before Remmi climbed into the driver's seat.

"OK," Asher said as she climbed into the car.

"Where are we going?" Asher asked.

"Drakes," I said.

"Oh, yeah," Asher said as she punched in the address on her phone for directions. Apparently, she'd been given it when the Daemon sent her there the first time.

"She's cute," Tara said as she looked at Asher. Then Tara looked at Remmi. "Her mate is too. Are you planning on recruiting them, James?"

Remmi and Asher glanced at one another.

"Not the time, Tara!" I growled as we sped off into the night.

Rhi and all of Asher's people were waiting in the parking lot of Drakes as we pulled up. From all the suitcases, it looked like they had packed their whole house!

As we started to get out of the car, the first tremor hit. It shook the entire area with enough force to cause all of us to stumble. Some buildings were swaying, and a few looked like they were starting to crumble.

"Quickly, get inside!" I yelled as I headed towards the door to Drakes with Shae still in my arms.

Remmi and Asher were right behind me, while their friends were trying to catch up.

"Pinch it off, Rhi; we gotta go!" I said as I passed Rhi and Tara locked in a tearful kiss. Tara had been out of the car and in Rhi's arms before I'd even gotten the car door open.

Asher's friends kept slowing down to ask if she was OK, even though Asher repeatedly reassured them she was fine.

"Move it!" I shouted from the door. I tried the doorknob, but it didn't move. "Rhi, I can't open the door!"

This finally split Rhi and Tara apart, and they moved to the door.

"Is she red?" One of the women asked as Tara, still wrapped in a curtain, passed her.

"Not now, Angela!" Asher yelled as she continued to pull Remmi towards the door.

Rhi grabbed the door handle and pushed. She looked at it again and then tried to pull, but the door didn't move.

"Maybe it's locked?" Asher volunteered.

Rhi glanced back at Asher with an annoyed expression. She turned and kicked the door with enough force that it crumbled in on itself and went flying to the other side of the building.

Inside was nothing except girders and wiring.

"No!" Rhi screamed.

Rhi sprinted into the building and dashed around the large empty space at speed.

But I already knew what had happened.

"The portal's not here, is it?" I asked.

"The Drakes system must be offline," Rhi shook her head as Tara wrapped an arm around her.

I racked my brain for other options, but there just weren't any. I slowly turned to face Asher.

"I'm sorry. This is how we were planning on escaping, but it's gone," I said with genuine remorse in my voice.

"The door that went to that weird techno club?" Asher asked.

I nodded. "Now, we're as trapped here as you are."

Another earthquake, stronger than the last, chose that moment to hit. It lasted long enough that everyone grabbed onto something to keep from falling over.

Car alarms and sirens filled the air. At the end of the street, I could see people running in all directions.

"Lou," Shae whispered. "Call Lou."

"Lou's gone, Shae," I said. "He died the same day you did." My voice was anything but joking.

I saw Asher silently mouth the word "Died?" to Remmi.

"It says he's there," Shae mumbled, sounding delirious. "I'd do it, but my net's offline," Shae said, then coughed.

I didn't know what "it" was, but I had nothing else, so I opened up my neural cockpit and sent the ping to Lou's dead gen code.

"There's nothing," I said a few moments later and shook my head slowly.

The wind picked up suddenly. It was hot and tasted of pennies. Meanwhile, the dark skyline was quickly getting brighter.

"Is that?" Asher asked, looking at me.

"It's the living fire. It's almost here," I said.

I looked, and all of Asher's people were holding one another. Some were crying, while others stood in shock. Asher and Remmi had joined them.

Rhi and Tara rejoined us. As soon as they were close enough, they wrapped themselves around Shae and me.

I pulled Shae a little tighter to my chest.

The air was noticeably hotter, and it was getting hard to breathe, so I stopped. Then, I took one last breath to say something cheesy. Luckily, that's when my neural cockpit chattered to life.

Hit the deck. This is going to be close!

I didn't recognize the voice in my head at first. From the reaction of everybody else, they'd all heard it and were dropping to the ground.

A sound I'd hoped never to hear again tore at my eardrums. It sounded like the ripping of a sheet and ended with a boom that shattered what few windows were left around us.

The four of us, as a unit, were sent flying as something impacted the ground near us with terrible force. The breath I'd taken to speak was stolen from me as we hit the ground.

"Don't fight the straps!" Viola yelled over the sound of the roaring wind. This time, her voice came from speakers somewhere above me.

I glanced up in time to see a massive AUG towering over us. When it landed, it had crushed the building next door. It had several transport pods mounted to it, the same type Beth had used when she kidnapped us from the Alamo.

Multiple tentacles reached out from each pod and grabbed at everyone around us. Several reached out and picked the four of us up as one before hauling us up into the air.

Try not to struggle, Dad. Doing this with one arm is a bitch! Viola said with obvious strain in her voice.

I tried to hold still, instead focusing on keeping Shae steady. But when the living fire crested the horizon, it was both blinding and terrifying.

Fuck! Viola said.

Then we were rising into the air, Viola having taken off already. We hadn't been pulled into the transport pods yet, but we were out of time. I watched in horror as the wave of living fire raced towards us.

Then, we were engulfed by darkness.

Chapter 16.5

BETH

I stared at nothing, still not believing what my neural cockpit had just shown me.

I wasn't supposed to be still connected to the Behemoth network. I'd disconnected forever and a day ago to keep Behemoth from finding me. But the request had somehow still found me.

When you're attached to a wing as its commander, all your subordinates' communication is routed through you. Anything that goes out beyond your wing must be approved by the commander.

But when you transfer wings, you're removed from the previous one, so you can be tied into the new one.

I'd been removed from Shae's wing months prior to their deaths when she had taken over as commander. The only communique I'd ever received from them since was the lunch requests Shae had sent me. But those were always personal messages, nothing official.

But there it was, still in my command queue:

SABLE:
Emergency relay request to Blank Designation: LOU

SINCLAIR:
Emergency relay request APPROVED

I hadn't approved the request. It had been done automatically per my previous settings. I'd trusted Shae's wing enough that if they had put in an emergency request, it was an emergency. Therefore, my standing order was to approve all emergency requests without question.

But I was out of their loop, and they were all dead! Someone had to be using James's gen code. But that was impossible. A gen code couldn't be faked; that was the whole point.

So, either someone had found a way to fake his gen code, or James was somehow still alive.

"Everything OK?"

I shook myself free of the shock of the message and focused on Shelby as she was putting down a drink for me and sliding into the booth beside me.

"I'm not sure," I said, quickly changing my presets so I'd be notified if something like this happened again. Instead of auto-approving, I'd be prompted to decide what I wanted to do.

Meanwhile, part of me desperately wanted to ping James's gen code. But doing so was ridiculous. He was gone, they were all gone. Even if someone had found a way to spoof his code, my pinging would send up a giant flare on Behemoth's network about where I was. Or was this all just a Behemoth trick to try and get me to reveal my position?

Luckily, the auto-approval hadn't come from me, but the preset still in the Behemoth system. I'd only received the notification that it had happened, and even that had been routed through a deadhead relay.

Could I route something through the deadhead to James's code that wouldn't give me away? I pondered this and tried to figure out if it was safely possible.

Shelby's snapping fingers in my face drew me back to the here and now.

"Hello, Beth," Shelby said.

I blinked several times and focused on her again.

"Sorry...just...sorry," I said and took a sip of the drink she'd brought me.

"Must be something serious to pull you down a rabbit hole," Shelby said.

"I'm not sure..." I frowned and tried to push it to the back of my mind, but it wouldn't budge.

"You ever hear of someone spoofing a gen code?" I asked.

"Can't be done," Shelby said automatically. "That's the whole point. They can't be faked, not even if you had an identical twin or something silly like that. It's been tried before, but since it all goes through Behemoth, it can tell the difference."

I frowned. "What if—"

"Can't. Be. Done." Shelby shook her finger at me.

"But—" I tried.

"No. Now tell me what's going on," Shelby said.

I sighed and took a large swallow from my glass.

"I just got a message from a ghost," I said.

"Cool," Shelby said.

"Cool?" I asked.

"Yeah, ghosts are cool," Shelby said.

"I'm not talking about those leftover EM creatures. They don't have a gen code," I said.

I'd taken Shae to the ghost book store once. But those creatures were little more than the echoes of living beings. And they sure as hell couldn't use a neural cockpit, which is the only place that a relay command could come from.

"And before you ask, no, a neural cockpit can't be spoofed either," Shelby said.

I still didn't know a lot about Shelby. While she was kind and had taken me in, she hadn't shared a whole lot about her past. While she knew way too much about me and wouldn't say how, she was still a mystery to me.

"So, if I received a message from a gen code I know is dead..." I started.

"Then that person's not dead," Shelby said with a nod and took a drink.

"Not dead..." I repeated.

Don't do it, my minder snapped as I formatted the

message. *It's too risky.*

I have to know, I said as I pushed the message out through every filter I knew that could protect me.

If James was, somehow, alive out there, and I could get a hold of him without Behemoth finding me. Then he'd be able to tell me what happened to the others.

Or Behemoth would come kicking in the door to kill me any moment now.

I stared at the door and held my breath as I pushed the send button.

Chapter 17

JAMES

"How is Asher's family dealing with it?" Shae asked as she took a sip of her cup of soup. She was propped up on the couch, wrapped up in a blanket beside me.

"Actually, they aren't her family," I said. "Aside from Terri and Patty, none of them are related."

I'd gotten the whole story from Asher earlier. Her mom, the only real family she had, was in the military and was deployed all the time. Asher was left with Sinjin and Angela during the deployments until she was old enough to move out and live on her own.

Asher's mom had still been downrange when we escaped the Bio Hab, so she'd been left behind.

"They're still trying to cope with the change," I said as I bit into the grilled cheese sandwich. It was warm and buttery, just the way I liked it. I glanced over at Viola, who was still at the stove making more sandwiches. "This is really good, Vi."

Viola just smiled and returned to flipping another sandwich.

"That's not really what I heard," Rhi said as she leaned back in her chair at the small kitchen table. We'd turned the couch around to face the kitchen so everyone could be comfortable.

We were in a hidden backroom training room we'd never been to before. Viola had brought us here to recover after escaping the living fire and had the forethought to revive our honeymoon cabin.

It had only been a few days, but Shae was nearly back to full health, and Tara was practically bouncing off the walls with how healthy she was.

"Oh?" I asked as I dipped my sandwich into a cup of tomato soup.

"Seems they're more worried about what body augment to get," Rhi said as Viola set a fresh sandwich and cup of soup in front of her. "Thanks, Viola."

Viola smiled and returned to the kitchen.

"I thought they just found out they were having to go to the low-tech Bio Hab. Coming from a modern society, isn't that a big deal to them?" Shae asked. It was warm inside the cabin, but she kept curled up in her blanket. I wasn't sure if it was for comfort, warmth, or both.

Rhi laughed tightly. "I think they forgot about that part after they were told they could have body augmentation."

I felt it, so I was sure Shae did as well. Anytime Rhi talked to or even looked at Shae, her anxiety level shot through the roof. Something serious was going on with her, but now wasn't the time to hash it out. Everyone was still enjoying the glow of being back together again. I didn't want to upset that right now.

"Why can't they go somewhere else again?" Tara asked as she glanced over from where she sat, looking out the window.

"They got tagged by Behemoth when we escaped," Viola said. "It's my fault, really. If I hadn't had to use that captured AUG, Behemoth wouldn't have known. I'm just glad I still had Lou in reserve. Otherwise, I never would have found you guys."

Viola, Cr'eon, and Hess had eventually escaped the firefight Rhi and I had left them in, but Viola had lost an arm, and Hess had been hurt badly enough that she'd required time in a healing tank.

Cr'eon was with Asher's people, trying to help them adjust to the abrupt change.

Viola's body had been repaired somewhere, somehow, in the few days since she'd rescued us from Asher's Bio Hab. There was still a lot about Viola I didn't know or understand.

When I pinged Lou, he'd been in mothballed storage somewhere. Thankfully, my signal had been relayed to Viola, who commandeered an AUG and rescued us in the nick of time. Unfortunately, Viola hadn't had the time to be picky and had chosen an AUG that was still connected to Behemoth, so there had been complications.

"It's a good thing you thought to contact Lou, Mom; otherwise, y'all would be toast," Viola said, pouring up more soup. "How'd you know Lou was one of mine anyway?"

Shae glanced up. "Well, back then I thought he was an AG plant...and that was really just a gut feeling. He had some mannerisms that stuck out to me.

"What clinched it, though, was when he was able to override Behemoth's lockdowns of our gate engines at the battle of Austin," Shae said. "I originally thought he was just an AG plant. It was my minder who told me he was one of yours and told me to try to contact him."

I shuddered again at the thought. Shae and Tara both had minders now. The same autonomous AI program that Beth had in her head, they now had as well. Each AI was an individual and supposed to solely look out for its host, but it was still creepy. That, plus when I imagined a minder, all I saw was some weird snake-like thing coiled up in their brain. I knew it wasn't how it worked, but my imagination didn't care.

Beth's minder had manifested as a snake on her body. So far, neither Tara nor Shae had theirs manifested. Viola said it took a while, but it would happen eventually.

Apparently, the eyes that had been on the sides of the biopods had been the minder's defense programming, watching out for them.

Regardless of how I felt, without them, we'd all be dead right now.

"I still can't believe Behemoth put a minder in Tara, though," Viola said. "Daemons don't have minders. That's only to look after everybody else."

"Don't ask me; I only work here," Tara said as she came over and sat down at the table where Viola was putting down another sandwich and cup of soup.

"Just another voice in our heads," Rhi smiled at her and squeezed her hand gently.

Rhi and Tara's arm tattoos had resumed filling in the day they were reunited. As a matter of fact, they had moved to their shoulders and upper backs now. Strange characters and patterns were once again mirrored on each other's skin, and they couldn't be happier about it.

"I'll be honest, I've never trusted the minder program," Viola said. "Don't get me wrong, I think it's a great idea to have a quasi-shrink in your head to help you out and all. But the fact that it's only supposed to look out for the host, regardless of Behemoth's wishes? I just have a hard time buying that, and I've seen the code!"

"The code is solid?" Shae asked.

"As far as I can tell, it's everything advertised. No Trojan horses or anything," Viola said.

"Well, that's good," Shae said. "I always worried about Beth and hers."

"Why would Drake help the AG kidnap us?" Rhi asked.

"Perhaps he didn't know who was in the biopods?" Viola suggested.

"That doesn't track," Rhi said. "Salrip said those pods were so rigged up that anyone would know how important they were."

"Maybe, maybe not," Viola said, tilting her hand side-to-side. "He could tell they were MEG priority, but not necessarily their contents. Besides, Drake was designed to be a part of the same resistance that the AG are part of. Why wouldn't he help them out?"

"I guess that makes sense," I added, but Rhi didn't look convinced.

"So, exactly how long do we have to live on the renaissance fair Bio Hab?" Rhi asked around a mouthful of sandwich.

"It's not a renaissance fair Bio Hab," Viola sighed as she sat down with her own plate of food now that everyone was fed.

The current plan was for all of us, including Asher's crew, to hide out in a backroom Bio Hab. Supposedly, this was a safe haven that had once been used by one of the "other" Behemoths for hand-to-hand and martial weapons training. From how Viola described it, it was a cross between a fantasy and a steampunk novel.

Personally, I couldn't wait to see it. Rhi, on the other hand, wasn't as enthusiastic.

"And as for how long, does it really matter? You live, like, forever," Viola said.

"That's true, but there's something to be said for modern plumbing!" Rhi chuckled.

Viola rolled her eyes. "I already said I was going to take care of it, so just chill, Mom, geesh!"

When Viola explained her origins to Shae and Tara, they seemed to take it in stride. I guess stranger things had happened to us.

Shae and Tara pulled our memories to see what had been going on with Viola before all this. Shae basically accepted her as a daughter, while Tara treated her more like a little sister. But then again, it had only been a few days.

Rhi was still staring at Viola.

"I'd say, at least 10 years," Viola said and took a bite of her sandwich. It sounded like she'd arbitrarily thrown the number out there. "I'd say that in 10 years, things will have settled down, and I'll have been able to scrub the databases by then," Viola said around a mouthful of sandwich.

"Good," I said.

"Good?" Shae asked.

"Yeah, good," I repeated. "I'm done with Behemoth's bullshit. It's already cost me two people I love. I'm out, no more!" I said and washed my hands of the subject.

Shae patted my arm gently.

"Who knows, maybe you'll like this new Bio Hab so much you won't want to come back?" Viola suggested. "It really is a pretty nice place."

Rhi made a disgusted sound and shook her head.

"It'll be fun!" Tara said as she took Rhi's hand. "It'll be just like home." She beamed at her wife.

Rhi's face softened then.

"Is there a reason there are so many similarities between Bio

Habs?" I asked.

Viola looked at me and cocked her head to the side. "How do you mean?"

"Well, after talking to Asher, it seems our two Bio Habs have a lot of the same traits, even some of the same people...more or less," I said.

"OH, that's easy. Behemoth uses a group template," Viola said.

"A what?" Shae asked.

"Behemoth will create a series of Bio Habs from one template," Viola explained. "Then it lets them develop and watches what happens."

"So, there's like five of Asher's Bio Hab out there that are identical?" I asked.

"That's an oversimplification, but yeah," Viola said. "Each one is its own animal, so while some things stay the same, others change over time. Then throw in the whole multi-dimensional mess and there's even more variation."

"Thinking about that makes my head hurt," Tara said and touched her temple.

"So, Asher and crew are all getting body augments?" I asked, trying to fend off my own developing headache by changing the subject.

"I offered it to help soften the blow. At first, I was just offering them the standard 'tune-ups.' You know, age reversal, health regen, stuff like that," Viola said. "But then the boy asked if there was more that could be changed. Apparently, he plays fantasy games, and the fact that we were going into a Bio Hab with that sort of setting..."

"He wanted to become an elf or some shit?" I mumbled.

"Pretty much," Viola nodded and took a bite of her sandwich. "Plus, the mechanics of that Bio Hab allow for paranormal physics."

"Para-what?" Rhi asked.

"Paranormal physics," Viola started. "Uh...a magic equivalent. Anyway, that pretty much sold him. I doubt he'll ever leave."

"Plus, using neural training, you can spin them up on local

skills and abilities," Rhi said.

"It will be a real-life role-playing game for them," I said.

"You'll be there too," Viola said. "Don't get jealous. I can get you some augments too...well, I can try. Who knows what would happen with your chaos engine?"

"I think he's fine just the way he is," Shae said as she put her head on my shoulder.

"Awwww," Tara sighed.

"Gross," Rhi said, dropping her sandwich onto her plate. "So much for my appetite. Hey!" Rhi protested when Tara snatched the remainder of her sandwich.

"You didn't want it!" Tara said.

"Give me that," Rhi said, snatching her sandwich back.

I chuckled at the antics and looked around at my reunited family. I couldn't explain the feelings that filled me as I looked at each of them. We'd been through so much together. I never wanted to be apart from them again. The thought of the years we'd spent apart caused me to shudder.

Shae's hand on my thigh chased the bad thoughts away.

"When do we have to leave?" I asked.

"I'd say we still have a solid day here that's safe," Viola started. "We'll need two days at an off-site neural hub to get everyone spun up and another two at an augment center, depending on what all they choose. Then we'll be able to head out."

"So, we'll be bouncing around for the next week?" Rhi asked.

"I'm afraid so. Behemoth knows you're all active right now, so it's been trying to track you down, more so than normal. The AG are as well, but they don't have the same resources. Plus, I still have those loyal to me in the AG who will help out. But it's best to keep moving, just in case," Viola said.

"So, we've got the day to ourselves then," Shae said.

"Seems like it," I said and turned to her. "Whatcha wanna do?"

"Oh," Shae started with a grin I didn't recognize. "I've got a few ideas, mo shíorghrá."

Alt F4 – Book 4

Epilogue

RHI

OK, yeah, so...if you hadn't noticed...this is where the cross-over starts. Yeah, that's right, he's collaborating with Ren Silver, who's writing the Asher series. So, the gestalt and Asher will be entwined for a bit.

But there's a catch.

Asher's series is adult-only smut!

You're surprised, right?

Well, it shouldn't come as a surprise that this series used to have a bunch of smut scenes in it as well...since I mentioned them way back in what, Book 0? Anyway, it wasn't until he went mainstream that he cut those all out.

So, gestalt Book 5 will be just like the other gestalt books in the series and boringly smut-free. It will tell the story from the gestalt's point of view, just like it always does.

But if you jump over to Asher's series, starting with her Book 2, you'll get the story from her perspective...plus some seriously hardcore smut, if that's your thing. You don't have to read her first book if you're just looking for the gestalt crossover stuff.

Don't worry, you can still get the main story by sticking to only one series. But if you've been wanting to catch the gestalt in a lot of compromising positions, check Asher out.

Nuff said...for now.

ABOUT THE AUTHOR

Do you really want to know?
I mean, if you've read this far, you've pretty much read the others.
Not a lot has changed…just paying for the privilege of pushing
more of these stories out for the unsuspecting public to read or
ignore.

ABOUT THE AUTHOR'S CAT

7 6vcdx
-0 []6t=y\[c5 huj yu

INTERESTED IN MORE OF THIS UNIVERSE'S INSANITY? CHECK US OUT ON FACEBOOK AT

"MUGZ INK BOOKS"
OR
FOR ASHER'S SERIES
"REN SILVER, AUTHOR"

www.ingramcontent.com/pod-product-compliance
Lightning Source LLC
Chambersburg PA
CBHW050023180626
46810CB00002B/542